Village Fortunes

REBECCA SHAW

An Orion paperback

First published in Great Britain in 2013
by Orion Books
This paperback edition published in 2014
by Orion Books,
an imprint of The Orion Publishing Group Ltd,
Orion House, 5 Upper Saint Martin's Lane
London WC2H 9EA

An Hachette UK company

1 3 5 7 9 10 8 6 4 2

A CIP catalogue record for this book
is available from the British Library.

ISBN 978-1-4091-2099-5

Typeset by Deltatype Ltd, Birkenhead, Merseyside

Printed and bound in Great Britain
by Clays Ltd, St Ives plc

The Orion Publishing Group's policy is to use papers
that are natural, renewable and recyclable products and
made from wood grown in sustainable forests. The logging
and manufacturing processes are expected to conform to
the environmental regulations of the country of origin.

www.orionbooks.co.uk

INHABITANTS OF TURNHAM MALPAS

Ford Barclay	Retired businessman
Mercedes Barclay	His wife
Willie Biggs	Retired verger
Sylvia Biggs	His wife
James (Jimbo) Charter-Plackett	Owner of the village store
Harriet Charter-Plackett	His wife
Fergus, Finlay, Flick & Fran	Their children
Katherine Charter-Plackett	Jimbo's mother
Alan Crimble	Barman at the Royal Oak
Linda Crimble	His wife
Maggie Dobbs	School caretaker
H. Craddock Fitch	Owner of Turnham House
Kate Fitch	Village school headteacher
Dottie Foskett	Cleaner
Zack Hooper	Verger
Marie Hooper	His wife
Gilbert Johns	Church choirmaster
Louise Johns	His wife
Greta Jones	A village gossip
Vince Jones	Her husband
Barry Jones	Her son and estate carpenter
Pat Jones	Barry's wife
Dean & Michelle	Barry and Pat's children
Revd Peter Harris MA (Oxon)	Rector of the parish
Dr Caroline Harris	His wife
Alex & Beth	Their children
Tom Nicholls	Assistant in the store
Evie Nicholls	His wife

Johnny Templeton	Head of the Templeton estate
Alice Templeton	His wife
Dicky & Georgie Tutt	Licensees at the Royal Oak
Bel Tutt	Assistant in the village store
Vera Wright	Retired

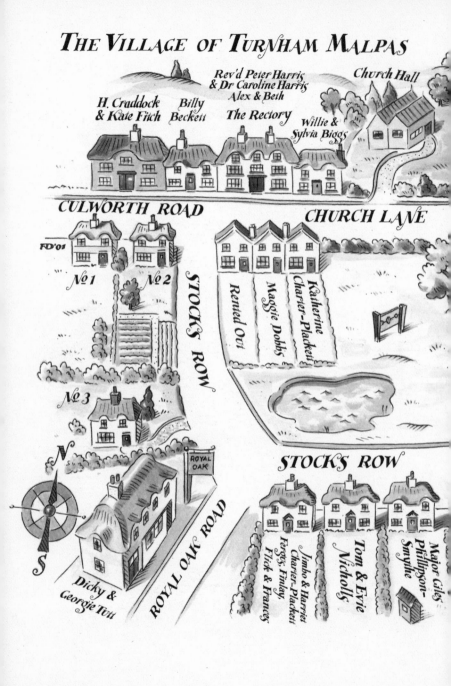

Chapter 1

The news of the arrival of a second son for the Lord of the Manor was round the village in no time at all. The two main centres for spreading the news were the usual Saturday coffee morning in the village hall and Jimbo's Village Store. Jimbo was mentally rubbing his hands with glee, as the longer customers stayed to talk about the baby, the more they were inclined to shop; and the frequent ringing of the door bell and the pinging of the cash register delighted him. Being in a celebratory mood, the villagers were buying slices of gateaux and some indulged themselves by purchasing sparkling wine to toast the baby. Fran had been twice into the wine store to bring out more bottles, and was as excited by the pinging of the cash register as her father. She gave him a wink and he winked back.

'Dad! What a morning. It's like Christmas! Want your coffee? We can't be long though, as Tom can't manage by himself.'

'Ten minutes. The post office's not that busy.'

'Or do you prefer a bottle of orange juice?'

'No, I need coffee. It'll give me a boost.'

'I'll get it. Dad! If you rush that chocolate biscuit down at that speed, you'll have indigestion all morning.'

'You're right. Sorry. Get the coffee, please.'

Fran had to set up the coffee machine again, and while she did she couldn't help but hear the conversations going on around her.

'Imagine! Another boy. A pity that. Still, there's always time.'

'So long as he's healthy, that's what matters.'

'He couldn't be more beautiful than little Charles. I've never seen a more beautiful baby than him.'

'Oh! I know, but there's always that fragile look, round his eyes.'

'I hadn't noticed.'

'Oh! There is.'

'But he's full of life and walking really early.'

'I know he is, and I'm glad. I wonder what they'll call this new one? In the past it's always been Tristan, Ralph or Bernard. I don't like them names, but it's all about tradition with these old families, isn't it?'

Fran didn't like the family names either, and when she handed her dad his coffee she said as much. 'They're still talking about the baby. They've moved on to names now. The traditional ones are dreadful. No self respecting baby would want them, not nowadays.'

'Ralph wouldn't be too bad. It could be pronounced Rafe if they want to be really posh.'

'I don't think "posh" bothers Johnny at all. He's the nicest man anyone could hope for. I could marry him myself.'

'I thought you always said you wouldn't get married. "I'm not having a man telling me what to do," you used to say.'

Fran grinned. 'Still do. Another coffee?'

'I'll get back to work and give Tom a chance to take a break.'

'I'm coming; I'll eat this gateau later.'

'No need for you to slave like I do, Fran.'

'Ah! But there is. I want a viable business to take charge of if I finally decide to take it over.'

Jimbo paused and turned back to ask, 'Decided not to go to university after all, then?'

'Thought about going, but no. Waste of time. Then I think ... maybe ... perhaps.'

'It's not been a waste of time for the others.'

'Go and relieve Tom, Dad, and leave my life to me.' Fran

laughed and pushed him out of the door in front of her. All the same, she thought, three years enjoying life might be a good idea before she fell under the spell of retail business. But one glance round the storeroom with its carefully organised stock and her dad's straw hat abandoned on top of a pack of jars of marmalade showed Fran this was where she belonged. She picked up Jimbo's straw hat, put it on her head at a jaunty angle and marched back into the front of the store to roars of laughter from the customers. Their laughter was music to her ears. She was good at customer relations, and getting people to buy was seventy-five per cent to do with relationships in a village store.

'Next!' Fran called out from the till.

'Just like your dad you are, Fran. Always got an eye for the money.'

'But I'm lovely too, Mrs Dobbs. Always friendly, never snappy, always got a smile.'

'Just like when you were at the village school, such a happy little girl you always were.'

'Is it still as lovely at the school as when I was there?'

'As the school caretaker, I can honestly say we miss your lovely smile. Don't you ever lose it. That my change? Thanks.' As Maggie Dobbs strode off she remembered Fran's first day at school with her scrawny pigtails and her uniform too big for her, and she smiled. Fran had got into more scrapes than any child she knew. She was always in the kitchen having her knees cleaned up or her elbows and once they'd had to ring her mother, Harriet, to tell her Fran had broken her elbow. It took a long time to heal and hours of physiotherapy to get it functioning again. As Maggie wandered back to her cottage with her shopping she recollected when Fran fell from the top of the climbing frame in the school playground. That was a worry; a huge lump came up on her head and they thought she was unconscious for a while. That was another hospital job, but

Fran always kept that lovely smile of hers, a smile that made Maggie smile too when she thought about it.

Now she must be nearly twenty. Surely not. No! She was ... she was almost twenty-one! How the years had flown by. She was the one most like her dad. Keen on the business, and had the right attitude too. Not a bit of edge to her; Fran was always courteous and helpful, eager to go to any lengths to get you what you wanted. Lovely she was. The other three were off out into the world without a backward glance at their dad's business. Would Fran stay with him? Was that what she wanted? If Maggie had asked Fran the answer would have been, 'Yes!!'

Now she could drive, Fran had been secretly looking in other towns and villages for premises where her Dad could start up a new business and put her in charge. That was what she wanted. A village store with herself in charge. But she felt too that she'd better hold back her ambitions for now and get more knowledgeable before she struck out on her own. Fran had considered doing a course of some kind, or working for a big company like Marks and Spencer to learn their trade secrets. She imagined her own smart stores all over the country, selling good food at reasonable prices. Bur for now she had to be practical. Jimbo's Village Store was busy and Fran knew she was a vital cog in the machinery.

'Good morning, Mr Fitch. Long time no see. How are you?'

'How am I? All the better for seeing you. When you go to university we shall miss you. Or at the very least your dad will. When do you go?'

'I'm not sure that I will. All I want to do is work alongside my dad, and so maybe I shan't bother. Some degrees nowadays aren't worth the paper they're written on, I hear.'

'It isn't set in stone that you should. I never did and it done me no harm.' Mr Fitch hesitated. Perhaps if he had he wouldn't be living in that appalling Glebe House, all of it designed in such terrible taste that it made his flesh creep. Even the utility room hadn't escaped the vast slabs of garish marble that featured in almost every room. And now he faced the pain of seeing what had once been his very own absolutely beloved Big House being restored by an incredibly wealthy young man, namely Johnny Templeton. Mr Fitch's heart lurched at every bit of restoration that was being done. If only he'd been more sensitive to the needs of the Big House ... He'd always known that dratted swimming pool was a mistake and that he'd only gone for planning permission for the pool because he liked the idea of getting his own way despite the enormous opposition there was to it. Those days were well and truly over. The cut and thrust had gone from his life now, no business, no Sir Ralph to get the better of; just himself, Henry Craddock Fitch. The only delight in his life was his darling wife Kate. Just the thought of her made him smile.

'Don't forget your shopping. Mr Fitch?' Fran's voice brought him back to earth.

'Sorry, dear, day-dreaming. Thank you.' Mr Fitch wandered off towards home, and on passing the school on his way to Glebe House he hoped he might get a glimpse of Kate, but the school was quiet, with not a soul in sight. A sudden shout of laughter came from one of the classrooms and the spontaneous, joyous outburst warmed him.

His Jack Russell, Sykes, was waiting for him behind the front door, dark brown eyes full of joy and his tail wagging. While Mr Fitch put his shopping away in the fridge, Sykes went to get his lead and stood as close to Mr Fitch as he could, which meant Sykes frequently got his feet trodden on, but he didn't care. The trick worked and within minutes Sykes and Craddock Fitch were walking down Jacks Lane and on to the field alongside the beck which led them through the woods. Sykes scampered about, loving every moment while Craddock, lost in thought, plodded steadily on. He decided to go through Sykes Wood and then into Home Park past Turnham House and down the mile long drive, before turning home towards Glebe House. If it did nothing else a long walk would keep him fit and Sykes would love him for it. It was months since he'd been all the way round, and Craddock felt it would do him good.

Sykes Wood. Haunted, they all said; more so since Venetia's body had been buried there. Maybe he ought not to ... No, he was being ridiculous. He'd only been her lover for what? Perhaps two or three months, and then it had all fallen apart when he found out he was playing second fiddle to that rogue – what was his name? Couldn't remember! But Venetia was found buried in the deepest depths of the wood, stabbed times without number, and at the thought Craddock found his eyes brimming with tears. He shrugged his shoulders to pull himself together. That was no ending for the feisty sexy woman she was. She wasn't worth his grief though; she'd betrayed her husband with numerous lovers time and again, and she was without a conscience. But she had been beautiful nevertheless.

The extreme cold penetrated Craddock's Barbour jacket and he wished he'd put on a sweater underneath. Passing Turnham House he spotted Johnny getting out of his 4×4.

Craddock hurried to catch him before he disappeared inside. 'Johnny! Johnny! Any news?'

Johnny cheerfully shouted, 'A lovely son arrived safely during the night.'

'Wonderful news! Wonderful! So glad for you. My best to Alice.'

'She'll be home tomorrow, if all goes well.'

'Good! Good!' Craddock waved his goodbye, Sykes stopped his enthusiastic greeting of Johnny and hurriedly followed after Craddock, and the two of them set off down the drive towards home. Lucky man, two sons, Craddock thought.

It occurred to him that one day long ago he'd been lucky too and had two sons. Why had he never kept in touch with them? How old must they be now? They were born not long after he stole that shovel that had become the start of his empire, and so they must be forty or so. Just as they reached the first of the beech trees that lined the drive Craddock was overcome with a powerful longing he'd never experienced before. If he could find them, if only he could find them. Perhaps they'd be married by now, or at least living with someone; and perhaps there might even be grandchildren he could cherish. His heart felt as if was almost bursting. He must try to find them. After all Craddock Fitch wasn't a common name, not like Jones or Smith, and so it should be easy to search for. Craddock knew the dates of his sons' birthdays; they were written down in an old diary he'd never thrown away. Now, he thought about that diary and wondered why he'd kept it all this time. Had he secretly been longing to find them but never acknowledged it before? Well, this time he would look for them. He couldn't let Johnny have everything, and he himself be left with nothing. Johnny with his money, Johnny with his vast hotel business, Johnny with the house that Craddock had loved so passionately (and still did) and now Johnny with his two sons. Craddock decided he wouldn't tell anybody about his search, although he would tell Kate as soon as he had any luck. The very second he had any luck.

Usually he had coffee before trying to find something to keep him busy until lunchtime, but today he didn't need to look for something to do as now he had an important mission to accomplish. He was going to find his two sons.

Chapter 2

After Craddock Fitch had left the store, Fran had worked all day alongside her dad and Tom, keeping the customers happy and satisfied. She could never understand why she found working in the store so satisfying. Maybe her genes were predominantly her father's and that was the reason; but whatever it was she loved the cut and thrust of the store, and the gossip.

But was she now also the target for gossip? Had someone seen her out and about with the new man in her life? Perhaps someone had seen her tonight, and then the balloon would go up. Please God, no, not yet.

Fran glanced at the clock on her dashboard and knew there would be an inquisition the moment she opened the front door. Her father appeared to be totally unaware that although she still lived at home she was an adult and could come and go as she pleased. Fran saw it was even later than she'd thought, and so she pressed a little harder on the accelerator. He'd be up, waiting, pretending he was working late on the accounts and that her arrival was a matter of no significance whatsoever. But her dad couldn't fool her. She knew him inside out. It was all because he loved her, she knew. He loved all of them, but the ones who'd left home and were out of sight didn't bother him so much now. But Fran Charter-Plackett still lived at home; she was the youngest, and because of that ... Two more miles and she'd be there. Why was she worried? She told herself she wasn't. Of course she wasn't. She was doing nothing wrong. Nothing at all.

She parked the car in the drive, locked it, opened the back

door to find her father waiting. 'I heard your car. Do you know it's two o'clock?'

'Yes.' Fran kissed his cheek to help calm the situation, but tonight it didn't work.

'It's a working day tomorrow. How can you possibly be ready for a good day's work when you arrive home at this time?' Jimbo rubbed his hand over his bald head and waited. She was special to him, so special he hardly dared let her know how much.

'Dad. I'm almost twenty-one. I can do as I like. Have I ever let you down? Not been there when the store opens? Made mistakes? Been rude to a customer because I'm too tired to care? Never. When I let you down you can sack me. And quite right too, as I shall deserve it. Goodnight, Dad. These late hours won't do you any good either, you know.' Fran stretched her mouth into a smile, kissed his cheek again and fled upstairs before he could ask any more questions.

Showered, moisturised, electric blanket switched off, Fran put on her favourite winter pyjamas and slid under the duvet. For five minutes she sifted through the events of the evening and then slipped gently off to sleep.

True to her word she was up, dressed, breakfasted, and in the store at six-thirty to start on the newspapers. For one brief moment as she dragged the papers in from the porch at the front door of the store where the van had dropped them off during the night, Fran regretted her late night. But one big lungful of the frosty country air revived her and as she heaved the newspapers up onto the counter to sort them out, she knew she was in the best possible place for Frances Charter-Plackett. None of this hectic nightlife Jimbo's other three children had, scrunched up in city apartments with scarcely a breath of fresh air even when they were outside. Not a single sight of rolling countryside, grazing cows, bleating lambs, frisky horses; only buildings, buildings, buildings, as far as the eye could see.

With the papers neatly stacked on the shelves, Fran set up

the coffee machine and drank the first gorgeous steaming cup of the day leaning against the open door looking out across the Green. The geese were already waking; the young ones born in the summer were beginning to take on an adult look, and Fran smiled at the thought that all of them were descendants of geese that had been in the village for centuries. This was miles better than dragging through the early-morning rush in the City: squeezed on to packed trains, smelling other people's armpits. Nothing could be as fresh or revitalising as staring across the Green and seeing the old oak tree still surviving and the stocks sturdily standing tall through the long winters. No! It was Turnham Malpas for her.

Fran heard Malcolm's milk float coming along. Though he wasn't supposed to, he delivered a supply of milk to the store as well as the houses. Fran remembered it was payday and carefully unlocked the safe to take out his money.

'G'd morning, Malcolm. Drop them there and I'll move them. Here's the money.'

'Your dad not about then?'

'It's my early morning. We take it in turns, Tom, Dad and me.'

'I meant to tell him this morning that this is my last week.'

'Your last week, after all these years? Why? I thought you liked delivering milk, the early mornings and all that? All that fresh early morning country air you used to boast about.'

Malcolm removed his peaked cap and scratched his scalp. 'I do, but there's not enough business to make it worth it, nowadays. They're all buying from the supermarkets now. Thirty years ago I delivered to every house in the village and beyond but now ... Well, it's not worth it.'

'Oh, I am sorry. You'll miss meeting everyone, and I'll miss you.' Fran patted Malcolm's shoulder. 'What are you going to do?'

'Early retirement. That's me. Early retirement.'

'You're too young to retire, Malcolm.'

'Got my sheep to look after, you know.'

'Sheep? I didn't know you had sheep.'

'Two hundred.'

Amazed by this revelation because she thought nothing happened in Turnham Malpas without her or her dad knowing about it. 'Two hundred? Where?'

'Fields the other side of Little Derehams where I live.'

'Well, I never. They'll keep you busy then.'

'I can see 'em from my front windows. Lovely sight, it is. Been building 'em up for four years, waiting for when the milk round collapsed. Well, it has. Must crack on. Tell your dad.'

His van grunted into action and away he went, and then Fran's first customer appeared in the doorway.

'Good morning, Willie.'

'Hello, Fran, love. My usual, please, and half a pound of that bacon my Sylvia likes best. You know the one.'

Fran suddenly saw Willie in a new light. Whatever had happened to that vigorous brisk seventy-year-old she knew and loved. His back was bent, his legs appeared slightly crooked and his voice had weakened. She kept her lovely welcoming smile, served him his change and went to open the door for him. But as he passed her, he said sadly, 'I'm not the man I was, little Fran. You're not little though, are you? Not now. You're a young woman and a real help to your dad. Thank you for this.'

Willie dropped his newspaper and couldn't bend down to pick it up so Fran bent down, glad to hide the sadness in her face. 'Here we are. Can you manage home?'

'Got to, if only to let my Sylvia know I'm not about to kick the bucket.' He struggled over the step and set off somewhat unsteadily for home. It occurred to Fran that when Willie went there'd be no more Biggses living in the village. Ever. And there'd been someone with the name of Biggs for centuries, just like the geese. Dying and leaving behind no children to carry on the line was an awfully sad position to be in, Fran thought She'd need to make sure that somehow she had children – well at least one – so her genes would carry on. Enveloped in gloom, Fran began the routine of setting up the store for the day's business. That terrible headache she'd woken with was lessening, thank goodness.

Tom came to work at eight o'clock, Jimbo arrived five minutes later and at eight-thirty her mother arrived, along with Greta Jones, who was still in charge of the mail-order office. Her dad gave Fran a sharp look, he then proceeded to give every single shelf intense scrutiny followed by a detailed examination of the freezers and the chilled shelving. His eyes had reached the corner reserved for customers to sit and make use of the coffee machine, and he took a paper cup filled with coffee and two sugars, and tested it. The taste appeared to please him and then, and only then, he retired to the back office for an in-depth discussion with Greta about the possibility of extending their mail order to include fresh meat.

He irritated Fran no end when he did that scrutiny of the store. She knew how particular he was (and for that matter so was she), but to have to witness him doing it every day had seriously begun to annoy her.

She followed him into Greta's sanctum. 'Look, Dad, I like everything looking smart just . . .'

'Not right now, Fran. Talk to me later.'

'Dad! When you've finished in here, I need a word. OK?'

Jimbo nodded. 'Right. Now, Greta. About the meat idea I had . . .'

'Not in here. It isn't suitable. There isn't enough room. There's no refrigeration, there's nowhere to put the special paper and plastic wrapping, there simply isn't enough room for proper hygiene. And it would have to be chilled and I'd freeze to death and there's no room for scales for weighing it all. Sorry, no can do.'

Greta reached up to pick out two jars of Harriet's Country

Cousin Peach Jam ('peaches from our local greenhouses') for the order she was putting together. She considered the discussion at an end, but Jimbo hadn't finished.

'I've had a better idea. You would be in charge here but also in charge of the meat packing and orders in the new space I'm creating in the Old Barn.'

Greta shrugged her shoulders. 'I can't be in two places at once. You know full well what will happen: your advertising will be so tempting that the meat packing orders will be three times bigger than we ever envisaged, and I'll be working nights as well as days and my union steward will have something to say about that. Believe me.'

Talk about unions always switched Jimbo into rocket mode. 'Union steward? Are you a member of a union? Because if you are it's out that door faster than you've ever moved before. Well? Are you?'

Seeing that she'd finally got him to listen to what she had to say Greta secretly smiled. 'No. But my steward is that chap I've left snug in bed at home. His name's Vince Jones.'

Harriet burst into peals of laughter. Fran shrieked her amusement, and Greta winked at them both in turn.

Eventually Jimbo had to laugh too. 'I didn't mean that. I meant you supervise and I get a junior person straight from school to work in here; and your Vince could do the meat, and you could supervise him too. He could lend a hand when necessary, and between the three of you you could manage. And then when it takes off – there's loads of room in the Old Barn for expansion isn't there?' He nudged her in a friendly way. 'So what do you think? Eh!'

He got no reply.

'I might even move the whole of the mail order to the Old Barn, if and when such a time came. There's air conditioning there too. You're always complaining in the summer about the heat.'

Greta extracted a beautifully printed sticky label from a pack she kept conveniently to hand, wrote the customer's address on it in copperplate handwriting and stacked the parcel in a plastic crate labelled 'Ready for Posting'. Not until then did she turn to answer Jimbo. 'I'd need a rise. My Vince would need to know how much you'd pay him; and I want to interview the junior alongside you.'

'I don't know about that, the final decision would be mine. Vince'd have to go for training, food hygiene and such. Wear the right uniform, fancy hat and that.'

'You're on. I'd insist on the proper equipment for the meat. Get organised like it is here. The only way I get through the work is by *organisation*.'

'I have to say I admire your organisation, very much. I don't know where we'd be without it.'

Greta threw him a look to check if he was pulling her leg but realised he wasn't; his compliment was genuine. He meant it. From that moment on Greta became his devoted slave. If he'd said she had to have the mail-order office on the moon, she'd have booked a season ticket with Virgin immediately.

Fran had to admit her dad could persuade anyone to do anything at all; she just hoped she had the same skill. She also hoped that he would never find out what she was up to at the moment as, knowing him, he'd bring in every argument he could to persuade her otherwise, and so she stood in the corner by the tinned soup shelves and sent up a silent prayer: he must not find out.

'I'm taking my break, Dad, OK?'

'Of course. You could always step in if the junior didn't work out, couldn't you?' Jimbo saw the astonishment followed by the resistance in her eyes; he backed off. 'Temporarily, for a day or two, just until I got sorted.'

'Temporarily, that's all. Not my cup of tea at all.' Fran saw the advantage in her of being willing to do the kind of work

14

she hated. 'But yes, help out, of course I would.' She smiled at him. 'I'm better working with the customers, as you well know. Does your mind never stop thinking up new ideas? Taking on meat by mail order is a whole new ball game, speed of delivery to the customer, who would be flexible enough to provide the meat, etc? Doesn't matter if the jams and chutneys get delayed for a day or two as nothing goes off. But meat ...'

Jimbo mock punched her jaw. 'Can't stand still. One door closes another opens.' The two of them laughed and Fran relished their compatibility. She had a far closer relationship with her dad than the others, mainly, she supposed, because they were the same kind of people. Fran went to find her mum who was applying herself to the icing of a wedding cake of the old-fashioned kind; three tiers, sugar flowers, artificial orange blossom and, waiting on her worktable, were the plastic bride and groom for the very top. It made Fran cringe.

'Mum, it's such bad taste. I don't know how you can bear to do it.'

'They're *paying* me to do this, and this is what they want and so this is what they will get. Just because you think it's in bad taste ...'

'Mum! You agree with me.'

'I know I do. But what they want to make their day perfect is what they will get. I can't wait for the day when I can ice a wedding cake for one of my own children. Those three up in London are having a far too exciting life to settle down to marriage and babies, but I'm hoping you might decide on a more normal life. Will you, do you think?' Harriet skilfully finished another icing flower and laid it to dry out on a sheet of greaseproof paper. Getting no reply she looked up at Fran and saw she wasn't going to get one. A shut-down look had come over her daughter's face, and she was already leaving. 'Going for my half-hour break as I've been cracking on since half-past six. Back soon. You're clever with the flowers, Mum.'

Fran was glad to escape. Why did everyone appear to be intent on probing her about her life? Her life was her life and no one else's. She'd taken an old wholemeal loaf from one of the wheelie bins at the back of the store and was about to feed the geese. This morning there were mallards too and, unusually, a couple of coots. She supposed the cold weather had persuaded these strangers to try elsewhere for food. Just as the loaf was almost finished Peter came across the grass from the direction of the church. Now this was another person she didn't really fancy talking to. She wasn't in the mood for his piercing blue eyes that seemed to be looking right into your soul; she'd had enough of inquisitions for today.

'Good morning, rector. Cold, isn't it?' He towered above her, but not threateningly so, nevertheless she needed to escape.

'Good morning, Fran. Taking a break?'

'Well, I started work at half-past six this morning like you always do, and so I take a break about this time.'

'It's always surprises me that you didn't go to university like your sister and brothers did.'

'My choice. I just wanted to follow in Dad's footsteps and so I didn't want to go. Nowadays it's so easy to work hard, get a degree, and then it leads absolutely nowhere.' Fran squinted up at Peter to see the effect her comment had made.

'True, very true.'

'Time I went back to work.' It wasn't, but it suited the moment to tell a fib.

'Fine, that's where I'm heading.' So instead of getting rid of him he escorted her back to the store.

Now Fran had stopped going to church it embarrassed her to be seen with Peter. As a child she'd adored him, but now she'd put away childish things.

He opened the shop door for her as though she was some kind of fragile Victorian creature. The doorbell jangled joyfully as always and even that annoyed her. With a brisk nod and a smile to say thank you to Peter, she vanished into the back, washed her hands thoroughly and then began to restock the bacon display, which she'd noticed, as she stormed in, was looking empty. Absorbed in her work of restocking any item that needed it because she liked the displays to look tempting, Fran's objective was really to keep out of everyone's way, especially Peter's. Why had she so surprisingly found talking to Peter so difficult? In her heart she knew very well why. It was because he was a totally honest person. In fact, *shiningly* honest. And she wasn't.

Chapter 3

By the middle of the afternoon, Fran was her charming self once more. After all she was an adult now, and was doing only what adults did, so why should she feel so guilty? Mr Fitch had come in to get some bits and pieces his wife Kate had forgotten to include in her weekly order. While she packed Mr Fitch's carrier bag for him she decided to ask how he liked living in Sir Ralph's old house, having now had plenty of time to settle in. 'How long is it now, two years?'

'Almost. Never will, but as Kate would say, beggars can't be choosers.'

'Oh! Come now. Beggars? I think not.'

Mr Fitch, slightly surprised by the frankness being displayed by the girl at the checkout – Fran was it? – contemplated his answer while he put his debit card away. 'Perhaps not by today's standards, I keep thinking up all kinds of ideas for starting anew, but then I change my mind when I think of the expense and the effort.' He picked up his carrier from the counter top and swung away, saying as he left, 'Be seeing you soon, no doubt.' He went out to untie his dog Sykes and set off for home. He paused by the school wall to watch the children leaving for the day. There was far less chaos with the two minibuses taking the children home to the outlying farms and villages now. To think he'd been rich enough to pay for it himself at one time and then later had been relieved when the council took over when he couldn't afford it any more. Sykes began scrabbling at the wall asking to be lifted up. So he grabbed him under his ribcage and hoisted him up. Some of the children out playing came to have a word.

'Hello, Sykes. You've been out for a walk, your legs are all muddy.'

'Hello, Mr Fitch. Why do you call him Sykes? Funny name for a dog.'

'Because a long time before you were born an old man called Jimmy lived here and had a dog called Sykes named after the big wood no one likes.'

'It's haunted, that's why.'

'Well, that's as maybe. But then Sykes died, and not long after that a little dog came to the village following a huge accident on the bypass, and he was so much like the first Sykes that old Jimmy kept him and called him Sykes too. Then he disappeared one day and never came back, and so that's why I called this one Sykes. In fact when I went to choose a puppy I chose this one because he looked so much like the first Sykes.'

'He's a nice dog, he never growls.'

'He does when he sees a cat. Can't abide cats, can't Sykes.'

The children ran off to find their mothers or to climb on to one of the two waiting minibuses, leaving Mr Fitch with only Sykes for company.

Hearing the hubbub outside that always meant the end of school, Fran thought there was only another hour and then she would be finished for the day. After her late night and early morning she was ready to leave. The doorbell jangled vigorously and in came the Lord of the Manor, Johnny Templeton, and on his face there was a broad grin.

'Fran. I'm just back from the hospital.'

'The man of the moment! We all know your news. Wonderful, everyone's so pleased! Everything OK?'

'I should say so. He's beautiful, and Alice is thriving. He's had his first feed and he's as fit as a flea.'

'So no doubts about the inheritance then? Two sons now to take over after you. You must be chuffed.' Fran went round the end of the counter, kissed Johnny and gave him a hug, shouting as she released him, 'Dad! It's Johnny.'

Jimbo dashed in from the back office and slapped Johnny on the back as he congratulated him.

'Wonderful news. Everything all right?'

'Everything's fine, thank you.'

Tom came out from the post-office cage to congratulate Johnny; and then Harriet, hearing the commotion, came in from the back to hug Johnny and add her congratulations.

'Is Alice all right? It all went well did it, no hitches?' Harriet asked.

'He's a big baby and the delivery was fast, but she's doing great.'

'Ah! Does he have a name?'

'Not decided yet. I'm keen on one of the traditional Templeton names. I know they're not very fashionable, Bernard and Ralph, but I do like the sense of tradition.'

Fran laughed and then said, 'Well, with your good looks, there's one thing for certain, he'll be handsome.'

Her mother joined in the teasing. 'Good looks run in the Templeton family; you only have to look at your brother Chris to know that. Is your other brother in Brazil just as handsome as the two we know? You know, the blond hair and the dark brown eyes, and the aristocratic nose?' Harriet winked at Fran as she said this to let everyone know she was only teasing Johnny. Except it was true, they were an outstandingly good-looking family.

Johnny looked embarrassed. 'Well, I have to admit Nicholas is quite good-looking.'

Harriet said, 'By the sound of that modest admission Nicholas is definitely very handsome.'

They all burst out laughing. Jimbo, putting an innocent expression on his face, said, 'How about James for the new addition? Charles and James Templeton sounds good, doesn't it?'

'Only because it's your name, Dad!' said Fran. 'But it does sound good, I'll admit, Charles and James. Give Alice our love, Johnny, and tell her how pleased we all are, won't you?' At the same time Fran made a mental note to get out all the spare stock of 'Welcome to your new baby' cards for boys. She groaned inside, thinking she was getting more and more like her dad the longer she stayed here. Maybe going to university would be a good idea after all. She'd think about that another day, but at the moment a nice cosy evening watching the TV and then off to bed early to catch up with her sleep was the only decision she intended to make. Fran didn't want her dad to find reason to criticise her for being tardy, not right at this moment in time. She needed to keep him sweet.

Fran was about to leave when the bell signalled the arrival of another customer. It was Chris, Johnny Templeton's brother. Since he'd arrived about eight weeks ago he'd been a fairly frequent visitor to the store and they all knew him.

'Good afternoon, everyone. Johnny! Isn't it wonderful news, everybody, about the baby? He's coping very well. Flowers. I've come to buy flowers for the new mother. Have you got any?'

Fran didn't offer to assist him but Jimbo did, acknowledging the smell of money that surrounded the Templeton brothers. 'Here we are, Chris. This is what we have left. If we'd known . . .'

'I'll take the lot. Make them into a bouquet, would you? I'm going up there to see my newest nephew. I expect you've all heard the news. Johnny was like a man walking on hot coals all yesterday but I told him time and again that everything would be fine. And here we are, with another strong healthy baby boy who has just joined the human race! Brother Chris knows, and I've been proved right once again.' He thumped his chest like a gorilla in acceptance of the approval he got. 'It seems we Templetons can do nothing but breed boys. Nicholas has two, there's three of us, and now Johnny has two.'

Chris slapped Johnny on his back and rather ostentatiously

gave him a great hug. They were all used to Chris's larger than life reactions to everything, and took it as being part and parcel of this younger brother up at the big house.

Meanwhile Jimbo had got himself in a tangle with the bouquet and Fran had to rescue him. 'Look, Dad, I'll see to it. Leave it to me.'

'OK. OK. I will. Chris will you allow me to give you a bottle of champagne? To wet the baby's head?'

Fran, her face shielded by the sheet of coloured cellophane she was using to wrap the flowers, smiled, recognising her dad's business technique for what it was.

'That's mighty generous of you, James, mighty generous. Thank you. I'm sure Alice will be able to have a sip, just a sip I know, but it'll make all the difference to her. Can't leave her out of the celebrations, can we, when she's done all the hard work? Thank you, Fran, you've made a gilt purse out of a sow's ear, well and truly.' As Fran handed the bouquet to him Chris slipped an arm round her shoulders and chastely kissed her cheek. 'Beautiful, just beautiful. Thank you.'

'I've just had a thought, I don't think the hospital allows flowers?'

'They will, I'll make sure of that.' His supreme confidence in his ability to flout hospital rules amused them all. They just knew he'd get round them some how; he was that kind of man.

Chris left in a flurry, opening the back door of his vivid red sports car and carefully placing the bouquet on the back seat, laying the champagne on the front seat; then he tooted his horn several times and left. Everything always felt flat once Chris had gone. Fran went off home, Tom took his afternoon break, Jimbo cleared away the buckets the flowers had been standing in, and silence fell.

Jimbo sat on the seat provided for the person in charge of the till and contemplated *money*. Obviously Johnny had money; money of his own, and also the money and properties left him by Sir Ralph. It seemed to Jimbo that Chris had money too, but all of his came from the hotel business they owned back in Brazil. Money on a scale that no one in the village had now nor ever would have, not even Craddock Fitch in his prime. Jimbo liked Johnny and when Chris joined him up at the big house he'd imagined it would be like having two Johnnies instead of one. But it wasn't. Chris flaunted his money and wanted everyone to admire him in a way that Johnny never did. Chris's personality was bigger and more brash, louder and less likeable. But at the same time one couldn't help liking him, and yet one resented him too. Johnny was safely and happily married. But Chris was a loose cannon and one never quite knew what he would do next. Johnny came to church frequently, but Chris, Jimbo imagined, probably didn't even know where it was. Johnny endeavoured to be part of village life, Chris lived in the village with Johnny and Alice, but as for taking part in it ...

You kind of knew where you were with Johnny, but not Chris, thought Jimbo. This roving creature supposedly looking for a hotel chain to buy in Britain disappeared during the week and then turned up sometimes at the weekend and then did his disappearing trick again on Monday morning, or sometimes he wouldn't leave until Wednesday or even Thursday, and so no one knew where he was from one minute to the next. Jimbo was drawn to Chris's sharp business acumen but at the same time he couldn't trust him and he couldn't put his finger on why not. Johnny obviously thought the world of him, so maybe he ought to accept him, and Chris was certainly one of his best customers. That was what the free bottle of champagne was about, keeping Chris on-side for the money he brought to the store. Every couple of weeks he would come in and buy expensive items of food to take back to the big house as his contribution to the housekeeping. He bought the very best of everything. Ordered special items for collection on Friday and more often than not the bill came to well over a hundred pounds. How Johnny, Alice and Chris managed to eat all he bought Jimbo couldn't imagine. It must have lasted well into the next week when Chris wasn't even there to help consume it. Still, if that was what he wanted, Jimbo wasn't one to complain.

Customers were few that half hour. Two people came in with parcels to post, hoping they hadn't missed the last collection; and one for a birthday card, and could Jimbo lend him a pen to write it while he was there, and had he missed the post? And he'd need a stamp, please. Well, one thing was for certain, Jimbo wouldn't get rich on that little lot. But he could get rich on Chris, and so maybe he'd better change his attitude to Johnny's dearly beloved brother, Jimbo acknowledged to himself.

While Jimbo was sitting at the till, Chris was at the hospital charming the nurses. He'd swept into Maternity where he'd been mistaken, twice, for a new father before they finally connected him to Alice; and twice he'd been told he couldn't leave the flowers as they were banned. But he'd cheerfully listened and then begged so humbly to be allowed to at least show them to his sister-in-law that he had been allowed to do so on the understanding ... 'But of course I will, I wouldn't dare disobey. Room four you say?' and smiled so sweetly that the previously grumpy nurse fell under his spell.

'Alice! You clever girl. Let me give you a kiss. Excellent work. Johnny's like a dog with two tails. Where is this beautiful new nephew of mine?'

'Right beside me, in the cot.'

Chris bent over the cot and gently kissed the baby's forehead, tenderly cupping his face in his hand. For one brief moment Alice saw the real Chris, then he disappeared as quickly as he'd come. 'My word, Alice, he's a beauty and not half. Still, with a beautiful mother like yourself, what else could he be but handsome? He's a typical Templeton, isn't he? Like us three:

24

good-looking and full of himself. He's strong, look, he's holding my finger. What a grip and not yet a day old. My word.'

Chris turned his attention to Alice, sitting himself down on the bed, holding her hand and bending over to kiss her. 'Wonderful job you've done. I understand from Johnny you were extremely brave.'

'I don't know about brave, I just did my best.'

'I'm sure you were brilliant, exhausted but brilliant. I won't stay long, I'm not very good with hospitals and illness. Do you know that I've never spent a single night in hospital? Always been fit and well all my life. Broke my arm once playing polo but I refused to stay in overnight and made them sort it out there and then so I could sleep at home. I've brought my brave girl champagne, see. No, don't protest. Just one little sip with me, and then we'll give the rest to the nurses. I insist. Can't have you missing all the fun.'

Alice, who had understood what made Chris tick within five minutes of first meeting him, said, 'OK then. Just one little sip.' She made to struggle out of bed to get a glass from the washbasin but Chris wouldn't allow it.

'Stay right there, I've borrowed glasses from the nurses.' He inspected them as though making sure they were clean. The cork popped and hit the ceiling making a slight dent. 'Don't worry, they'll never notice, and if they do you must claim complete innocence. Those gorgeous blue eyes of yours will do the trick.' He poured a full glass for himself and just a drop for her. 'There we are! To Johnny, to Alice and to whatever it is you're going to call him.'

'To Johnny and to our second son.' Alice sipped the champagne.

Chris, being Chris, swallowed his in seconds. 'You know, Alice, I'm looking after Johnny so don't fret. He's the sort of man who needs looking after. So stay here as long as you feel you need, or as long as they will allow you to, because your other half is being well taken care of, and little Charles too. He's an absolute delight, believe me.'

Alice knew exactly what that meant. Chris would spend a lot of time telling Johnny how wonderfully Johnny coped with his domestic responsibilities, how well he cared for Charles and how wonderfully his cooking skills had improved, but never lift a finger himself to help. Decorative was how Alice described Chris in her own mind, and he was certainly that. She'd thought Johnny was handsome but when she saw Chris and Nicholas at the wedding, resplendent in their morning suits standing either side of Johnny, she knew it was Chris who won the prize for good looks. What's more, he knew it.

'You are giving Johnny a hand, aren't you? There's such a lot for him to do. Charles is still a baby and needs a lot of care.'

'Of course I am. I'm running about like a scalded cat as my mother would say. About your flowers, they tell me they're not allowed in the wards, but I've persuaded them to put them on the windowsills in the corridor, well I will have before I go.' Chris began to fidget. She knew he wanted to leave so she declared herself exhausted and said she'd better get some sleep while the baby slept, and so would he mind ...?

So Chris kissed her again and trundled away with the flowers and the champagne, glad to escape. Unattached, unencumbered women were the ones he liked the best. All the domesticity Johnny had so eagerly taken on board wouldn't suit him at all. He liked the fun side of life, not the responsible side of it. Heaving the pushchair into the car, changing nappies, up in the night when he longed for uninterrupted sleep (which was his due), wasn't for Christopher Templeton. No thanks.

Chris went to charm the nurses into placing the flowers where he wanted them. They agreed to put the flowers on the windowsills, though it was strictly against the rules, and the nurses thoroughly enjoyed their illicit champagne while persuading Chris to reveal all about his wonderfully exciting life in

Rio. Chris played the glamorous chap from distant shores to the very best of his ability. He really was good fun, they said. And Chris thought they were too.

By the time he got back Johnny was giving Charles his bedtime bottle and calming him down ready for bed.

'Hi there. You look a picture of contented fatherhood, Johnny. The baby is great, so like Charles. I've done my duty, kissed and congratulated the proud mother, and done my uncle bit with the nurses to make sure Alice gets lots of attention. You're a lucky man, you know that? You've certainly chosen a beauty with Alice.'

'Yes, I know that.' Johnny put little Charles over his shoulder and cuddled him. 'Chris, what about this hotel chain you're out looking for? You never say anything. Not seen one suitable?'

Chris flung himself down on the sofa. 'One or two, but none that make me want to stay there. I think that's always a good sign about the hotels if you yourself actually want to do that. Saw four in Cornwall, Land's End way. But they'd all need refurbishing and I mean *completely* refurbishing. And they were asking a ridiculous price.'

'But they might be the ones to go for. Got any brochures?'

'Yes, I'll get them out. When will dinner be?'

'Going out?'

'I'm hoping to.'

'Won't be long. It's in the oven. Here hold Charles for me and don't let him wriggle down on to the floor now that I've put his clean pyjamas on. Right? I'll go check the dinner.'

Rather ungraciously Chris agreed to play uncle. Then the warm, comforting presence of Charles's body against his own surprised him. He hadn't expected to be stirred by a small boy who had decided that standing on his uncle's thighs and jumping up and down provided him with some much-needed exercise. He brought Charles's face close to his own and for a brief moment they both stared at each other, Chris was moved to kiss his nephew, which motivated Charles to head-butt him.

'Ouch! That hurt!'

Johnny came back in with the oven cloth in his hand. 'It's ready. I'll take Charles and put him in his cot, and then we'll eat.'

'He's just head-butted me. He's going to be a rogue is this one, and not half. Here you are.' Chris handed his nephew over and examined his forehead in the mirror. 'No bruise yet but there will be, I'm sure. Why in heaven's name don't you have some domestic help? Heavens above, you can afford it.'

'I know we can, but I had great difficulty in persuading Alice to live here and so I'm taking it one step at a time. If I rush things and get help when she doesn't agree, the balloon could go up.'

'I've never known a woman who wouldn't be glad to hand over all the hard work to someone else.'

'Alice isn't like the normal run of women. Well, not your kind of women, anyway.'

'Well, at any rate, it's you doing all the work and not me, and I'm perfectly willing to let you do it.'

'As ever. Won't be long.' Johnny tossed the oven cloth to Chris. 'Here get the casserole out, the vegetables are ready drained.'

Though the oven cloth was scrupulously clean Chris took hold of it as though it was covered in thick grease. 'OK. Got the message. Dining room? No watching TV while we eat?'

'No, I've already laid the table.'

Chris shrugged and departed for the kitchen. He opened the wine and approved of the label, got the casserole out of the oven along with the man-sized baking potatoes, took them into the dining room, fished out the plates warming in the oven. He stood back to check the table. Serving spoon? Which drawer? He'd no idea.

While the two of them ate the casserole, which he had to

admit was delicious, Chris posed a question. 'So you've been outmanoeuvred, that's not like you. You're normally the one who does the outmanoeuvring. Like when you got this place back.'

'True. But the difference is I love Alice like I've never loved a woman before, and that makes the difference.'

'Got it bad then?'

'I suppose I must have.' Johnny laughed and then asked, 'And you, what about you? I'm thirty-four and you're only two years younger. Isn't it time ...?'

'And Nicholas is twenty-nine and already married with two children. You get more like mother every day.'

'How is she? I heard you speaking to her earlier. Really, how is she?' Johnny waited for the reply.

'Right now? In remission.'

'Good. That's good news.'

Chris offered to refill Johnny's wine glass for him.

'No, thanks.'

'I've known the time when you'd have opened a second bottle when it was just the two of us. Economising?' The mocking look on Chris's face reminded Johnny of their younger days.

'I may have inherited pots of money besides what I earn from the hotels back home, but that doesn't mean I have to *throw* it away. Unlike you I have commitments: employees' wages to pay, a house to restore, the estate to bring up to speed, the farm to modernise, children to feed, school fees to think about. This woman I suspect you're seeing? Someone I know? Who is she?'

Chris shot to his feet. 'Lovely meal. No time for the pudding. You eat it. Got to go, running late. Alice home tomorrow?'

'I expect so.'

'You'll have lots to do then. I'll be late tonight.'

'Got your key?'

'Yep.'

Johnny caught sight of Chris checking his appearance in the

hall mirror. So he was right that Chris had a woman in tow. Johnny watched Chris starting up his car. God, he was a prepossessing man and probably would still be when he was in his sixties, no wonder women found him magnetic. Well, it wouldn't be long before someone in the village spotted them together, and then the news would spread like wildfire. Just *who* was it?

Chapter 4

Barry Jones pushed open the heavy outer door of the Royal Oak and hurried in to get out of the cold. As he opened the inner door the heat of the fire blazing in the saloon hit him with a welcoming blast, and he went over to warm himself by sitting in the only chair in the inglenook fireplace. Holding his hands out to its warmth he called across to Georgie behind the bar, 'G'evening, Georgie. Icy cold out there. I reckon there'll be a deep frost tonight.'

'Good evening to you, Barry. No Pat tonight?'

'No. A do on at the Old Barn. My usual, if you please. The others not in?'

'Zack and Marie have a B and B guest they're not too sure about so they're staying in; Vera's got a heavy cold; Dottie might be in, Vince and Greta will be in later, I know for a fact. Shall I bring it across?'

But Barry was already making his way to the bar.

'Everything OK at the big house?' Georgie enquired. 'Baby home yet?'

'He is. Johnny's thrilled to bits, and the baby's grand. Stronger looking than little Charles; more robust, you know.'

Georgie protested. 'Don't say that. Charles is a beautiful boy, there's nothing wrong with him, always so happy, and walking at ten months. That's going some, you have to admit.'

'I know he's beautiful. I know nothing about little babies, having none of my own, but this second one ...'

'Have they given him a name?'

'Not yet. Can't make their minds up.'

'Don't forget your change.'

'Ah. Right. Thanks.' Barry went back to sit in the chair in the inglenook fireplace, grateful it was still vacant. He'd been working outside almost all day putting the new fencing up at Home Farm and he still felt chilled right through. He contemplated the cost of the fence. He'd thought Craddock Fitch was wealthy, well he had been, but this Johnny Templeton was in a different league. He didn't spend money foolishly but he did spend it where it was needed. The fencing could have been bought for half the price Johnny had paid for it, but it wouldn't have lasted as long nor looked so good; and for a craftsman like Barry, the satisfaction he got from building the fence was enormous. There was nothing quite like working with quality wood. The fence would still be there looking good when Charles inherited, and there was something special about that idea, a permanency that hadn't been there when Mr Fitch was the owner. And not just for the estate, but for the village too.

Vince and Greta Jones came in and Greta settled herself at a table while Vince went to the bar. 'Vince! Greta! I'll come and join you if that's all right!'

'Of course!' Vince ordered their drinks. 'Our usual, please, Georgie. And whatever Barry's having.'

The three of them chose to sit at the old oak table with the settle down one side; it was the best table in the entire saloon bar and their favourite.

Vince paid for the drinks, saying, 'It's quiet in here tonight, Georgie.'

Georgie looked grim. 'It is, more's the pity. I don't know where everyone gets to these nights.'

'No money, that's the trouble.' Vince carried the drinks across and sat himself down.

As Greta and Vince relished their first sips silence fell, and then Barry raised his drink. 'To the new baby. Got to wet his head, haven't we?' So the three of them clashed their glasses together and said it again.

Greta said, 'Makes me feel all medieval, it does. A new baby up at the Big House. Hang all these wealthy industrial people taking over our stately homes, flesh and blood is what counts.'

Vince picked up his glass again, examined the clarity of his ale out of habit, and said, 'They know how to conduct themselves, they do. It's instinct.'

'Exactly,' said Barry, 'everything Johnny Templeton does for the estate is carefully thought out, and then he strikes. Beautiful wood I'm using for the fencing. It gives a craftsman pride in his work and no mistake.'

Greta chuckled. 'One thing for certain is that you'll be pleased you didn't lose your job. I remember you sitting here one night, in that very chair, convinced you'd be losing your house and be out of a job. But now look at you.'

Barry had to admit that Greta was right. 'It all seemed so certain and Mr Fitch was too, don't forget. He'd no idea that Sir Johnny had fooled him in to thinking it was that residential home company that was buying it. Mr Fitch laughed when he found out how he'd been misled. Laughed like he hadn't laughed for years.'

Greta questioned what Barry had said. 'I couldn't understand that. Why did he find it funny when he'd fought so hard to stop Johnny buying it?'

Vince sighed with impatience. 'I'll tell you once again, and then that's it. He enjoyed the idea that someone as upright and as moral as Sir Ralph had a nephew, albeit a bit distant, who was as ruthless as he himself was, Craddock Fitch that is. That's what made him laugh.'

Greta laughed too. 'Oh, I see. Well, I think so. Right, now you've explained it proper instead of laughing like a drain so I couldn't tell what you were saying. Yes, it is funny. He's hating not living in the Big House, you know. I feel quite sorry for him.'

'You've never felt sorry for him before. He couldn't do a thing right for you for years.'

Greta smiled ruefully. 'I know that, don't remind me, but I do feel sorry for him now.' She contemplated Mr Fitch for a moment and then added, 'Once, at one of his parties, I caught him smoothing his hand over the banister rail of the main staircase and you could see he loved it, treasured it, kind of. I bet he didn't smooth his hand over all that red marble when he lived at Glebe House; and now he's renting Sir Ralph's old house, that's a come down and not half.'

Vince brought a dash of common sense to their conversation. 'No. But it's no more than he deserves when you think about all the trouble he caused us all.'

At this moment Dottie Foskett came in, glanced round, spotted them at the best table in the saloon bar, and came across. 'Evening everybody. Mind if I join you?'

'Be our guest, Dottie.' Greta pulled out the chair at the end of the table for her.

The three of them watched her at the bar ordering her drink. You couldn't help but like Dottie, added to which she cleaned at two of the most important gossip-worthy households in the village so she was a useful friend to have. And she was always good for a laugh. To their surprise, just recently Dottie had changed her favourite drink for the last four years from half a pint of home-brew ale to vodka and tonic; and now she sat down with one in her hand. She placed it carefully on the nearest drink mat and looked round at them, her eyes sparkling with interest.

'Well?' the three of them asked in unison, knowing she was bursting with news.

Provokingly Dottie replied, 'Well?'

'What's the latest news?' asked Greta.

'Who says I've got some news?'

'Your eyes do. Come on, come on.'

34

Dottie smiled. 'I was at the rectory, cleaning the bedrooms, when I saw ...'

'Yes?' urged Vince.

'Sir Johnny and ... Mr Fitch coming to Sir Johnny's house next door but one, what was Sir Ralph's before. They went in for a while and then I heard them in the back garden. So I went in to the back bedroom and looked out, and there they were, viewing the garden.'

'Why?' Barry asked.

'Well, funnily enough I got the answer sooner than I imagined I would. I mean, was he looking at the house on behalf of someone else, or was he looking at it for himself? Was Sir Johnny selling it to him, or renting it to him? Either way, what was Mr Fitch doing with Glebe House if he moved? Selling it because he needed the money and renting Sir Johnny's what he inherited from Sir Ralph, or selling it to him?' Dottie's complicated question intrigued the three of them and there was silence for a whole minute.

Dottie drew in a deep breath and followed her unanswerable question with another one. 'And who was it who came to the rectory door and knocked five minutes later?'

Vince declared himself tired of puzzling unanswerable questions. 'For heaven's sake, *tell* us.'

'Mr Fitch!'

'Go on then,' urged Greta.

'The rector opened the door asked him in and they stood talking in the hall. I couldn't 'elp but hear.'

'Just a minute,' said Vince. 'I thought you never told a single secret you learned when you were working at the rectory. Secretive you've always been, like MI5.'

'I couldn't help but hear, they were standing there in the hall, I wasn't listening at no keyhole. Apparently he's seriously thinking, Mr Fitch that is, of moving into Sir Ralph's old house, renting it because Sir Johnny's refused to sell, because Mr Fitch 'as got a buyer for Glebe House.'

'Well, I never. The money'll come in useful for him. Who's buying it then?' asked Barry.

'Fancy that,' said Greta.

'That Glebe House is so flashy I wonder who in their right mind wants to buy it? I mean, I certainly wouldn't.'

Rather sarcastically Greta said, 'You certainly couldn't, even if you wanted to. It's way out of our reach.'

Vince pondered. 'Well, who is buying it?'

Dottie made a pretence of being occupied with her vodka and momentarily ignored their questions. But then she couldn't help herself. She had to tell them, and she couldn't hold on any longer.

'It's someone who used to live in the village and had to leave, and now they're coming back.'

'Coming back? *Tell* us. We can't think.'

Complete silence greeted this declaration.

Georgie who, having no customers, was free to listen to the latest gossip made a guess, 'And they moved house in the middle of the night?'

Dottie nodded.

With one voice Vince and Greta, Barry and Georgie shouted, 'Not Merc and Ford Barclay?'

Dottie nodded.

'Well, I never,' added Georgie. 'That's a turn up for the book, and not half. I thought he'd gone to prison.'

Dottie agreed he did. 'He's out now, and it appears Mr Fitch has been in touch with them ever since they left.'

'No! Really? Doesn't sound like something old Fitch would do.'

'They must have liked the red marble then, if they're coming back.' Vince had to laugh. So did the others. The red marble in Glebe House was a standing joke in the village.

36

Greta liked the idea of them coming back. 'They are lovely people, even if he has been to prison. So generous they were, and Merc so clever with her embroidery. Remember, Dottie? I bet the embroidery group have missed her on Monday afternoons.'

'We have missed her and not half. She was brilliant at it. I'm OK for slaving at the dull repetitive background, none better, Evie says. But for sheer talent you can't beat Merc Barclay. Her embroidery is absolute bliss, and she's so good with colour. I'm glad they're coming back.'

Greta asked, 'Do you know exactly when, Dottie?'

'No. But they are.'

Greta decided she too was glad they were coming back. He was a good spender, was Ford; he liked the good things in life and was generous to a fault. Though perhaps now he'd been in prison the money wouldn't flow so freely as it had before. And anyway the village had Johnny now, and he'd enough money for all of them put together. Still, Merc and Ford would be good to have around, even if they weren't rich. Greta remembered Merc's overdone make-up and startling clothes, and Ford being overweight. Would he have slimmed down in prison, or eaten far too much to compensate for missing Merc, because they all understood how much he loved her?

'Well, Dottie, I think you've topped the gossip stakes well and truly tonight. Best bit of news we've had in months, except for the new baby at the Big House,' said Vince. 'I can't wait for 'em to arrive. Nicest chap there is, Ford, even if he has been to prison.'

Greta added, 'Sometimes I think that some people are in prison that shouldn't be, and Ford is one of those. I reckon he was innocent, but couldn't prove it.'

'Well, I for one couldn't understand why he was in. There couldn't have been a kinder, more frank sort of person than him in that prison. He never seemed to me to have secrets he shouldn't have,' ventured Dottie.

'There must have been something a bit iffy about him though, otherwise why would the law have accused him?' asked Greta.

'Buying stolen scrap metal, they said. But how could you know,' argued Barry, 'which was stolen and which wasn't, when they came and tipped it off a lorry morning, noon and night. Church lead didn't have it stamped on every yard or so, "this lead belongs to St Whatever's", did it? Or copper piping, "this came from forty-seven Withering Lane and has been stripped out by Ted and Terry while the builders nipped off for lunch".'

'Another one?' Barry asked.

'Yes, please,' they all said, and settled down to the further detailed examination of the latest village news.

It seemed as though everyone had only just heard the news about the return of their old neighbours when they appeared in the village. In truth, it was six weeks to the day since they'd been discussing it in the bar when Ford and Merc moved in. This time it was the middle of the morning when the furniture van arrived, and the two magnificent royal blue pots which Merc had placed each side of the front door when they first lived there reappeared at the front door once again, and declared to the world in general that they were *back*. Many net curtains were gently pulled aside by anyone who happened to be at home at the time. And before Ford and Merc had time to begin instructing the removal men where the furniture needed to be put, gifts were arriving, pleasantries were being exchanged and a general hubbub of greetings filled the garden of Glebe House.

Grandmama Charter-Plackett invited the pair of them to lunch. 'I expect you've been up since dawn, so shall we say noon for lunch in my cottage and then we can talk? *Really* talk.' She strode purposefully round to the store, collected one of the larger shopping baskets and began planning the meal. She had to admit Merc's fashion sense appalled her, and she found her lavish, colourful make-up intolerable, but nevertheless she liked her. In fact it was more than liking really, as she held Merc in great affection and was glad to have her back. As for Ford, he reminded her of her late husband. He was just enough of a rogue to delight her like her husband had, and he was ultra charming with it.

As the clock in her sitting room chimed noon, Grandmama propped open her front door and hurried back into the kitchen to check the vegetables. She hoped they wouldn't be late or the leeks would be mushy and the chicken pie crust sacrificial. Then she heard the brisk footstep which characterised Ford, and the pair of them were calling through the open door, 'Can we come in?'

Merc opened wide her arms in welcome and enclosed Grandmama in them. 'So lovely of you to invite us. Food is the last essential on our list, and I was beginning to wonder what we would do as both of us have arrived here with scarcely any money in our pockets, having forgotten to call at the cashpoint before we set off. Just one of those things.' She turned to look at Ford who was hanging about behind her, hesitating over whether to come in. 'Ford, for heaven's sake, we're amongst friends, come in, come in.' And so Ford followed her in.

It was only when they were in her kitchen that Grandmama noticed the change in Ford. 'Why! Ford. You've lost weight. You must have been very disciplined. How much have you lost?'

'He's lost four stone. Doesn't he look different?'

'Different, I should say he does! What a change.' Then it occurred to Grandmama. 'Was it prison, was that what made you lose it?'

Ford nodded. 'It was. The food, I couldn't eat it. Nothing wrong with it, in fact it was rather good, but I just couldn't eat it. Thanks for the invite; we didn't quite know how people would receive us.'

'How people would receive you? Why with open arms, of

course. We're all delighted. You've served your sentence and that's that, all over and done with.' Grandmama squeezed his arm to reassure him. 'You're out now. Come and try my home-made chicken pie with jacket potatoes and buttered leeks. Sit down. What would you like to drink? I've got cider, orange juice or wine. Which is it to be? Merc?'

'Orange juice for me.'

'And me. We don't drink at lunchtime, as we're trying to cut down.'

'Orange juice it is. Oh, you've no idea how glad we all are that you're back where you belong. Bring us up to date with the news, then.'

Merc helped herself to the home-made chicken pie, buttered leeks, and a jacket potato, and picked up her knife and fork. She loved every mouthful. They were home at last, and it seemed there'd be no recriminations about prison or anything else. Ah! Most important. She had to know. 'Is the embroidery class still going? Evie's, you know.'

'Of course it is! More pie, Merc? They can't wait for you to join them again; they've talked of nothing else since we first heard you were coming back. Another jacket potato? Ford, what about you? Help yourself to the leeks. I hate leftovers.' Ford was remarkably quiet and not his usual chatty self at all. Maybe he'd feel better after a few days. Moving house could be a great strain. Somehow Grandmama found that the thin, strained-looking Ford didn't suit the chap she'd known who'd been so full of himself and full of energy when he was fat. Ford, thin and withdrawn, didn't seem right. He was, well, really a very different man. Outspoken as she always was, Grandmama ventured to be up-front with her comments. 'You've nothing to fear, you know, Ford. None of us care one jot that you've been to prison. We all consider it a big mistake.'

Merc looked up and swiftly intervened when she realised Ford wasn't prepared to reply. 'He is innocent but we just couldn't prove it.' She reached across and patted Ford's nearest skinny leg. 'It's made life very difficult, you know, not being able to prove it.'

'I see.' Grandmama was stunned. She'd been very prepared for being magnanimous about his guilt and being in prison, and here they were claiming he was innocent. Well, maybe he was. Barry from the estate had said how difficult it was for Ford to know whether the metal he'd bought was stolen or genuine.

'Help yourself to more juice if you wish, and I'll clear the table. Then we'll have pudding. It's lemon passion with fresh cream.'

Merc and Grandmama chattered on about what had happened in the village since they'd done their moonlight flit but still Ford hardly said a word. He enjoyed the pudding and had two cups of coffee, and then out of the blue he said he must go. 'Got to supervise everything. You never know.' He left a big silence behind him. Eventually Merc said, 'He's taken it all very badly. But now we're back where we love to live, he'll soon pick up, I'm sure.'

'I'm sure he will. Everyone is delighted you're back and by Monday afternoon you'll know I'm speaking the truth. By the way, they're starting a new project, the embroidery group are, this very Monday. They've been very secretive about it.'

'Come back at the right time then, haven't I?'

'Yes, you certainly have.'

After Merc had gone, Grandmama cleared the kitchen, set her dishwasher going and then hurried over to the store to see her favourite daughter-in-law. Well, her only daughter-in-law, Harriet. She found her in the kitchen at the back, as she guessed she might, making things to fill up the dessert freezer at the front of the store.

'Trifle? That looks wonderful. Single portions? What a good idea. I'll take a couple when I go. I love trifle.' Grandmama established herself on the chair Harriet used when she'd been on her feet for too long, and before she could say a word Harriet asked, 'Enjoyed your company?'

'Well, really, you can do nothing in this village without everyone knowing before you've even thought of it yourself. Yes, I did. Apparently ...' The two members of staff who were assisting Harriet stopped working and came to listen. 'They claim that Ford was innocent and he went to prison when he shouldn't have. Ford has lost four stone in weight. I don't know what that is in new money; you young girls will know I expect. But whatever you calculate it in, it's a lot of weight. Very quiet he was, not himself at all. You won't recognise him. Merc's just the same though, and dying to get back to embroidering again.'

'They all say that. "A miscarriage of justice" it was, he's entirely innocent of any crime. Oh yes.'

'Harriet! How unkind. I've no reason to disbelieve them.'

'Makes everyone feel sorry for them though, and it let's them slip back into life as respectable people when they are patently not.'

'Harriet! You're working too hard, you must be. You need a holiday. Tom's good at being in charge and so you persuade Jimbo to fly you somewhere exotic. By the way, how's my Fran? She hasn't been round to my house for weeks.'

'No. We scarcely see her nowadays. Always out.'

Grandmama sat up attentively. 'Boyfriend?'

'Yes.'

'Who is it?'

'No idea.'

Grandmama shot to her feet. 'No idea? Hasn't Jimbo questioned him about his intentions?'

'We haven't met him.'

'*Not met him*! Huh! Whyever not? You should have.'

'You don't do things like that now, Katherine.'

'I suppose not. Still, Fran has always been very sensible. I expect he's thoroughly respectable.'

42

Harriet didn't answer straightaway, and when she did Grandmama was not reassured.

'We will meet him, I expect, all in good time,' Harriet said.

'I think you sound worried.'

Harriet finished the last of the individual trifles with a glacé cherry and looked up at Grandmama, who, having known her daughter-in-law for almost thirty years, recognised the underlying worry in Harriet's eyes. 'Tell her I'm feeling lonely and need some company. I want to see her,' said Grandmama.

'Will do. Can't promise she'll come though.'

'If she doesn't, I shall come to her. Right, I'm going. Bye, everybody.'

Not seen the boyfriend. It sounded very suspicious, and as though Fran was ashamed of him. And then, as though the spirit world had called Fran up for her, Fran appeared from Church Lane just as Grandmama was crossing the road from the store. She was on the old bike Jimbo kept for local deliveries. Fran slid to a halt but stayed on the saddle. 'Hello, Grandmama, fancy seeing you.'

'Seeing as I live just round the corner from the store ...'

'Well, yes. I've been busy.'

'Delivering?'

'Yes, someone down the Culworth Road is just home with a new baby and I've delivered a present from a friend. Groceries and such.'

'I see. I've just been saying to your mother that I haven't seen much of you lately and she says that could be your boyfriend's fault.' Grandmama left a significant pause, hoping for a revelatory reply.

Fran shrugged. 'You know what it's like.'

'I don't. I haven't got a boyfriend. Those days are long gone.'

'Well, yes.'

Drat the girl. Her honesty had always been the stumbling block between them. 'I have to be honest, Fran. You and I have always been frank with each other and that's why we didn't get on well when you were younger. Is he so *disreputable* that you daren't let me meet him?'

'No, he is not. Got to go. Busy, busy. Bye, Katherine.'

If there was anything more calculated to anger Grandmama, it was one of her grandchildren addressing her by her first name, and, as she was angry to begin with, she was steaming with fury as Fran cycled off. Using her first name was a sure sign that Fran was being defiant. Obviously the boyfriend wasn't suitable for her, and she didn't want the family to find out who he was. That's what came of her not getting into the independent school her sister went to. Grandmama had always known that comprehensive school in Culworth was totally lacking in moral fibre. Well, if Fran thought she was going to keep it a secret, she was very wrong. Her Grandmama had time on her hands, even if her parents hadn't. She'd find out.

Chapter 5

An impromptu party took place that very night in the saloon bar at the Royal Oak. It had been in Georgie's mind but it hadn't really materialised until the habitués of the old table with the settle down one side had rung up one after the other, and suggested it.

'Shall we, Dicky?'

'Why not? Best be prepared, you know what they're like round here. Any excuse for a party.'

The village telephone network went into action and the information was passed round the houses, from right down the Culworth Road, along Church Lane, past Glebe House, down Shepherd's Hill, as far as Dottie Foskett's and Stocks Row, and finally down Royal Oak Road, until everyone knew about the party to welcome Merc and Ford back to the village. Grandmama was put in charge of making sure that Ford and Merc, no matter how tired they were after moving, had to be inveigled into the bar by nine o'clock. Prompt.

Grandmama was only too willing to undertake the mission, and was dressed and knocking on the door of Glebe House by eight-thirty. 'I've come to insist that you let me buy you a drink tonight in your favourite watering hole. And I won't take no for an answer.'

'We're not tidy at all, but come in.' Ford ushered her in and shut the door behind her. 'I don't think Merc is able to come out; she's absolutely knackered.'

'So would I be if I'd just moved. It took me weeks to get

over it when I moved into my little cottage. But please, will you come? Just one drink and then I'll let you go.' She knew full well she was lying but she was determined they would go to the pub that night, even if they never went again.

Merc's kind heart couldn't resist Grandmama's pleading and she agreed to go. 'I shall fall asleep after one drink, I'm sure, but yes, we'll come.'

Grandmama rubbed her hands together with glee. 'I'm so glad. You're a pair of angels.'

'Give me a chance to tidy up and get changed. These old trousers won't do at all.'

'No need to get all done up. It's always quiet on a Monday night. In fact there may only be us there.'

'Sit down, Mrs Charter-Plackett, I'll be as quick as I can. Ford, you don't need to change, you look absolutely fine.'

'Please, Merc, call me Katherine. We're old friends you know.'

'Katherine it is then.'

Being asked to call her Katherine meant to Merc that she had been included once more in the intimate echelons of village life, and she felt greatly encouraged by Grandmama's kind gesture. So they had done right to come back here where they'd first felt so welcomed and were obviously so well liked still. Thank heavens it had all worked out right and at last they could settle down to living their normal lives again just when she thought they never would. Like Katherine had said, it was Monday night and it would be quiet, and so they could edge their way in to village life quietly.

Quietly? Someone, namely Dottie, was on look-out and the moment she spotted the three of them coming round Stocks Row she called out, 'Hush everyone!' Every single seat was taken apart from three at the table with the long settle down one side, because they were being reserved especially for Merc and

Ford. Everybody sat motionless and silent, waiting. Suddenly the outer door shot open and before they knew it Grandmama had pushed open the inner door and ushered in Ford and Merc.

A great cheer went up and everyone got to their feet, shouting, 'Welcome back!' in one great thrusting voice.

Merc burst into tears of joy, and Ford, after a moment of emotion, called out, 'Nobody here on Monday nights! That was a whacking great fib you told us, Katherine. Good evening, everyone.' He bowed low in appreciation in every direction and surreptitiously wiped away a tear.

'Now you've to sit here, look, on the best table in the bar and your first drinks are, according to Dicky, on the house. What would you like?' Grandmama was delighted that her scheme turned out so well.

'A gin and tonic for me, please, and I know Ford would like a half pint of Dicky's home brew. He's been longing for that for months. Haven't you, love?'

'Indeed I have. Lovely to be back, and thank you all for making us so welcome.'

Ford sat down no longer needing to squeeze himself in as he used to do. They were all surprised at how thin he was and how quiet. Maybe he was exhausted after moving, or perhaps embarrassed about being an ex-prisoner. But whatever was the reason, he certainly had lost that big personality they'd all grown accustomed to, and loved.

The people who'd come to welcome Merc and Ford back to Turnham Malpas were queuing to buy them their next drink, or eagerly hovering around to bring them up to date with the latest village news.

When she could get a word in, Grandmama wanted them to know about the changed circumstances up at the Big House. 'Sir Johnny has pots of money, believe me, and the alterations he's doing on the estate, well, they are costing a fortune. But it doesn't bother him. He's rolling in money.'

'He's married you say?' inquired Merc.

'Oh, yes. He married Alice. You remember, the music teacher, and they've just got their second son yesterday. We don't know his name yet.'

'What about Craddock Fitch? We haven't seen him,' asked Ford.

'Well, he's moved into Sir Ralph's old house. Renting it from Sir Johnny. But he's gone up north doing some research they say. But what on earth he has to research I don't know. He'll be back in a day or two.'

Their impromptu welcome-back party was in full swing but not everyone there was as enthusiastic as Grandmama.

One of the less keen was Harriet. Jimbo, thinking of future trade that Ford and Merc might bring to the store, had insisted on her attending the party. But she only decided to join him because otherwise she'd be in the house alone as Fran was out with her mysterious boyfriend.

'It's all very well is this, Jimbo. But I don't normally socialise with ex-prisoners.'

'Hush. For heaven sakes! They'll hear you.'

'And if they do, I've a right to say how I feel. I didn't lie, did I? It's the truth. He is a liar.' Harriet glared at Jimbo and raised her eyebrows. 'Isn't he? Go on, admit it.'

'Yes. But now's not the time.'

'Be honest, you're only welcoming them because it's good for trade. I haven't been married to you all these years without knowing what makes you tick.'

'Well, for now, *hush*, and try to look as pleased as everyone else is.'

'Are they really? I wonder. I can't say Ford looks particularly pleased. In fact he looks as though he'd rather be at home with the door locked against the chance of unexpected visitors.'

'You're talking nonsense, Harriet; he's always a very sociable

48

kind of man. Mother's thrilled to bits they're back, and she's a good judge of character. She always has been.'

'I'm not talking nonsense. Anyway I'm going home as it's late and I've a lot to do tomorrow. I need an early start.'

'It'll look very obvious if you go now. There's another hour to closing yet.'

'Sorry, Jimbo, I'm off.' Harriet got to her feet and called across to Merc and Ford that she was leaving. Merc tried to persuade her not to go, but Harriet made the excuse of a bad headache coming on and disappeared, leaving Jimbo feeling an inconsiderate fool of a husband. Maybe she was right. After all Ford had been found guilty of condoning theft. He'd made a lot of money at it too, no doubt, if he could afford to buy Glebe House. But Jimbo hadn't finished his glass of home brew yet and he decided he'd leave when his glass was empty.

Harriet stood for a moment as she enjoyed the sight of the village in the light of a brilliant moon. The thatched roofs and the gleaming white walls of the cottages around the green appeared more spectacular than usual, and she savoured the privileges that living in such a beautiful rural place afforded her. She spotted Fran's bright yellow mini creeping gently round the green and felt relieved her daughter was home safely.

Harriet raised her hand thinking Fran might have noticed her standing there in front of the pub, but her wave wasn't returned. Behind Fran came a bright red sports car which Harriet instantly recognised. The driver paused to give Fran a wave and then pulled away leaving Fran to park. No wonder Fran refused to tell them whom she was seeing. He was much too old and much too sophisticated for a girl of Fran's age and experience. Harriet couldn't think what to do. If she went home right now Fran would know she'd seen his red sports car and there'd be no avoiding a confrontation. And Harriet couldn't face this. In fact, she decided, she'd pretend she'd seen nothing at all, she wouldn't even tell Jimbo. She'd ignore it. Blot it out of her mind, and then one day when the time felt to be right, Harriet would let Fran know she knew and give her some motherly advice. Of all people. Chris Templeton!

Chapter 6

Finding no one at home Fran went straight to bed in order to avoid both her parents. Being out, they wouldn't know what time she'd come home, and so as long as she kept her eyes shut if Mum came in to say goodnight she'd be all right. Fran wondered where they'd gone. Usually they shared all their news with her but tonight they hadn't. Maybe they'd had an unexpected invitation somewhere. Well, she certainly wasn't going to worry herself about them, they were grown-ups after all. Instead she'd lie warm and snug in her very own bedroom, and *think*.

About Chris. Jimbo and Harriet would be certain to disapprove. He was too old for her, wildly sophisticated, with a much broader knowledge of the world than she had. All she'd done was go to school, have a few holidays abroad in well-civilised places in Europe, and work in a village shop (which by his Brazilian hotel standards was minute and pathetically local). And what had he done? Been to the Arctic on a school expedition, nearly been killed in an avalanche on some mountains somewhere in South America, canoed down the Amazon at a back pack and tent level. He always had loads of money available, and had actually lived with two girls, although not at the same time of course, before he'd come to England.

Fran Charter-Plackett had been a virgin until she'd met Chris and by comparison she was totally inexperienced in all aspects of life. Why he fancied her she didn't know. But fancy her he did and she loved every moment of the time they spent together. He could arouse her with one gentle touch of his beautiful hands on her bare arm, and when— Fran heard the front door slam.

Drat it. That sounded like Dad coming home. Just in case her dad could read her mind she decided to shut out all thoughts of Chris, which was stupid. But the thought of her dad, and worse, her mum knowing who she was seeing ... No, it wasn't Dad, it was Mum. Definitely Mum, because she was coming upstairs. Fran's bedroom door opened and Mum said, 'Hello, darling. Been home long?'

Fran pretended to stir slightly.

'Sorry, we'll talk tomorrow.'

Fran waited till the door had closed again and then she sighed. She had all this brave talk about being an adult and being able to come and go as she pleased, when all the time she couldn't face up to her parents. At almost twenty-one. If she was at university she'd be doing exactly as she liked. With one bound Fran was out of bed, pulling on her dressing gown and heading downstairs.

'I thought you were asleep. Cup of tea?'

'Please. Where's Dad?'

'Finishing his home brew in the pub. They've had an impromptu welcome party for the Barclays, and Dad insisted we went.'

'Right. I've been up at the Big House.'

'You have?' Harriet turned away so she wouldn't betray what she'd just found out.

'Seeing Chris.'

'Ah. Right. Nice man.'

'You approve?'

'It's not for me to approve or disapprove.'

'Come on, Mum, tell the truth.'

Harriet placed a mug of tea on the worktop and nodded to Fran that this was for her. 'Yours.'

'What are you having?'

'A whisky.'

52

'You never drink whisky.'

'I can do as I like.' Harriet took a sip of her medicinal whisky.

'Like I do, you mean?'

'Apparently.' Harriet turned to face her. 'Let's stop fooling around. He's too old, too smart, and he'll soon tire of you.'

'Mum!'

'I'm right and you know I am, and that's why you didn't want to tell us who you were seeing.'

'He isn't. He's lovely. He's kind and considerate and amusing, and interesting, with an unusual slant on life. He finds the English absolutely hysterical.'

'Hysterical? That's not very good manners on his part.'

'You're being stuffy, just like he says we all are. It's time we all relaxed, he says, and see the funny side of ourselves. And he thinks that class distinction, no matter how much we deny it, is still present in every level of English society and that it's hilarious. And come to that, I think so too.'

The front door slammed shut and Fran knew her dad was about to find out the most precious, most important secret she had ever kept from him. Damn it, she wasn't ready for it.

Jimbo strolled into the kitchen, looked from one to the other of them both and asked, 'What's the matter?'

Fran decided to go for it. 'I've just been telling Mum.'

'What?'

'Who it is I'm going out with.'

Very casually Jimbo replied, 'Oh. That. I've known for a while.'

'You have?' Harriet was shocked. 'You never told me.'

'She's old enough to know what she's doing.'

Fran, who'd been expecting him to explode into one of his notorious tempers, was at a loss to know what to say. 'You don't mind then?'

'He is the most unsuitable man for you to be consorting with that I could ever have imagined you would find time for. But you're a young woman now and it's time for you to make your own choices.'

'Thanks, Dad, for treating me as a grown-up for the first time ever. Thanks, I appreciate that. So that's all right then. If Dad's all right about him, you don't mind, Mum, do you?'

Harriet, staggered by Jimbo's calm and the fact he'd known for weeks, answered, 'Apparently not. I'm off to bed. See you in the morning.' In fact Harriet was completely nonplussed. She and Jimbo never had secrets from each other. It was one of their golden rules and yet here he was, calm as you please, when Fran was cavorting with a man so unsuitable that if Harriet had made a list of unsuitable characteristics for a boyfriend of Fran's, he'd match up to every unsuitability. Was there such a word? If there wasn't, Harriet Charter-Plackett had just invented it.

Harriet brushed her teeth with such vigour that any lingering bacteria would have fled in haste halfway through the process. She flung her clothes on the carpet, careless of where they fell, and leapt into bed still infuriated by Jimbo's attitude. Not for one moment did she imagine that a man of Chris's temperament had not wanted to go the whole way with Fran. Well, at least she knew Fran was bang up to date on contraception and so hopefully no worries on that score.

Harriet caught the sound of Jimbo's footsteps on the wooden floor of the hall as he crossed from the kitchen to the stairs, and she hurriedly pulled the duvet right the way up to her chin and pretended to be asleep. On the other hand she couldn't have fallen asleep in such a short space of time, so that trick wouldn't work.

When he came in from the bathroom a few minutes later, she said, 'Shut the door, Jimbo, please. Now tell me how long you've known about Chris and Fran.'

'I found out quite by chance really. Remember that time about six weeks ago when I went to that committee meeting of the Rotary Club in the pub the other side of Culworth, when they wanted to ask me about having a big dinner party and entertainment afterwards at the Old Barn? Well, I saw Fran and Chris coming out of there. I was so surprised I hid in the gents until they had time to drive away.'

'Why didn't you tell me?'

'Because.' Jimbo got into bed.

'I said, why didn't you tell me?'

'Because I knew what your reaction would be, and while I was hiding in the gents I decided the more we opposed him the more her resolve would harden and that she'd never listen to common sense. But it's gone on far longer than I'd anticipated, I imagined it would be short lived. You have to admit he is a very attractive man.'

Harriet studied his last sentence and admitted that she found Chris attractive too. 'He is, but she isn't his type. Too young, too inexperienced, she's a child by comparison.'

Jimbo groaned. 'I know that, but if we oppose her seeing him ...'

They lay in bed side by side, each with their own thoughts. Finally it was Jimbo who broke the silence. 'You'll have to have a word with her.'

'Me?'

'Yes. It's a mother and daughter job, is this.'

'Oh, is it? And what is her father going to do about it?

'Best if I stay out of it, and then if things get really serious I'll have to come in with the heavy guns. With him. Man to man.'

Despite her anger over the situation Harriet had to laugh. 'Heavy guns! Chris Templeton would make mincemeat of you.'

'Thanks for the vote of confidence.' Jimbo paused for a moment and then said, 'I can't think what he sees in her.'

'The only thing I am grateful about is that Fran knows about contraception. I saw to that. And the school did too of course.'

'That's not quite the point though, is it? Him having his way with my daughter. Sounds old-fashioned, but I don't like the man any better for it. Coming in here and pretending he barely knows who she is.'

Harriet remembered the day Alice's baby was born and the flowers Chris bought, and the way he kissed Fran for making them into a respectable bouquet. 'Kissing her as though he scarcely recognised her when all the time ... That was deceitful and not half. He's not nearly so pleasing as Johnny.'

'You're in the mood for crossing people off your visiting list, aren't you? That's three just tonight.' Jimbo reached over to turn off the bedside light. 'Merc and Ford Barclay, and now Chris.'

'He's taking advantage of her, that's what I don't like. I mean, what does a sophisticated wealthy man like him want with her? Only one thing. I'm going to tell her right now, in fact. I'll go wake her and tell her. She needs to know.'

Harriet flung the duvet off, dropped her feet to the floor and was about to set off for Fran's bedroom when Jimbo caught hold of her wrist. 'Get back in bed and let's have another think.'

'I'm going. Let go.'

'Please, Harriet, not now. Tomorrow. It's her day off, do it then, not when you're already furious. Talk to her when you're calm. You could do more harm then good right now. Please.'

Some of the anger went out of Harriet at that moment. 'Of course tomorrow would be more sensible.' She got back into bed saying, 'I'll never sleep a wink all night. We've a right to be angry, haven't we? Oh, Jimbo!'

'Don't worry, darling. She has to learn about life somehow, hasn't she?'

'But with him? You see, he knows at bottom it isn't right. Otherwise he'd be more open with us about his feelings, wouldn't he?'

Fran always stayed in bed at least until eleven or even twelve o'clock if her day off was during the week, and this was no exception. She lingered in the bath instead of showering and then she rolled downstairs just in time for her lunch.

'Mum? Oh, there you are.'

'Thought we'd have lunch here in the kitchen, because I need to work this afternoon and I've no time for sitting around. Big bowl of extra-nourishing home-made soup, with rolls, then cheese and biscuits and some lovely fresh fruit, all neatly chopped into a salad. Sound OK? Cream?'

'Lovely. Thanks.'

Harriet didn't mention their conversation last night, hoping Fran would do so first. And she did. 'You know, Mum, Chris is lovely, really lovely. I wish you knew him better.'

'Invite him here this weekend. Why not? There's no one else here. The others aren't coming home.'

'Are you sure?'

'Yes. Sunday. For lunch. Is he vegetarian or anything?'

'No, he's easy to please.'

'Is he?'

This loaded question halted Fran in her tracks. 'Don't pry.'

'Can I say something, and then I won't utter another word about him until he arrives on Sunday.'

Fran nodded.

'To begin with, he's too old for you, too adult, too experienced in the ways of the world, too smooth. But he is *gloriously* good-looking, I can't deny that, no one can.'

'He is, isn't he? A perfectly splendid specimen of a man.'

'But, Fran—'

'I can't help myself, Mum. He's so interesting, such fun. Please like him for my sake. Please, Mum.' Fran looked her mother straight in the eye, begging her approval; and Harriet found she couldn't deny her daughter the pleasure of knowing her mother approved.

'I'll reserve my judgement until Sunday. If he remembers his manners and knows how to eat peas nicely I might begin to like him.' Harriet grinned to ensure Fran knew she was joking.

Fran smiled her appreciation. 'He's done such fantastic things. He nearly got killed in an avalanche, you know.'

Harriet, ashamed of herself because at that moment she heartily wished he had, smiled. 'He's lived dangerously then.'

'That's what makes him so exciting. I wish I'd done dangerous things, I've done nothing at all really. Absolutely nothing.'

'You could have gone to university, done some dangerous things there.'

'Yes, but I'm doing what I want to do at the store.'

'In that case you are very lucky. Loads of people your age haven't even got a job, never mind one they like.'

'You'll like him, I know you will.' Fran stared into the far distance, lost in her thoughts, and briefly Harriet envied her.

Then Fran said, 'He's just *delicious*.'

Harriet knew from the way she said '*delicious*' that Fran had been far closer to Chris than she would have wished, and Harriet hated him for this. He wasn't such a fool as not to know how inexperienced Fran was. She'd kill him with one of her own kitchen knives. She would. Ten years in prison would be a small price to pay. With her qualifications she'd inveigle herself into the prison kitchens, transform the food, write a recipe book and be thanked for her sterling work in the interests of the prison population. In fact they might even find there was a sudden desire on the part of the prison population to turn over a new leaf, entirely due to the improvement in their diet, and they'd all strive to become first-class citizens. She glanced at Fran and was tempted to let her in on the secret just for a joke, but decided no. Not right now.

'Mum!'

'Mmm?'

'Chris isn't keen on shellfish, or curries. Just thought I'd tell you.'

'Right. Thanks. More fruit salad?'

'No, thanks. I won't be in tonight, by the way.'

'OK. Going somewhere nice?' But Harriet didn't get an answer.

Sunday came round all too quickly, for both Harriet and Jimbo, and also for Fran who, although delighted that Chris was coming to lunch, had unexpectedly now got serious misgivings about it. She was sure it wasn't, but could it possibly be a ploy on her mother's part to let Chris know how much her parents disliked the idea of the two of them together? But he was wonderful, absolutely wonderful, and the idea of going to Brazil to live with him was monstrously tempting to someone like herself who'd led such a sheltered life. Chris had never said those exact words, but how else could they continue their relationship if she didn't go back with him to Brazil? Chris had mentioned several times about 'when he went back to Brazil', as though getting her to warm to the idea. He did have a flat of his own, though he didn't seem to spend much time in it because he was always talking about the meals he ate at his mother's, and how his laundry was done by a maid who worked for his mother.

At twelve exactly the doorbell rang, the door opened and a voice called out, 'It's me, Chris Templeton, shall I come in?'

He looked completely and absolutely perfect. It was a winter's day, but even so, the sun was shining brightly on his fair hair. He wore a kind of tweed suit that looked superb, a far cry from the ones Sir Ronald Bissett wore for Sheila's sake. It was both very smart and casual at the same time, and Harriet and Jimbo knew for certain it would have cost the earth. Harriet liked his strong grip as they shook hands. Jimbo shook his hand too, but Fran got a discreet kiss on her cheek nearer her ear than her mouth, as though Chris was trying to impress on them that Fran and he were not intimate, although Harriet knew differently.

Jimbo, being the suave host that he was, wandered off with Chris to the drinks cabinet so he could choose what he would prefer. 'Take your pick. Fran has gin with whatever, and so does Harriet.'

'I'll have whisky, neat, if that's all right with you.'

Jimbo chose the same purposely. 'Glenfiddich?'

'Yes, please.' Chris took an appreciative look around the dining room. 'Lovely house you've got here. I'm slowly getting used to Johnny's old house. We've nothing like it back in Brazil as you can imagine. The architecture is exactly right for Johnny though. Wonderful solid old woodwork. Frankly I'm more keen on the modern stuff, but there we are. It wasn't me who inherited, so it's all worked out for the best. I'm amazed that though he *owns* the house he can't just tear it all out and modernise it. Still I suppose if you don't have rules about what you can and can't do with an ancient house, you wouldn't have any old houses left. But would that be a bad thing, I ask?'

'We like our old houses, and we don't want to lose them.'

'But we have to advance into the twenty-first century, and keeping the old perhaps means we allow ourselves to be held back.'

'What's wrong with being held back? The old houses are perfectly splendid and very comfortable to live in. The house Alice used to live in has an inglenook fireplace in the kitchen, and everyone naturally gravitates there.'

'Like the one Johnny has in the hall?'

'Exactly, but not as big of course. They have an inglenook fireplace in the pub; have you seen that?'

'No, I can't say I've noticed.' Chris offered to carry the tray. 'I've a good steady hand, even when I'm drunk.'

'We'll take the drinks into the sitting room, OK?' Chris followed Jimbo, carefully balancing the tray so as not to spill anything on Harriet's immaculate cream carpet.

'How's business? Given the current downturn?' Chris asked. In the absence of Harriet and Fran they chatted about the store and the old barn, and the variety of events he held there until Harriet called out, 'Lunch is ready.'

Harriet's food immediately drew flattering remarks from their guest. Even Harriet felt it was nice of him to make such pleasing comments when she'd slaved in the kitchen to make it all as appealing as possible. But after a while his compliments ceased to ring true, and Harriet began to wish he would stop. His brother Johnny, who during his bachelor days had been a frequent guest at their table, genuinely complimented her food beautifully, but he didn't overdo it. Where as Chris bordered on gushing with his compliments, as though she was the little woman who, for once rather surprisingly, had excelled herself.

Fran was very quiet and Chris almost entirely ignored her. After lunch Chris suggested a walk, an idea that Jimbo and Harriet declined, thinking Fran would enjoy a walk with him and that she certainly wouldn't want both her parents with them. So the two of them went off in Chris's sports car to a destination known only to themselves.

Jimbo gave Harriet some very useful help in the kitchen, and almost before they knew it they were seated in their favourite chairs, free to have a post-mortem of the lunch over coffee.

'Well, I'm sorry, I may be biased, but he is a pain in the proverbial. Honestly, the way he complimented me about the food, it was insulting.'

'I don't think he meant it to be. It's just his way.'

'Do you like him?'

'Not especially, no. Condescending, you know, about our business.'

'Jimbo, it is small compared to theirs. Let's be honest.'

'It is, but we don't half make a lot of money considering our size. You know, as a father, I don't see what Fran sees in him.'

'Neither do I. She's dazzled by his good looks and his lifestyle. He is very attractive to a young woman like Fran.'

'Can't see it, but there you are. I'm not happy about it. He comes across as less than truthful.'

'Can't you have a word with Johnny? He'll feel the same as us, I'm sure.'

'I might.'

'Not might. You must, Jimbo. For Fran's sake. Before we know where we are she'll be off to Brazil with him.'

'All right, all right. I will then. But what the heck I'll say I do not know.'

Chapter 7

As it turned out, it was Harriet who had the first opportunity to speak to Johnny, because he came into the store early one morning when Harriet was standing in for Jimbo who had a heavy cold and could barely speak.

'Harriet. Good morning. I want a bottle of that stuff you give to babies when they have colic. Do you sell it? I can't remember what we used to give to Charles.' Johnny snapped his fingers as an aide memoire, but the name wouldn't come to mind.

'Hi, Johnny. How's the little one? Apart from the colic, of course. Have you and Alice settled on a name yet?'

'Yes, finally. He's going to be a Ralph, like his grandfather. And funnily enough, I think it suits him.'

'A lovely name. Very traditional.' Harriet presented him with a bottle from the baby food shelves. Johnny sighed with relief. 'That's it, that's the one! Clever girl. We've been up since half-past three with Master Ralph. And of course when it's time for us to be up and Charles too, Ralph falls fast asleep with exhaustion.'

'Par for the course, Johnny. Here you are.'

Johnny handed over a five pound note, and obviously wanted to chat some more. 'There's something else I'll remember in a moment. How are things with you?'

'We had your brother to lunch on Sunday.'

'Of course you did. Did he behave himself?'

'If you mean did he know how to use a knife properly, yes he did. But Jimbo's a bit concerned.'

'He is?'

'Yes. Chris is a lot older than Fran, you know, and we'd rather ...'

'It's the longest he's gone out with the same girl that I can remember. I think he must be getting serious.'

'Ah, right. Does he talk about her much?'

'No, which is unusual.'

'She's very inexperienced with older men.'

'How old is she then?'

'Twenty-one next month.'

'I thought she was much older than that.'

'You wouldn't fancy having a word with Chris, would you?'

'You mean it, don't you? Like a big brother kind of word?'

'Yes.'

'I will, but he won't like it. Bye.' Johnny paused at the door and looked back. 'She seems much older than twenty,' he said again.

'Well, believe me, she isn't.'

'Better get back, just in case.'

Harriet remembered something else Johnny needed prompting about. 'Alice. She needs some domestic help, Johnny. It's too much, with two babies so close in age. Dottie Foskett who helps me one afternoon a week is very good. She was trained to clean by nuns, need I say more? And I know one of her clients died a couple of weeks ago so she has the time to fit you in.'

'You could be right. I'll talk to Alice about someone. After a night like we've had, she could be more amenable to the idea. Bye, Harriet, I'll keep in mind what you said about Chris. I will have a word, you know. Bye. Thanks for this.' Johnny held up the colic medicine as he held open the door for Willie coming in for his morning paper.

Johnny joined Chris at the breakfast table and his opening gambit was, 'I've been talking to an anxious relative.'

Assuming Johnny meant someone back in Brazil, Chris asked, 'Who was that?'

'Harriet at the store.'

'Ah!'

'They are concerned about the age gap, and the fact that Fran is too young and too immature for a man of your experience.'

'Huh!' Chris heaped marmalade on his toast and bit off a large square.

'Well? Should they be worried?'

Chris gave a wicked grin. 'I suppose so, but we're very careful.'

'So I should hope. In a village of this size ...'

'Don't give me the familiar sermon, please.'

'I will if I want. Your task was to find a chain of hotels in Britain which would fit in very nicely with what we have already, and which obviously, once purchased, I could supervise from here. But what happens? You find a new woman – well, girl – and you're here all week instead of working to expand our business. I'm sorry, Chris, it won't do.'

'You can't have it both ways, Johnny. Lord of the Manor and directing me about what I should and shouldn't do. Having inherited this place, and more or less given up any responsibility for our hotel business, you can stuff it. I shall do as I like. Nicholas is doing a great job in charge back home. Fran is a nice girl, good fun to be with and very ... Well, anyway, we're fine, and if we want to see each other we will. She's certainly very willing.' Chris drank the last drop of his coffee, placed the cup back on its saucer and leapt to his feet. 'Her parents fell for the Templeton charm on Sunday. They couldn't have been more delighted with me, and they're obviously more than pleased for us to be seeing each other. After all I am a good catch from their point of view, as their business is certainly very small fry compared to ours.'

'From Harriet's attitude, I gather they are somewhat concerned.'

'For God's sake, shut up. I'll do as I like. The big-brother stance can get very tedious, especially when you concern yourself with my love life. See you, I'll be in tonight for my fodder. About seven as usual. Hope you have a better day with Master Ralph; he certainly ruined my night's sleep.'

Chris drove straight from the Big House to the village store and burst in through the door, sending Jimbo's bell furiously hopping about on its bracket. He reached a hand up to stop the aggravating ringing and found himself facing someone behind the counter he didn't recognise. 'I'm Chris Templeton, brother to Johnny? Is Fran around?'

'No, it's her day off.'

'Has she gone out then?'

'I said she's not working,' the girl said frostily. 'I don't know what she's actually doing. You'll have to go round to her house to find out – if she's in, that is.'

'OK. OK. I'll do that.' Chris could feel her dislike enveloping him. What on earth had he done to deserve it? 'Not met you before. I'm Chris. And you are?' He held out a welcoming hand.

'I'm Bel Tutt. B-E-L. Short for Isobel. I work here part time. Nice to meet you.' She shook hands willingly but Chris found her grip was like being clamped in a vice from which one was very unlikely to escape. Before she released his hand Bel looked Chris directly in the eye, and he knew he had an enemy.

'Nice to meet you, Bel. I'll go round to the house and find her. Good morning.'

So, Fran thought no one knew, but that Bel obviously did. She knew and she didn't like him for it. Unused to being so obviously disliked, Chris had to shake himself to throw off the animosity. If she knew, how many more people knew? Not that he cared. As he walked along Stocks Row to Fran's house Chris determined he wasn't going to allow a bunch of useless villagers to influence his actions. No. He was above that kind of thing.

When he got to Fran's house he rang the bell and in a moment the door was flung open. There she stood, looking so beautiful she took his breath away. Even though her shining dark hair had not been brushed, and she was wearing old jeans and a woolly jumper that had seen better days, her eyes were filled with such love. And it was all for him. They stood looking at each other for a long minute.

It was Fran who pulled herself together first. 'Come in,' she said in an oddly squeaky voice. Before today, except for lunch last Sunday, they'd never met like this before, in broad daylight for the world to see. And Fran wasn't sure it was a sensible thing to be doing.

'I thought you'd be working. I met this old battle-axe in the store: tall, uncompromising, with a handshake made of steel.'

'That'll be Bel. She's lovely.'

'She is not. Anyone at home?' When Fran shook her head he added, 'Kiss?'

Chris kicked the front door shut behind him with his foot and, putting his arms around Fran, he kissed her and soon they were both overwhelmed with passion and couldn't stop. Fran, at first trying to escape him, as the sensible part of her brain told her this wasn't right, backed off. But Chris followed her and she became trapped between him and the wall and she gave in to him. A minute or two later she was saying, 'Not here. Not here.' His mouth on her neck, he muttered, 'Upstairs then.' And together they climbed the stairs. Fran guided him into her bedroom, still held tightly, still being smothered with kisses. Chris shut the door behind them with his foot.

Jimbo's grandfather clock clanged ten o'clock and jerked the pair of them into consciousness with a short sharp shock.

Fran, back in the common-sense world she usually lived in, said, 'You've got to go. Now. Right now.'

'OK, OK.' Chris paused to kiss her again.

'No, I mean it. Right now. Please.'

'Tell me, was it the best ever? It was for me.'

It was Fran's turn to pause. 'Yes. But ...'

'There are no buts where love is concerned. It was the best ever, like I said. I'm going.' Chris began dressing himself. 'Tonight. Usual place? Shall we eat or not?'

'Not.'

'I'm gone. Seven-thirty it is then. You're so beautiful, Fran. So beautiful.' Before he left the bedroom Chris gently cupped her chin with his hand and kissed her lips. She lay there listening to his footsteps fading away down the hall, and she heard the slam of the front door. He hadn't parked outside the house, had he? She leapt to her feet and rushed into the front bedroom grateful to see him, still charged with energy, marching along Stocks Row towards the store. He looked fabulous, so very much in possession of himself. She was so lucky. Then guilt took its place. It wasn't as if they hadn't done it before. But this time ... in her bedroom.

The one overwhelming thought was relief that neither of her parents had unexpectedly come home while he was there. The thing was that she was now two people. The one who struck out to be an adult and do as she wanted, go where she wanted with whom she wanted, and her old non-rebellious self. What had just happened felt like such an invasion of her existence that she decided she must have another shower. A complete fresh start to the day. Every item of clothing clean on, and she'd spray with the air freshener where he'd been because Mum was always quick to know if strangers had been in the house. Harriet claimed they left an alien smell about, which wasn't the Charter-Plackett family smell at all. Five minutes after Fran had sprayed everywhere as her final gesture towards family harmony, she heard her Grandmama's voice in the hall.

'Fran? Where are you, darling?'

'In the kitchen, putting the coffee on.'

'Excellent. That's what I've come for. How did you know I was coming?'

'I didn't; it's my normal time.'

'I must say the house smells lovely and fresh. You are a good girl.' Grandmama embraced her in a huge bear hug. 'When your mum and dad work so hard, they need someone like you to help.'

Fran sneaked a quick glance at her Grandmama. Surely she didn't know, did she? 'Sit down here in the kitchen, I don't want to mess up the sitting room. You don't mind, do you? There's the sugar. Biscuit?'

'Yes, please. Two please. Biscuits that is. Thank you, dear.' Grandmama bit into her biscuit with her usual vigour, crunched it for a moment, and then asked, 'What are you doing tonight? I thought perhaps you might come and sit with me an hour. It seems quite a while since you had a spare evening.'

'Not tonight, sorry.'

'I see. Boyfriend, is it?'

'You could say that.'

'Well, either it is or it isn't.'

'Yes, it is.'

'Am I permitted to know who? Or is it whom? I never can get that straight in my mind.'

In an attempt to legitimise him, Fran replied, 'He came for lunch on Sunday.'

'I wish I'd been there to meet him but I'd been invited to Merc and Ford's for lunch, and we had quite a party. So, tell me who it is?'

Fran didn't answer for a moment and then she said, 'Chris Templeton. But don't tell anyone; it's still a secret.'

'He seems a charming young man to me. Bit old, isn't he though? What is he thirty, thirty-five?'

'Thirty-two actually.'

'A bit old for you, darling, surely? A whole twelve years older.'

69

'I shall soon be twenty-one. It doesn't *feel* as if he's a lot older.'

'Well. I'm not having you charging off to Brazil with him. It simply won't do. Of all places.'

'He isn't poor, you know. They have lashings of money, so if I went I'd be well looked after, believe me.'

'So it has crossed your mind, then, the possibility?' Grandmama looked horrified.

'Well, it does, doesn't it, when you're in love.'

'My dear, it would break my Jimbo's heart. You are his favourite, his absolute favourite.'

'He's got the others: Finlay, Fergus, Flick.'

'But they're not *you*. Think of Harriet, too. You're her youngest little chick, still at home, helping her and your dad to run the business, and I'm proud of you, so proud you've no idea.' Grandmama picked up her mug as though to hide her feelings, and Fran realised how distressed she was as it was rare for Grandmama to display deep emotion. Anger and disbelief, yes, but not love. Fran took hold of Grandmama's hand, saying, 'I know they love me, and I know you love me too. But Chris, well, he loves me as well. He says so.'

'He's serious, is he then?'

'Oh yes. Very serious.'

'I see. How long have you been going out?'

'Five weeks and three days.'

Grandmama was amused by the exactness of her statement. 'Not long. Don't make any promises yet, you need longer than five weeks. That's what life has taught me: don't rush things as that's when mistakes are made. Look at me with your granddad. Met and married inside four months. With hindsight if I met him now it would probably be four years not four months before I married. Anyway, I'm going now. Thanks for the coffee. And if he lets you down tonight come round and I'll have a box of tissues handy.' Grandmama patted Fran's shoulder, kissed her on each cheek, and rushed out to catch the bus into Culworth.

As if. Chris wouldn't let her down. If he said they were meeting up, he came for her on the dot. Typical Grandmama, feet well planted on the ground and trusting no one. But she and Chris were different. They were in love, and it was beautiful. Fran had had crushes on boys at school and although at the time she'd thought it was serious, she knew now, with Chris, how unreal the crushes had been, and how very real it was with him. Fran thought about what had happened this morning; he must love her for that to happen when she most certainly was not looking her best. If he could love her at her worst, well then.

The phone rang and Fran hoped it was Chris, but it was Harriet. 'Frances, Mum here. Can you come? We'll give you a day off later in the week, but Bel was terribly sick ten minutes ago and looks dreadful, and so could you take her home and then come and help out? Dad still isn't back.'

'OK. I've nothing else on, I don't mind. Be there in five minutes.'

Hurriedly Fran slapped some make-up on, checked herself in the hall mirror, locked up the house and whizzed round to the store in her Mini. When Fran saw Bel she couldn't believe how awful she looked. Bel could barely stand, and she was the colour of sludge.

'Handbag, Bel? Where is it?'

'In the mail-order office with Greta.'

'I'll get it. Coat?'

'Same place.'

Safely tucked into the front passenger seat of Fran's car, Bel opened the window. 'I need some fresh air; I hope you don't mind,' she said. But before they'd got round the green Bel flung the car door open and was violently sick out on the road as Fran tried to pull up in double-quick time.

'Oh, Bel! Is it something you've eaten? That was terrible.

You must feel awful. Should we go straight to the doctor's, do you think?'

Bel shuffled down in the seat so she could rest her head on the back of it. 'I just want to get home.'

'Yes. Right. Two minutes. Shall we ring your Trevor?'

Bel shook her head.

'Dicky? Someone should be with you.'

'It could be catching, I'd rather not. Just get me home.'

Fran pulled up outside Bel's house and dashed round the car to help her out.

'Trevor fitted a little cloakroom in downstairs when we moved in and so I'll sit down here. It's blinking cold. Please can you put the fire on?' Bel slumped down on the sofa and rubbed her arms to get some warmth in them. She watched Fran scurrying about sorting things out for her. 'You must go as there's only your mum to serve and do the post office with Tom off ill, and your dad's not there. I'll be all right. Honestly.'

Fran put a jug of water on the coffee table along with a glass. 'You must drink, or you'll get dehydrated. Please let me ring your Trevor.'

'If I get worse I'll ring him. Honestly I will. I can't ring Dicky 'cos it's Georgie's day off and she's already gone out. This is terrible.' Bel's English-rose complexion was now even more sludge-coloured and Fran hesitated about leaving her.

'Just go.' Bel flapped her hands at Fran to hasten her out. 'Go!'

'Look, Bel, let's put your mobile handy and then you can ring without even getting up.' Fran fished it out of Bel's handbag for her and laid it on the coffee table. 'If there's a lull I'll be back. OK?'

Bel scarcely nodded her acknowledgement; she closed her eyes and didn't say another word. Fran poured out a glass of water for her and headed back to the store. Of course it turned out to be an extra busy day. Fran had mastered the post office years ago and now she was glad she had because it seemed as though every household in the three villages needed to make use of it. So while Harriet served at the till Fran never left the post office cage at all, and eventually she became seriously claustrophobic and had to rush outside for a gasp of fresh air. The locked cage was necessary for insurance, but it did feel like a prison to her after a while. She stood out in the winter sun enjoying the breeze, until she turned to have a look through the window and saw she had a queue of four waiting for her. She went back inside and locked herself in again.

'Don't see you in the post office often, Fran love. Shorthanded, are you?'

'You could say that. Dad's out on business, Tom's ill and I've just taken Bel home. Sick as a dog, she is.'

'Oh! Not another one, surely. It's certainly going the rounds. Little Derehams is rife with it, they say. Louise and Gilbert have three of theirs down with it, and Gilbert wasn't looking too clever when I saw him setting off for the office this morning. Really seedy he looked and believe it or believe it not he had a *cardigan* on.'

'A *cardigan* on?' This phenomenal piece of news went down the queue.

'Gilbert with a *cardigan* on?'

'Wearing a cardigan. That must be a first. In fact it is a first.'

'Never! He must feel bad.'

'One third of the children at the school are missing this week,' said Maggie Dobbs. 'Been a long time since that happened, believe me.'

'One third. Heavens above! What've we done to deserve this?'

'Could be your hubby being fined and banned from driving for three months after he overtook an ambulance on the brow of a hill.'

'Or you, for that matter, when Georgie turned you out of the pub for behaviour unbecoming to a gentleman.'

'No such thing.'

'That's what I heard. You shouldn't have attacked poor Dicky. The size of him compared to you. He's only a little tiddler, is poor Dicky. But powerful with it.' The customer who said this nudged her neighbour and they both sniggered, heads close together.

Bel's sickness had added a new dimension to the conversation in the store and Fran had to smile. At least, thank God, they weren't gossiping about her and Chris. She laboured away the rest of the morning wishing her dad would come home soon. When he eventually did, he took over the post office and released her so she could take her lunch break. So, for a change, she went home and enjoyed her lunch sitting in the kitchen alone, thinking about Chris and what a brilliant beginning to the day she'd had. Chris really was wonderful in bed, and Fran spent a delicious few minutes recollecting their morning together.

Chapter 8

In the saloon bar of the Royal Oak that evening, those who considered the old settle and the table that went with it belonged exclusively to them were somewhat disconcerted to find it already occupied when they arrived around half-past seven. There were four people sitting at the table, all well supplied with drinks, for they each had a full glass already lined up for when they'd finished their first one. And sitting there? Johnny Templeton and his wife Alice, Chris Templeton, Johnny's brother, plus Peter the rector. They were so absorbed in their conversation that none of them looked up when Greta and Vince, Marie and Zack, Dottie and Vera, and Willie and Sylvia turned away to find another table.

'What do you reckon? Something's going on.'

'Sit at that table by the fireplace.'

'OK.'

Dottie muttered, 'Bit of a cheek really.'

'Tables in a pub are for anybody. After all them chairs haven't got our names carved on 'em have they?' reflected Willie.

'But everyone knows that's our favourite.'

'This table isn't big enough for eight,' said Dottie.

'Let's pull that other one up, then we'll manage.' Vince and Zack did as Sylvia suggested, and before long they were all seated with a drink apiece and were ready to hear the latest gossip.

'Me first,' said Dottie. She took a long drink of her current favourite, a gin and tonic, dabbed her mouth gently, and said softly, 'Last night that new friend of mine who lives at the back of my cottage, even though she's in Church Lane and I'm in Shepherd's Hill ... you know, the one who—'

'Yes, yes, we know who you mean,' said Marie impatiently.

'Well, she went to visit a friend of hers and they went to their local pub for a drink, and you'll never guess who she saw there.'

'Who?'

'Well, it was someone not a million miles away from us right now.' She glanced across at the settle and said no more.

'Go on then.' Sylvia, having spent all day in the house with Willie, and him not speaking much nowadays, was in urgent need of hearing some news; any news, for that matter.

'Chris. Chris Templeton that is.'

'Seeing as he's the only one for miles around called Chris, then yes it would be.'

Dottie nodded her head in agreement. 'In the Wise Man pub.'

'So, what's interesting about that? He's a free man,' said Marie. 'He can drink where he likes.'

'It's who he was *with* and what they were *doing* that matters.'

This statement of Dottie's finally caught their attention, and Vera declared that if she didn't find out soon what Dottie was talking about she, Vera Wright, would strangle her.

'Then you never would find out.' Dottie took a deep breath and revealed all: 'He was with Fran. Fran Charter-Plackett.'

'So? They're both free agents,' said Greta.

'And they were kissing, and he couldn't keep his hands off her. A full hour they were in that pub, and my friend said they were at it all the time. She was as bad as him.'

'He's much older than her,' said Sylvia.

'She's not daft, is she? I wonder if Jimbo knows,' commented Marie.

'What d'yer mean "she's not daft"? I don't understand,' said Dottie.

Marie gave a sly smile. 'Think about it. He's so wealthy he can't spend it fast enough. She'll do herself a good turn if she marries him. All that money. And he is so good looking, I quite fancy him myself.' Marie, who from where she was sitting had a clear view of the main door, suddenly covered her mouth with her hand, and muttered, 'Be careful! Jimbo's just come in.'

'What did she say?' Vera asked loudly, and repeated it, even more loudly, when no one answered her.

Sylvia sitting beside Vera whispered, 'Jimbo's just come in.'

All eight of them covertly watched Jimbo. They saw him go to the bar. 'Good evening, Georgie. Full house tonight. Whisky please. Make it a double.' Jimbo paid for his drink, picked up his glass, walked towards the settle and squeezed in beside Chris, saying a bright, 'Good evening. Sorry I'm late, got caught up.'

'He looks cheerful enough,' said Willie. 'I bet he doesn't know.'

'So anyway, my friend from Church Lane said they were still at it in the car parked outside when she left well over an hour later.'

'I mean, I bet Harriet will be annoyed.'

Sylvia added her piece of news to the conversation. 'I know for a fact he's had lunch at Jimbo and Harriet's, but I didn't realise it was because Chris and Fran were courting.'

'Had lunch there!'

'Oh, yes. Last Sunday. I saw him being invited in, and all dressed up he was. I thought he was just visiting Jimbo and Harriet, but obviously it was because of him and Fran. Well, good luck to her.'

'What. Living in Brazil. Wouldn't want a daughter of mine to be living in Brazil. Not likely,' Willie declared.

Dottie, determined to get the most value out of her juicy piece of gossip by aggravating Willie, asked, 'You contemplating starting a family, are you then, Sylvia?'

'For heaven's sake. As if.'

'That's what your Willie seems to be saying.'

'He might *say* it, but no, we're not. Well, not with me he

isn't, and if he finds someone else to start one with he'll be out in the street before he knows it, with all his blessed Second World War memorabilia too.'

This exchange made the others hoot with laughter, and the whole subject of the conversation changed from the contemplation of Fran and Chris's romance to matters of a more mature nature. Secretly, they wished they could hear what those sitting at the table with the old settle down one side of it were saying.

If they had been invited to join that group they would have been very interested indeed because Johnny was just saying, 'So, Stock's day is in June, followed by the village show in July. What goes on after that?'

Jimbo remembered the big bonfire nights. 'November 5th Bonfire Night. Well, the Saturday night nearest to it.'

'Why have a bonfire on November 5th? Is it some sort of winter solstice celebration?' Johnny asked.

'It's been one of our big nights. We all come. Massive fire in your grounds, we burn anything and everything: old furniture, whatever you like. It's commemorating the time when Guy Fawkes and his chums tried to set fire to the Houses of Parliament.'

'My goodness. Tell me more,' Johnny said.

By the time Jimbo had finished his graphic description of Bonfire Night in Turnham Malpas, Johnny was aghast. 'But to *celebrate* it. It seems to me the maddest thing ever. What happened to Guy what's-his-name?'

'He was condemned to death by hanging. Did you know about this, Alice?'

'Of course. I like eating scorching-hot baked potatoes by the fire, but we've not had a big bonfire celebration for two or three years. I've lost count. Not since Craddock Fitch's business began to go downhill. He provided most of the money, you see.'

Peter reminded them about the beer tent and the refreshments. Johnny carried on making notes. Finally he looked up.

'Well, that's plenty to be getting on with. It seems to me that the first big village celebration will be this year's Bonfire Night. I shall write a page in the church magazine outlining the starting up of all the village celebrations which have been allowed to lapse. Do we need committees and such? I expect so.'

Jimbo remembered Louise Johns' sterling work organising everything when Craddock Fitch had the money to finance it all. 'Louise Johns is the one to get all the info from. Now the children are growing up perhaps she might have the time to take it all on again for us. Brilliant organiser, she is. There was no one who organised it as well as she did. We had all sorts of different people doing it when she was having all those babies, but none of them were as good as she was. Am I not right, Peter?'

'You most certainly are, and if she doesn't want to do it, she has all the notes from before which would be a big help. She kept meticulous notes, except for the time when she had two lots of Morris dancers by mistake and they refused to perform together.'

Peter laughed at the memory of the Morris dancers' problem.

'Exactly. You haven't had much to say, Chris. Would you like a word.'

'Does everyone expect to come for free to everything?' asked Chris.

Jimbo volunteered to explain. 'Stock's Day is free to all comers, and we get a lot of outsiders coming to watch the natives playing at being fourteenth-century villagers. At the village show only people who are officially exhibiting in the different classes get in free; everyone else pays because there's entertainment to watch. The bonfire is free, except they pay for their drinks in the beer tent and for food in the refreshment tent. Mr Fitch used to pay for the baked potatoes, and the scouts distribute those to anyone who wants one. It's lovely watching the bonfire while eating a hot potato.'

Chris had listened carefully to Jimbo and then made his offer of help. 'That'll be my contribution, the baked potatoes. I shan't be here, but I'll leave money with Johnny for those and I'll also pay for one of the entertainments at the village show, except I shall possibly be here for that. Or possibly not. But I'll still pay my dues. English winters I cannot cope with, so I shall be leaving for Brazil shortly, once I can't go out without a coat on and warm gloves.' He grinned rather charmingly at all those seated around the table and they couldn't help but like him, despite his cowardice about the English weather.

Johnny decided to wind up the meeting by thanking everyone for attending, and for all their advice. 'I have pages of notes and will study them all, then I'll type out a proper list for each event, pass that to you, Peter, for correction, and then sort something out for the rest of the village to read so they know officially what is going to happen. We've got to get back to how things used to be, and make it a real village with a life of its own, instead of always having to rely on events outside the village to give us all a life. Thank you so much for taking the time to put me in the picture, I'm looking forward enormously to establishing everything all over again. We need it, don't we?'

Peter and Jimbo each went home, and so did Alice, who'd worried all the time about her two babies being left with her newly appointed babysitter. But Johnny and Chris stayed for another round of drinks. Jimbo didn't utter a single word at home about Chris returning to Brazil shortly, because the thought of Fran leaving home for distant shores was more than he could face.

Chapter 9

A week after that crucial meeting in the Royal Oak, Chris left for Brazil. He'd found two small chains of country house hotels for Johnny to follow-up on and had left all the details with Johnny, including his thoughts that the owners were in serious financial difficulties. And Chris also left behind a distraught but very self-controlled Fran.

He told her two nights before he left that he intended going home immediately but didn't happen to mention he'd booked his first-class seat on the plane that morning. Confused by his shock tactics Fran thought they were talking about her going to Brazil with him, but within moments she knew for a fact she'd misunderstood him. And so poor Fran went from extreme delight to shattering disappointment within seconds, although she was determined to behave like the very grown-up person she had become.

Fran took a sip of wine to steady her nerves and then commented, 'That's been a quick decision.'

'Well, you know me, if I make up my mind to do something, that's it. I've done the hotel job for Johnny. If there's one thing I can't stand it's an English winter: heavy coats, thick gloves, pouring rain, freezing temperatures, umbrellas. Not for me. Sorry.'

Fran felt justified in protesting, 'But you don't know, you've never been here in winter.'

'No, but I've read about it, watched TV, seen pictures of the snow and the traffic hold-ups. Drivers marooned all night. No thanks. Already it's getting too cold for me. I'm a shorts and sunshine man. And I've missed sailing.'

'I see. Well, I can understand it.' Fran hadn't meant to add, 'I shall miss you.' But somehow the words slipped out by mistake because the pain was so bad.

'And I shall miss you.' But there was no pain in the tone of *his* voice. Chris didn't say, 'Will you come with me?' either. Not a mention of that, and tonight he hadn't even booked a room at the Wise Man like he had before. That hurt Fran more than she could allow herself to believe.

She reached across the table and gently touched the back of his hand as he picked up his wine glass. 'Your mother will be glad you're going back.'

'Of course she is. Time I got back. Nicholas is a brilliant businessman, but there's too much work to get through for just one person. Yes. Got to go home.'

Chris noticed tears beginning to well in Fran's eyes, but he succeeded in not making a comment about them by asking if she wanted pudding.

'No, thanks. It must be a long flight to Rio.'

'It is, but it's very comfortable when you travel first class.'

'Of course.' Rather wistfully Fran added, 'I've never travelled first class.'

'You should one day, just for the experience,' Chris said, as though money grew on trees.

'No chance of me travelling first class.' Fran noticed he wasn't the least embarrassed by his riches; others would have been much more apologetic after what she'd said.

'You never know. Coffee, Fran?'

There didn't seem much point in prolonging her agony; all she wanted was to hide under her duvet and cry. 'I've had a busy day so I'd better get home. Be seeing you, Chris, some time when you come back. Have a good flight. Goodnight.' How she got to her feet, how she managed to kiss his cheek

82

showing no passion, no regret, she'd no idea. But she did, and Fran left him without offering to pay her share of their bill as she usually did. Without a kiss from him too, Fran thought as she walked firmly away from the loveliest, most wonderful love affair she'd ever had in all her twenty years.

Chris watched her go, grateful she'd managed not to make a scene in such a busy pub. But she wasn't the love of his life. He'd known that right from the very beginning. But he'd wanted someone, anyone, to be honest, and she was willing and good-looking and jolly. She was just what he needed. Rio here I come, thank God. Chris decided he'd leave this village without the slightest regret. All he had to do was pay his dues for the baked potatoes – honestly, blasted baked potatoes, of all things. What made him offer to pay for them, he'd no idea. And then he could shake the dust of the village off his feet and get stuck into his social life in Rio once more. With no regrets. None at all.

Fran managed to get to her bedroom without speaking to either her mum or dad. She locked herself in her en suite, and finally gave way to her feelings. Tears didn't come at first, but when they did they came in torrents. She felt hard done by. She'd become aware tonight, deep down, that Chris had never had any intention of taking her to Brazil with him, married or not. She was useful, available, convenient, with time on her hands, and maybe for moments together he had been fond of her. But she had sensed as he spoke about going home as though he meant immediately, that most of the time he'd simply made use of her. Or made a fool of her might be a more honest way of putting it.

Then Fran remembered the beautiful moments they had shared and she wept again. They had shared the same sense of humour, made up silly rhymes together, laughed at the same jokes, hated people who told lies, loved the same films, liked the same dramas on TV. Truly, they'd been very compatible and it would have been very pleasing to go to Brazil, where Fran could have given all those girls – well, women – a run for their money when they realised she had captured their perfect gem, namely Chris Templeton.

Fran cried until she couldn't cry any more. At last only deep searing sobs that tore her apart came out, and she wished they didn't because they made her chest feel raw. She wished Harriet would knock on her door, and say, 'All right, darling?' Then her mum would give her an almighty big hug to help heal the pain. Would the pain ever heal? Or would she have this pain in the middle of her chest for ever? The common-sense part of Fran came to the fore then, and she almost laughed at herself. One unscrupulous man who thought only of himself couldn't be allowed to harm her for the rest of her life. One thing for certain was that she'd be much more cautious a second time round.

There came the longed-for knock at her door, and Fran heard the words she'd wanted: 'All right, darling?' She rapidly dried her eyes, wiped her nose, leapt off the bathroom stool, shot out into her bedroom and straight into her mother's welcoming arms. 'Hug me tight.'

'I am hugging you tightly.'

'Just what I need.' Fran knew she was safe for ever in this pair of arms.

'Are you sure you're all right?'

'Absolutely sure. Is there any hot chocolate going?'

'There soon could be. Shall we make some? The two of us?' Fran nodded.

'Good idea.' Mother and daughter went down the stairs together. Harriet hoped Fran, in the close familiarity of their homely kitchen, would be able to talk about what was troubling her, because she was obviously very upset. But apparently the pain lay too deep for Fran to talk about yet. Fran and her parents watched the ten o'clock news, drinking their hot chocolates, munching biscuits and making general comments about the news. Fran was the first to go to bed, and it wasn't until Harriet and Jimbo had turned off their bedroom light that Jimbo told his wife what he knew about Chris.

'I already knew he was thinking of going back very soon.'

'You did? When did you find out?'

'In the pub the night of the meeting. It was just something he said. He said he dislikes the idea of being in England in winter. Too wet, too cold, he claims, for him. So perhaps he's told her tonight.'

'A big relief all round. She's obviously not going with him then.'

'Thank God.'

'The question is, Jimbo,' pondered Harriet, 'has he asked her and she's refused to go, or has he *not* asked her and that's why she's so upset?'

'Either way, she's obviously not going, and if she's so upset then I think he hasn't asked her. We'll have to treat her with kid gloves for a few weeks, poor Fran. Anyway, it's all turned out for the best, hasn't it? Certainly to my satisfaction anyway. Why don't you and Fran go on a week's holiday, two girls together, somewhere warm? It would give her something else to think about. You'd enjoy it too, wouldn't you?' Jimbo turned over as he settled himself for sleep, and remarked again how relieved he was that Fran wouldn't be disappearing off to Brazil with Chris. 'And good riddance to bad rubbish, I say.'

'He's not as likeable as Johnny, is he?'

'No, he isn't. And Fran is worth more than being someone to make use of. Which is what he's done. Only don't tell her I said that. It's true, just the same though. Goodnight, darling.'

'Goodnight, Jimbo. Love you. She'll get over it, and if she doesn't know now that's what he's done, she soon will when she's had time to think, after the hurt begins to lessen. But you're right; a holiday might help.'

Chapter 10

In his role as verger at the church, the first thing Zack did every Monday morning was to walk all the way round the outside doing what he called 'inspecting the fabric'. He ran a caring eye over every inch of the outside for any signs of vandalism, and not a single inch of the outer fabric escaped the scrutiny of his experienced eyes. No, it all appeared to be OK. Then for some reason he took another look at the roof. He inspected it on both sides, all the way along the ridge of the roof from the gable end to where the roof joined the spire. There was something not right. What was it? He shaded his eyes and took another look. No, it couldn't be. But he wasn't wrong, was he? No, he was right. The lead was missing! During the night some thieving, cheating rogues had climbed up and removed it, inch by inch.

Zack boiled with anger. He marched around looking for signs of a ladder being used and he found the imprints of the two feet of a ladder in the mud and trampled grass where they'd struggled with the lead. But where had the vehicle been parked? They'd have needed a vehicle, as lead was far too heavy to have been carried away in someone's hands. After a while Zack found heavy tyre marks of what might have been a lorry in front of the church hall. So they'd driven up the drive to the hall and then, yes, there were the footmarks, two sets of heavy prints going from the church to the church hall drive. Had no one heard them? Seen them? Had it rained during the night? No, it hadn't. At least then the church wasn't flooded. He had to tell someone. Sacrilege, that's what it was. Sacrilege.

He rattled the knocker on the rectory door and to his relief the rector answered his knock. Zack found he'd lost his voice he was so upset. So he signalled urgently for Peter to follow him.

'Zack! Are you all right? What's happened?'

Zack still hadn't spoken, but now they were standing on the path just beyond the lych gate and Zack was pointing upwards. At first Peter couldn't see what he was supposed to be looking at. Then he realised. 'The lead. No! Right the way along!'

'Can't believe it. Can't believe it.'

'Neither can I!'

'Our lovely old church. Desecrated. They need hanging. I'm so sorry.' Zack looked haggard.

'See here, Zack, you're not to blame. It is not your fault. You understand?'

'But I'm in charge, aren't I? What Willie Biggs will say I don't know.'

'Willie might be getting old but even he will know it's not your fault. Phone. Phone.' Peter tapped his pockets searching for his mobile. 'I've left it on my desk. I'm going into the house to ring the police. Why don't you make yourself a cup of tea in your shed? You can drink it while we wait for the police to arrive. And make one for me too, please. I won't be long.'

So they sat together in Zack's shed drinking tea, with Peter finding all sorts of excuses for why people stole lead, and Zack berating himself for what had happened. 'I'll have to sleep in the church every night. It's the only answer to this.'

'You will not, Zack. For heaven's sakes, man, even if you did sleep in the church you couldn't tackle men strong enough to climb on the roof to heave lead off and carry it down to a lorry. These are fit men, believe me, really fit. No, it's not possible.'

'We'll have to have men doing night duty then, like air-raid wardens during the war. They could use this shed. Or we could get Grandmama Charter-Plackett to do night duty. One word from her and they'd crawl away and never come back. By Jove, she's a strong woman and not half. I admire that, they don't make women like her nowadays.'

The police car took over an hour to arrive, by which time Zack had reached boiling point again. 'Where have you been? Keeping the rector waiting. An hour we've been waiting. A whole hour.'

The police officer looked up at the roof and tutted. 'Lead you say. It's the third church we've been to this morning. Every single one stripped.'

Peter stepped forward and shook hands with them both. 'Good morning. Thank you for coming. I don't feel too bad if we're the third you've been to.'

'Same tyre marks, sarge. Look.' The second officer pointed to the church hall drive.

'New to us is this. We get every crime you can think of in this area but never stealing lead before, and here we are now with three in one night. It's like a blinking epidemic. Someone's moved into the area and they've decided to make a clean sweep.'

Zack sprang to life. 'Moved into the area? Well, we all know—'

Peter rapidly cut short Zack's revelation. 'We'll have to get it repaired quickly, won't we, Zack? In case of rain.'

'Yes, sir, we will, but we know—'

'Zack! Why not make a start on your Monday-morning jobs, otherwise you'll get behind. I know you're more comfortable if you're ahead of yourself.' There was a forceful note to Peter's voice and Zack saw the truth of his statement; he would get behind, and he hated that. Never mind, he'd tell Peter later when the police had gone. On the other hand, the police ought to be told, and so he turned back. But Peter, standing behind the police officers, gently shook his head at Zack.

So Zack swept and polished inside the church, all the time fuming and cursing about the heathens who'd stolen the lead. That Ford Barclay had only been back about two months and it looked as if he was already up to his old tricks. After that fuss they all made when he first came back, and how delighted Ford and Merc said they both were to be back.

Zack even rang Marie on her mobile and told her who the police said it was. 'Are you sure, Zack? Did they say his name?'

'Well, not exactly. But then police wouldn't, would they? They said it was someone who'd recently moved into the area. Well, who is there but 'im? Scrap-metal merchant by profession.'

'Well, now look here, just be careful what you say and to whom you say it. We don't want any bother, do we?'

'No.'

'So not another word about it being Ford. Promise?'

'All right.' But Zack decided to go to the Royal Oak that night to find out what everyone else thought. He waited until most of the regulars had taken their seats before he began. When he'd questioned everyone he could, Zack found that most of them were in the same mind as himself: Ford Barclay was at the bottom of the whole scheme. He may not have climbed on the roof and done the stealing, but he'd found someone to do the dirty deed, and he was the one selling it on. They were all outraged.

'We've been duped into thinking he was innocent, but all the time he wasn't. He was as guilty as hell,' Willie declared.

Zack nodded. 'Let out of prison because there wasn't enough evidence to charge him. Oh yes!'

'Well, I must admit it does seem a very odd coincidence. No lead stolen in this area ever, and he hasn't been back more than about eight weeks, and wham! Three churches in one night, the police say. And each one had the whole lot taken. The whole lot! Not a scrap of lead left,' said Marie.

'It does seem strange, but it could be a coincidence,' Barry offered with Pat's encouragement.

'Coincidence! Yes, an almighty coincidence, I must say. Have the police been round there yet? Questioning him? Do we know?' asked Vera.

Zack had to admit to himself that he was offended by Peter being so determined that Ford's name was not to be mentioned to the police when it was as plain as the nose on your face. 'Well, I never mentioned him to the police because the rector wouldn't have wanted me to.'

'I can't imagine Ford would be that daft as to come here and encourage no good thieves to steal lead and take it to him to sell. He hasn't got a yard where he could store it, has he?' said Pat, who liked Ford and Merc very much and was glad to have them back in their lives. To say nothing of the racing tips he passed round to the embroidery group each Monday. Not that Pat went to the group as embroidery wasn't her kind of thing; but Dottie was good at passing on his tips when they worked together on one of Jimbo's events, and Pat had added up the other day and knew for certain, that though she didn't win every week, she did win a lot more than she lost. Eighty-five pounds the week before last, for a start. It would come in handy with Christmas looming.

Barry offered to get the next round of drinks in and he went off with his order to the bar. Resting his foot on the brass rail, Barry detailed the order to Alan Crimble, who introduced him to Mary-Lee, the new barmaid. Barry decided she was a good addition to the bar. American, she said she was, and she flirted with him for a moment. He could tell she liked people. Barry, feeling he should talk to Alan in a civil manner for once in his life, said, 'Tried to work out the other day just how long you've worked for Georgie, Alan. It must be twenty years at least.'

'Nineteen actually at Christmas.'

'Don't you ever feel like a change?'

'No.'

'Why not?'

Alan replied with a question. 'How long have you worked up at the Big House?'

'Well, actually almost twenty years too come to think about

it. Same as you.' Barry grinned at Alan, and was rewarded with one of Alan's rare smiles.

'So that's sixteen pounds fifty-five. No sorry, *seventeen* pounds fifty-five.' Alan leaned over the counter a little and confided to Barry, 'Don't offer too often to buy the drinks because that lot'll carry on drinking as long as you're willing.'

Barry acknowledged the truth of what Alan had said with a nod and a grin, and he went back to their table to hand out their drinks. They were still, except for Pat, agreeing that Ford was at the bottom of the thefts of church lead, when to their surprise Ford and Merc arrived, right there in their midst before they'd had a chance to change their subject of conversation.

Willie was speaking about Ford as they materialised beside him. 'This village is no place for a chap like him. It stands to reason it isn't.'

Jovially Ford asked, 'What stands to reason?'

With refreshing swiftness of mind Marie said, 'Chris going back to Brazil. Chris Templeton, that is.'

An almost audible sigh of relief went round the table. 'Oh, right,' said Ford. 'We never actually got a chance to meet him. All right, was he?'

'Not as nice as Johnny, but just as good-looking,' said Pat. 'Here, let's move the chairs round a bit, and then you can join us.' She was glad to have an end to the supposition about Ford's involvement. Sometimes this lot were like gramophone records, on and on and on about the same subject. Pat wondered if it would be a good idea if she and Barry didn't sit with them, and when she saw the tray of drinks, and roughly added up what the cost must have been, she decided she was right.

Ford and Merc had been to the races that afternoon. 'That's why we're a bit later coming in,' Ford said. 'Lovely day for being on a racecourse: brilliant sunshine, blue skies. Here's your apple juice, Merc. And now I can have the best ale in the world, Dicky's home brew. The beer at the races wasn't a patch on this.' Ford took a deep pull on his pint and as he put down his glass, Pat burst out with, 'Did you win?'

'I didn't,' said Merc, 'but Ford did.'

They turned to Ford in the hope he'd tell them how much he won, but he just winked and didn't answer, so they knew he'd done rather well. 'I was at the youth club committee meeting last night, by the way,' he said. 'They are a grand set of young people, you know. They deserve treats.'

Marie asked what he'd planned for them. 'I know they've missed your outings while you've been away.'

'Well, before we went away I'd promised them we'd hire a canal boat and have a week somewhere, but of course ...' He cleared his throat and then continued, 'Anyway, I couldn't at the time, but we can now. I've booked a fourteen-berth boat for a week next summer on the Kennet and Avon canal and cleared it with the appropriate authorities.'

'That'll cost a lot, a fourteen-berth boat.' There was a hint of interest in Vera's voice which Ford didn't miss.

'You wishing you could go, are you, Vera? You can if you like, then Merc can stay at home, and you could do the cooking instead. We shall need someone to organise the food and you'll take up a lot less room on a boat than my Merc.' Ford had a big grin on his face, and Vera had to laugh.

'No, thank you,' Vera replied. 'Couldn't stand it. Who else is going to be in charge with you? Now there's no Venetia?'

'Merc and me, and Kate Fitch of course from the school. Anyone else like to offer because we need one more? Preferably a man good with ideas and a real commitment to teenagers; they're a lively lot.'

The silence that followed that request told Ford volumes. But suddenly out of the blue Barry spoke up, 'I could spare a week in August, if I'd be any help.' Barry displayed his strength by flexing his muscles and everyone was very impressed. 'For winding the locks, and that.'

Ford Barclay was delighted. 'My word, Barry, you're just the sort of chap I'd be thrilled to have on board. Do you mean it?'

'Oh yes. Pat won't mind. Would you have me?'

'I certainly would. You'd be excellent at keeping the boys up to scratch. Thank you very much indeed.' Ford leaned across to shake Barry's hand. 'You'd better come to the next committee meeting. I'll be in touch. My word, I'm so pleased. Thank you.'

In an aside to Sylvia, Dottie whispered, 'More likely he'll need 'im to drag the boys out of the girls' bedrooms. Or is it cabins on a narrow-boat?'

The two of them had a quiet giggle, which irritated Ford because he took his work with the youth club very seriously.

Ford's mention of Kate had turned the conversation towards what had happened to Craddock Fitch. 'He disappeared off up north, Kate said, doing research of some sort. Then he came back for a week or two and now's he's off again. Anyone know what he's up to?' asked Sylvia.

There was a chorus of 'don't knows' from all round the table, except Zack, who did say he thought Mr Fitch was trying to find his two sons. 'I overheard a conversation he was having with the rector in the church one day, and it sounded as though he was asking how he could get access to marriage records and the rector told him how to do it using that internet thing all the young ones go on about now. The rector wrote some things down on a piece of paper and Mr Fitch took possession of it as though it was pure gold. '

'Really?

'I never knew he had family.'

'I knew he had two sons. But his wife left him and took them with her, and he hasn't seen them since.'

'Hardly surprising, considering. Miserable old toad that he is,' said Vera.

Ford said, 'Well, he was difficult to get on with. But if you faced up to him and said what needed to be said, he was all right. I got on OK with him once I'd told him I knew he wasn't superior to me.'

'Whoops!' said Barry. 'That was risky 'cos he thinks he is.'

'It was all a front he wore to make himself feel superior,' declared Willie. 'He's better to get on with now his business has crashed and proved him not to be infallible. More normal, yer know.'

Slyly Zack decided to blow the whole pleasant evening sky-high by saying, 'Had you heard, Ford, there's been a load of lead stolen from two churches in Culworth as well as ours here. Made a clean sweep of it. Last night it was. It was me who discovered it this morning, first thing. The rector's very upset about it and he rang the police straightaway. They said it was the first time it had happened in this area. I thought perhaps you wouldn't have heard, having been at the races all day.' With his eyes intensely focused on Ford, Zack awaited a reply.

Merc nearly died on the spot, her heart beginning to beat painfully fast. Ford went rigid with shock. Before answering he took a long drink of his home brew and then said as casually as he could, 'No, we hadn't heard. We were off at the crack of light this morning.' Ford went right the way round the table catching the eye of anyone who was daring to look at him. 'If any of you are thinking I'm the guilty party you are very mistaken. It has nothing to do with me. Nothing at all. Pure as the driven snow I am. And always have been.'

So this, thought Ford, was what had caused the atmosphere to be so unwelcoming when they first came in tonight; he'd sensed it immediately. It was a very different atmosphere from the night they had been thrown the surprise party to welcome them back. So very different. Some people couldn't even look him in the eye tonight. No one answered him, although a few looked sheepish. Pat leaned forward and patted Merc's hand to reassure her there was at least one person on their side.

Ford felt so badly let down he wanted to leave immediately.

He glanced at Merc and saw she too was badly affected by Zack's obvious suspicions. Ford drained his glass, stood up, helped Merc to her feet, and the two of them left the bar, calling out a cheerful 'Goodnight!' to Alan and Mary-Lee.

Arm in arm they silently walked round Stocks Row and into Church Lane. Ford got his key out and they went into Glebe House. Merc retired to the kitchen to make a bedtime drink, but Ford went straight into his study, slammed the door and sat in his chair, braced his elbows on the desk and put his head in his hands. He'd thought he'd put all that trouble behind him, and here it was rearing up in the one place he had foolishly imagined he would at last be free of it.

Merc's pounding heart began to calm down, but because of Ford's distress her hands trembled as she measured the spoonfuls of Ovaltine into their mugs, and they trembled even more when she tried to pour the hot milk in and she found she hadn't enough hot milk to fill the two mugs, so she served two three-quarter filled mugs. She forgot the biscuits and went back to get them. Then she sat in silence in Ford's study, waiting for him to speak.

'How could they?'

'Not enough to do, that's their trouble, Ford.'

'I could kill 'em.'

Merc spilled some Ovaltine down her chin, dabbed it dry and declared she was heartbroken. 'I do have your word of honour that it wasn't inspired by you. Just tell me, tell me the truth. I need to know. At the appeal they said the evidence wasn't enough to declare you one hundred per cent guilty and so they let you out. But you haven't been daft enough to start up again, have you? Have you? You must tell me.'

'I can honestly say I have nothing whatsoever to do with lead being stolen round here. *Nothing*. That is the absolute truth. As God is my judge, you have my word.'

'Thank you for saying that.' Merc was completely satisfied

with her husband's reply, glad that at last it sounded as though he'd learned his lesson. They sat in silence drinking their Ovaltine, with only the occasional smile exchanged between them. Merc, drink finished, placed her mug on the tray. 'I'm going to bed now, but I doubt I shall sleep. Goodnight, Ford, love. Goodnight.'

Ford went up to bed about an hour later. When Merc heard him closing the door of the en suite and felt the mattress move as he climbed into bed beside her, she wiped away her tears and turned over to face him to give him an ultimatum. 'I really cannot cope with another upset like we had when you were arrested. Those months you spent in prison, the trial, the appeal; all of it was more than I could take. If ... *if* it all starts again I think it will, quite literally, kill me.'

Merc turned over and said not another word.

Finally Ford said, 'I promise you that I have no involvement with the lead theft that happened last night. Nothing whatso-ever, and I am speaking the truth. I know what it cost you ... your health, and that ... and it won't happen again. I promised that, and I meant it. I still mean it. I love you too much to allow myself to get embroiled in anything the slightest bit illegal.'

'I have your word on that?'

'Absolutely. You have my word.'

'So I can be happy again? Enjoy being back here in Turnham Malpas. Feeling settled. Feeling as though I belong? With no problems at all?'

'None.'

'So I can begin embroidering again?'

'Merc, I never wanted you to stop.'

'No, but what happened with you stopped me.'

'Not any more it won't.'

'OK. Thank you. I'm glad we've got everything straight again.'

Chapter 11

The embroidery group still met at 2 p.m. every Monday afternoon. They were expecting to begin work on a tapestry for a church in Culworth. To those outside the group it might have sounded small beer compared to the mural they'd just had hung in a cathedral in Hampshire; but the church was newly built in a stark minimalist style and was proving to be a very difficult challenge. Two designs had already been rejected, and Evie had decided they'd all have to go and visit the church and make their own contribution to the style and colours choices. The church committee wanted to attend but Evie, gentle, kindly Evie, had put her foot down and refused to tell them when they'd be going for their in-depth conference. So, instead of meeting in the church hall to embroider, they got into two cars and went into Culworth, parked outside the gates of the new church, walked up the path to the main entrance and went to stand in front of the piece of bare stone wall where the tapestry would be hung.

'It needs a big statement, something no one can pass without stopping to look. Eye-catching, that's the word. Eye-catching. Now we've got Merc back we can be eye-catching, can't we, Merc?' suggested Dottie.

Merc blushed. 'Don't know about that!' she said. 'I've done no embroidery since I was here last.'

'None?'

'No. I tried, but I couldn't, with the worry of Ford in prison and that; all my creativity went out of the window.'

'In that case then you'll be all ready for it to burst out.'

Merc laughed. 'It's wonderful being back in Turnham Malpas, believe me. I love it. Ford's loving it too. He ...' Quite a few of those gathered looking at that bare stone wall looked somewhat uncomfortable when Merc said that, and she noticed, and knew she hadn't to say that again.

Evie interrupted, saying, 'Thank you for coming back, you're an inspiration, Mercedes, a real inspiration to me.'

Merc opened wide her arms and enclosed Evie in one of her big hugs. 'Thank you for saying that. When we heard from Craddock Fitch that he wanted to sell Glebe House and did we want it now Ford was out of prison and not under a cloud, we were absolutely delighted. What a chance to come back to where we felt so comfortable, where we belong you know.'

'So that's decided then,' said Evie. 'Instead of trying to emulate the contemporary style of the church building we'll do the saint's arrival in heaven being welcomed by other saints, and all flamboyant and glorious and colourful, with God as a blaze of light. And if they're still not satisfied, I shall say we won't be doing it, but that they'll have to pay for the designs I've already done.'

Amazed at her standing up to be counted in this way, they all exclaimed with one voice, 'Evie!'

'Well, we can't be messed about any longer. I've spent hours on the designs already, which obviously they won't want to pay extra for, and we still have to do the work. I'm beginning to lose my enthusiasm.'

'Well,' said the weekender, Barbara, 'I back you up on that. We'd expected to begin embroidering three weeks ago, to us that's three weeks lost. You do right, Evie. Can I say something?' They all nodded. 'Well, this spot they've chosen, you do realise that every single person in the congregation will be able to see it, even if they're sitting on the back row. So, if they get bored with the sermon they won't want to be *struggling* to see it, you know, screwing up their eyes to distinguish things, they'll want to actually see it without having to peer at it. You know, see it. Really *see* it.' Barbara paused for a moment.

Someone said impatiently, 'Yes, so?'

'Well,' said Barbara, 'it needs to be colourful and obvious, not hiding itself in pale colours and full of teeny tiny things, so as no one can distinguish anything unless they're standing within two feet of it. Bold, kind of; strong and dazzling, kind of.' Barbara went to hide behind Dottie as she was so embarrassed by her own outburst.

A silence greeted this statement of Barbara's as it was very rare she said anything inspiring because she was always so downbeat and critical about everything.

Evie agreed. 'You are absolutely right, Barbara. Bold. Strong. Obvious. Colourful. Mind-grabbing.'

'I don't know about the rest of you but, frankly, after all this thinking I'm in need of refreshments. Cream tea, everyone, in the abbey coffee shop, like we said we would?' said Sheila, who'd agreed with every word Barbara had said, but couldn't for the life of her have found the words as Barbara just had.

The coffee shop, winding down towards closing time, was not as busy as they had expected. The best tables, the ones that caught the afternoon sun, were occupied but others in the shade were free. They found one they liked, ordered their teas and began chatting.

'Apparently we'll all be getting some info about the re-establishment of the village show, and Bonfire Night. Johnny's organising it all,' said Dottie. 'I'm so glad. It'll be like old times, and I can't wait.'

Barbara agreed. 'The village show, I love that. All the in-fighting and the secrets about how they grow such good garlic or something or other, confident they'll win first prize, and then their faces when they don't. I've decided I'm going to enter a few things. My Victoria sponge has to be seen to be believed.'

Evie interrupted the ensuing discussion about the person who always won the Victoria sponge class and did she actually make the cakes herself, by saying, 'I've asked to have some embroidery classes. Why not? I can't judge them myself, that wouldn't be fair. But I know someone in Culworth who would.'

'Oh, great,' said Sheila, 'just what we want. We'll run away with all the prizes!'

'It's Bonfire Night I like the best,' said Bel.

'And me,' said Evie. 'I like Bonfire Night the best too. The heat of the fire and the chill of the wind, and everyone so happy, and "oooh!" and "aaahh!" when the fireworks go up. And I love making the guy. I wonder if Jimbo will do the fireworks again?'

'I understand that Johnny is footing the bill for that. A professional company is going to be in charge,' said Sylvia. 'More tea anyone?'

'Jimbo always did a brilliant job, they couldn't do better than he did.'

Sheila said she'd like another cup too. 'He did, but he says he's too busy nowadays. The Old Barn is doing wonderfully well but, Dottie, you know more about that than me?'

'It certainly is. Three events last week and three this week. I'm not complaining. Fran had to help out last week it was so fraught. But seeing as Chris has gone back to wherever he came from, I expect she's glad to be busy. She's so good with people is Fran, she has them eating out of her hand in no time at all, especially if they're complaining about something. She smoothes their ruffled feathers and has them smiling and apologising to her for being awkward in next to no time. Though what there is to complain about I really don't know.'

Sheila raised her voice slightly so everyone could hear her saying, 'I felt quite sorry when Chris went back to Brazil without her. I thought they looked lovely together. We saw them just once in the Wise Man pub. They'd obviously been upstairs to the loo, don't know why they don't make the pub loos down-stairs, it would be so much more convenient, and they looked so lovely coming downstairs, not hand in hand, but very close. His blond hair and her dark hair and just the right height for her. They made a very nice pair.'

'I bet Jimbo didn't think so,' Dottie declared.

Surprised, Sheila replied, 'Whyever not?'

Dottie pulled a disapproving face. 'Too old he was, too so-phisticated, too, shall we say … well … *experienced*, for want of a better word.'

'O-o-h! Do you know something we don't know?' asked Bel.

'I don't know nothing.'

'If you don't know nothing then you must know something because two negatives make a positive,' pointed out Bel.

Dottie refused to rise to the bait and excused herself by say-ing, 'I'm off to the loo.' Then she left and didn't come back, and eventually they found her waiting by their two cars in the abbey car park.

'We've been waiting for you,' was the indignant reply to Dottie's humble apology.

Sylvia guessed it was something she'd heard in the rectory and that she had stopped herself from revealing it just in time. She squeezed onto the back seat beside Dottie and patted her forearm and smiled at her to show her approval of her reticence.

Dottie didn't speak all the way back to Turnham Malpas, fearful she might let out what she'd overheard Caroline and Peter talking about the other morning while she'd been digging about in the hall cupboard searching for the box of cloths for her cleaning, a box that had apparently gone walkabout. By staying silent she couldn't let out what she knew by mistake. It was nothing really but she'd overheard the doctor telling Peter how almighty glad Jimbo was that Chris had gone back to Rio, and that apparently the relationship was getting much too close for their liking; and how pleased they were that Fran had not been asked to go with Chris to meet his family. If Dottie had told them that they'd have all immediately come up with all sorts of gossip, of which possibly ninety per cent would be untrue. And she, Dottie Foskett, liked Fran and didn't want her to be upset by anything she'd done. How far had it gone then? All the way by the tone of the doctor's voice. And the reverend had nodded his agreement so positively that she guessed he knew more than he'd let on.

Chapter 12

The punters who sat so regularly on the table with the ancient settle down one side would have been fascinated to learn exactly what Craddock Fitch was doing all these days he'd been, as they described it, doing research.

He'd found himself tortured by being what his mother would have called being at a '*loose end*'. After thirty and more years slaving hard to build his business, expanding it to a size he'd never even dreamed of in the beginning, nowadays he found his compulsory idleness very hard to tolerate. His bones longed for the daily grind, the cut and thrust; even the severe exhaustion he'd had to face on a daily basis would have been welcomed. Passing his time shopping for Kate in the village and walking his dog in no way compensated him, although he found the absorption his new project brought him scarcely filled the gap. Except he did miss Kate in the evenings, a lonely dinner in a hotel no matter how tasty, or how beautifully presented, was no match for her presence.

But today Craddock Fitch had made progress. At last. His two sons had had their names changed from Fitch to Patterson in 1981. So now they were Graham and Michael Patterson, and their mother was Stella Patterson. Their stepfather, whom he loathed even though he'd never met him, was Cosmo Patterson. Of all the names. *Cosmo*! What on earth did that mean? Was his father an astronomer? Did it have any connection with the universe or was it something entirely different? He sneaked into the local library and went to the reference shelves and found a huge

Oxford Dictionary, but the nearest he could get was cosmos and that referred to the universe, so Cosmo must be the same, perhaps. Daft name. Daft man. What on earth had he done to his two boys with a name like that? Perhaps he'd sent them to a public school? Briefly Craddock Fitch swelled with pride, and then worried himself sick that he, their real dad, might not fit in with them. He hadn't enough polish, not enough learning, not enough *savoir faire*. His self-esteem took a staggering blow, almost as bad as the day he realised his business was about to fold.

It was only when Craddock was desperately trying to fall asleep (and had been for well over an hour) that it occurred to him that when he'd found the papers about the boys having their names changed along with preliminary papers regarding a divorce, it was a solicitor in Leeds whose address was on the paperwork. Maybe then ... Craddock got up and by the light from his bedside lamp he hunted through his briefcase and found he was right. Leeds then was where he would go tomorrow. With his mind made up he fell asleep within minutes of turning out the light.

A bright new Craddock bounded down to reception the next morning, informed them he would be leaving immediately after breakfast and wouldn't be staying on for that extra night he'd asked for. Breakfast had never tasted so good. He had a full English, knowing he shouldn't but he did, and he enjoyed every single mouthful. He left the hotel, woke up his satnav, and headed for Leeds.

It was a long time since he'd been in a big industrial city, and it made him relish the idea of Turnham Malpas and the gossiping lot of villagers who'd challenged him so many times over the years. He decided they were a grand lot and he rated Turnham Malpas the best place in Britain to live. He'd tracked down a hotel just out of the centre of Leeds on his iPad and pulled up there about half-past three. They had a room, non-smoking, and using the lift he headed for room 204. Not having Kate to unpack for him he debated whether or not to unpack, but then he remembered his suit. When that was hanging in the wardrobe and with his wash bag propped on the shelf behind the washbasin he decided to find the solicitor who dealt with the name change. Smith, Collins and Beresford in Greek Street. It wasn't until he arrived at the reception desk that it occurred to Craddock that the Mr Beresford he wanted to see might not even be there any more. Could even be dead. Craddock immediately fixed his mind on death and he shuddered at the thought. Had his boys become soldiers? Had they been killed in Afghanistan? Or, worse, injured beyond hope of a normal life? Right now was his first real chance of finding them and if excessive grovelling was necessary then grovel he would. No one living could grovel better than he when he chose to. It wasn't something he was accustomed to, but he would do it if he had to.

The receptionist, one of those brittle young women who'd chosen to be tough, especially to men, greeted him with a brisk, 'Good morning. Do you have an appointment?'

'Mr Beresford?'

She checked her screen. 'Your name?'

This was the point when he would have to lie. 'Craddock Fitch. I rang yesterday around lunchtime and was told to come as soon as I could.'

'Ah. That must have been in my lunch hour.'

Craddock wondered what she ate for lunch. Three lettuce leaves and half a tomato he guessed. With an espresso. No sugar.

He waited.

'I can't see you've been registered.'

'Well, I was told to come, so I've come. Maybe someone, not as efficient as you obviously are, forgot to make a note.'

She gave him half a smile that only just reached the corners of her mouth and said, 'We'll squeeze you in.'

Craddock decided to charm her. He gave her the kind of smile he reserved for Kate, did he see a slight blush on her cheek? No, he was flattering himself. 'Thank you, thank you very much. I'll wait here, shall I?'

'Take a seat. Won't be long.'

Craddock sank down into a very comfortable and very expensive-looking armchair, and thought that they must charge a lot for their services to afford chairs like these in reception. Indeed the whole office shouted money. The pictures of the partners, both old oil paintings and more recently photographs on the walls, were impressive; all of them solid northerners, two even with a gold watch and chain across their chests. He was gratified to see that Mr Beresford's photograph showed a man of stature and presence but was there a gentle twinkle in his eye that the owner had tried hard to disguise?

'Mr Fitch. Mr Beresford is ready for you now.' The receptionist made it sound as though it was at great inconvenience to both her and Mr Beresford that he'd been granted an interview. Anybody would think he was asking for it for free. Fat chance of that in this opulent place.

The strong grip of Mr Beresford's handshake impressed Craddock and he began to soften towards him.

He explained his mission, brought out the paperwork and then waited.

'You're from round these parts?'

'Yes, I am. A long time ago.'

'Thought so, there's still a hint of an accent. It never quite goes does it, try as you might.'

Craddock smiled. 'No, it doesn't.'

'As a boy?'

Craddock nodded. 'I went to Queen's Road School.'

Mr Beresford looked up, startled. 'No! Me too. I don't believe this. I don't remember *Craddock* Fitch. Now let me see ... I do remember a *Henry* Fitch though, definitely, perhaps he's a brother of yours? Fitch is such an uncommon name.'

'That's me. Henry Craddock Fitch. Dropped the Henry when I went into business. Thought it sounded a bit poncey.'

Mr Beresford laughed. 'After all these years. Well I never. Remember me? You won't, I was quite a few years younger than you. Bertie Beresford, that's me, you were a legend to us younger boys for the tricks you got up to. We all wished we were as daring as you. My word, what a coincidence. What a coincidence. Well, I must say.' He went back to the business in hand. 'And I dealt with your divorce, didn't I? It seems a long time ago now. But I remember. Mrs Stella Patterson. Of course. Beautiful, beautiful woman, as I recall. She could have been dressed in rags and she would still have looked splendid. A pity she never completed the divorce papers with us, I set the wheels in motion but then she never turned up for her appointment and that was the last I saw of her.' He put a stop to his recollections. 'Anyway, busy day, must get on. What do you want to know?'

'Do you have any information as to where they were living at the time? I mean, are they still clients of yours?'

Mr Beresford hesitated. 'Explain yourself.'

'When she left me and took our two boys I never heard another word except I knew she'd married this Cosmo fella.' He hesitated, decided it would not be helpful to do a character assassination on Cosmo and pressed on. 'I want to get into contact with my two boys, the ones here, Michael and Graham.'

'Ah, right. I've never heard a single thing about *them*, but Cosmo crops up now and again in the press.'

'He does? In what capacity?'

Bertie Beresford paused a moment as though weighing up if it was correct for him to tell the wronged husband. 'He's a Leeds councillor.'

'No! They still live in Leeds? What a stroke of luck.'

'He does, somewhere smart no doubt, but I don't know a thing about your wife, well, your wife that was, nor your boys.'

'Right.' Craddock waited for more information.

'Can't tell you anymore.' With a kindly helpful tone in his voice he added, 'But he will have a vote, won't he?'

'Vote?' What was Bertie Beresford talking about?

'He'll be registered to vote.'

Craddock smiled, the light had dawned. 'Ah, yes, I see what you mean. I could get their address that way.'

Mr Beresford cut him short; he'd said too much already. 'May I offer you some advice, Mr Fitch?'

Craddock nodded his head.

'Sitting in this chair for all these years I have learned that grown-up children may not necessarily be pining to see their real father.' He checked the paperwork Craddock had brought with him. 'Yours, you see, were very young at the time, and they'll have little memory of you, if any. They may have found themselves with a good and loving stepfather, and won't be able to see the need for you. So whatever you do, don't go in with blaring trumpets and gifts and expect a welcome. You'll more than likely get a puzzled look and the door shut in your face. So be aware. Don't expect too much. But good luck, Henry.' He smiled and Craddock saw the twinkle come back in his eyes.

'Thanks for seeing me, pure chance it was you, but I'm glad. If I have time would you care for a drink after office hours sometime, the two of us could trawl back over our days at Queen's Road School? Hear about how you've landed up here looking so prosperous.'

'Of course, just give me a ring next time you're in Leeds.'

'Might be sooner than you think.'

'Remember, don't expect too much and then you won't be disappointed. Good morning, Mr Fitch. You know where to find me.'

Later that same day Craddock was sitting in his car, a few yards from the house belonging to Cosmo. They were all very similar, with a sameness that told him they were 1930s-built: solid, expensive, confident. Depending on how much space was available to each house, some had double, some single, garages added. As he expected, Cosmo's garage was a double. A well-kept house with a beautiful garden to the front. Almost artistic, something rather more than a square of grass surrounded with plants and shrubs. Now Craddock knew where Cosmo lived, he had to retreat and plan his campaign with craft and guile, and he was good at that; but his campaign also needed Kate's empathy. He'd drive home and talk to her before he made a move. One false step and he'd lose his two boys and his beloved Kate; in the long term she had to be on his side.

Into his head sprang that comment Bertie Beresford had made so casually, what was it? *Pity for your sake she didn't complete the divorce papers.* It hadn't registered immediately, his head being so full of the boys' names and where they were. Did that mean then that Stella had never properly divorced him? Was he living a lie, thinking he was married to Kate, when in fact he hadn't been free to marry? The last thing on this earth he ever wanted was to be untruthful to Kate, for he loved her far and away above everything else in his life. At the thought, sweat rolled down Craddock's face, trickled down between his shoulder blades. Telling himself that potentially he hadn't deceived her on purpose wasn't the slightest comfort.

The following day when he returned to Turnham Malpas the first thing he did was ring Kate at school. He got a quick, 'Lovely, see you at half-past three, and then you can tell me everything. Make yourself a cup of tea, darling. Bye!'

Craddock went to stand in the front window and looked out at the village. There was no doubt about it, he loved this village, every stick and stone even if it didn't belong to him as he'd always dreamed it would. He felt the misty presence of Ralph Templeton invading his consciousness. For a brief moment the old Craddock crept back and smiled because he had the possibility of getting to know his two sons, whereas Ralph, for all his education, his glittering career in the diplomatic service and his title, had nothing. There was no one anywhere in the entire world to proclaim the name of Sir Ralph Templeton as their father. But he, Craddock Fitch, whom Ralph had despised, had two sons, and he had their addresses in his top pocket garnered from the same voting register as their stepfather. How Ralph would have sneered at the thought that he, wealthy businessman Craddock Fitch, might not actually be legally married to his wife. Or would he? Maybe, being the honest, kindly Ralph whom Craddock remembered, he would have been sorry at the trick that blessed Stella had played on him. But Stella ... Craddock trembled for a moment when he recalled her naked beauty. The nights of passion, the physical attraction he had for her had been overwhelming, and he remembered how at first he'd missed her so very much. He paused for a moment enjoying his memories.

He hadn't found Stella on the electoral register. He dwelt briefly on the reason why not. Died? Divorced? Separated? But that didn't matter; she wouldn't be interested in him anyway, and after all he had Kate, lovely flesh and blood Kate, who loved him just as much as he loved her. But now all of that might be ashes in his mouth. He'd have to tell her. This very day. He couldn't delay it. Why hadn't it occurred to him at the time that they'd never completed the divorce proceedings? He'd been too full of making his embryo of a business grow, that was his trouble; all those years, business, business, business, before everything else, that was why.

But he had a shock when he finally told her.

Kate's amusement at his news filled their sitting room with the joyous sound of her laughter. 'You mean to say we have probably been living in sin all these years? Well, I never. I'd better pack my bag, hadn't I? Hussy that I am. Hell's bells. You wicked man, tempting me into your bed with a marriage cer-tificate worth nothing.'

Craddock couldn't believe her response. Full-blooded laughter. No recriminations, no anger, no reproach. This he hadn't expected. His burden of guilt that had weighed so heavily upon him during the night quickly melted away.

'Well, there's one thing, Craddock, we needn't tell anyone, need we? I don't care. You don't care. You do feel OK about it?' Before he could answer her, she'd added, 'I know you do. Finding her and actually getting a divorce would waste so much time, so don't let's bother. Can you divorce someone in their absence?'

'You don't mind, then?'

'Mind? Well, it has come as something of a shock but what the hell! We love each other. Let's drink to living in sin, shall we?'

Chapter 13

Alice and Johnny had had a bad night with the baby, and when he heard someone ringing the doorbell and discovered it was only half-past four in the morning Johnny was not in the best of moods as he stumbled downstairs to see who was there. He undid the massive bolts, dragged the door open and his first words were, 'What the blazes are you doing here?'

Chris heaved his case in over the threshold, saying, 'That's not a very nice welcome to your brother, is it now?'

Johnny rubbed his hand over his forehead to wake himself up. 'Is there a crisis? What is it?'

'Let me get in. I'm hungry and thirsty and desperate for sleep.'

'Well, what's happened?'

'Nothing's the matter. I just wanted to escape the daily grind of running our empire, that's all.'

'I suppose one day the truth will come out. Alice and I are shattered. We've had almost no sleep, and it's already half-past four. You know where everything is in the kitchen. Help yourself. Same bedroom as before. We'll talk in the morning.' Johnny, too exhausted to care, left Chris to fend for himself. He couldn't remember the last time he'd felt so ghastly. There was more to Chris's sudden appearance than Chris was willing to let on, he knew. Damn him. Just damn him.

The grown-ups had their breakfast around nine. Alice had put the two babies, who'd breakfasted a while ago, on the dining-room floor to play while the grown-ups ate. 'So we don't know why's he's here then?'

Johnny shook his head. 'No, it's not just boredom, which he claims it is. There's something else. He'll tell us eventually. Just look at Ralph; spent half the night awake, and now he's as happy as a pig in muck lying there waving his arms about and watching Charles tottering around. They'll be a dynamic duo once Ralph gets on his feet.'

Alice smiled sympathetically. 'Sorry it was such a poor night. I do think it might be better if, for a while, you sleep in another bedroom, so at least one of us is fresh to face the day.'

'Absolutely not. They're mine as much as they are yours and so we take equal blame,' Johnny teased her. 'I shall be interested to hear Chris's story though. I hope it's not one of his women who's upset him; he takes it all so badly.'

Alice said, 'Mmm, I think that's all play-acting. He's not nearly so upset as he makes himself out to be.'

'Alice!'

'It's true. I got his measure almost the first day I met him. It's all show to illustrate what a sensitive so-and-so he is. But he isn't really; he's as hard as nails where women are concerned. I think it's Fran Charter-Plackett he's come back to see.'

'For goodness sake! She's a child in comparison with his usual women.'

Alice downed the last of her green tea, replaced the cup in the saucer, stood up and said, 'You wait and see, I shall be proved right.' She kissed Johnny's forehead. 'Love you.'

Chris eventually appeared downstairs around half-past ten. He ate his breakfast in the kitchen, assisted by Alice who was determined to find out why he was here so unexpectedly.

'More toast, Chris?'

'No, thanks, Alice. Where are my beloved nephews?'

'Johnny's taken Charles down to the lake to tire him out before his morning sleep, and Ralph is sleeping the sleep of the righteous in his cot having spent most of the night awake.'

Chris smiled at her. 'How do you manage to look so gorgeous after a night like that?'

'Your flattery will get you nowhere with me, Chris. What I want to know is why are you here?'

Chris favoured Alice with a deep calculating look, and then declared he was here because of unfinished business.

'Well, it certainly wasn't hotel business, because after a long struggle and a lot of running about on Johnny's part, the deal is going through next Monday for those country-house hotels on the verge of bankruptcy. So is it woman business?' She asked that question with a quizzical look on her face, her eyebrows raised.

Chris didn't answer.

'Is it Fran?'

After a pause Chris deigned to answer. 'Thought I'd been too abrupt with her. Young, you know; they hurt very badly.'

'Oh, my word. So, he does have a softer side then.'

Their eyes met and they both burst into laughter.

'Oh, Chris. Thirty-two and you still can't get it together. You need someone older and more sophisticated. She's a lovely, lovely, sweet girl with just the right amount of fire. She's not for you, Chris. Not for you.'

Chris looked hurt. 'Not for me?'

'No, and I don't want you lighting her fire again. It's simply not fair to her.'

Chris stood up, put the last piece of toast in his mouth, chewed it well, looked at Alice when he'd swallowed it, and said, 'I'll do as I please.' He headed for the door, opened it and turned back to say, 'Sounds like young Ralph's woken up. You'd better get back to what you're good at – changing nappies.'

Alice was livid at that final parting shot. So angry with him that she decided to phone the Charter-Placketts and let them know who was back in town. Forewarned is forearmed.

It happened to be Harriet who answered her call. 'Alice

Templeton here, Harriet. Got to be quick. Just thought I'd let you know that Chris is back.'

'Oh! Is he? Right. What is he—' was Harriet's reply, but she was too late as Alice had already put down the phone.

'Damn and blast,' said Harriet loud enough to alarm half of Turnham Malpas. She stamped her foot too and it hurt because the limestone floor tiles in the kitchen were so hard. That blasted man, just as Fran seemed to be getting over him. Well, appeared to be, at least. Not quite her bouncy self yet but getting there. Alice sounded angry. Why should she phone here? Did she know something Harriet Charter-Plackett didn't know? Why was he back again when he couldn't stand, he claimed, the English winter? Johnny had told Jimbo only the other day that the two small country hotel chains they were intending buying had at last faced the fact they were heading for bankruptcy and had definitely decided to accept the Templeton's meagre offer. So Chris wasn't entirely a waste of space, but right now Harriet could kick him hard enough to send him right the way back to Rio.

Winter had arrived in earnest about three weeks after he'd left. Icy-cold nights, frost on the ground, and the promise, according to the weather forecast, of a bitter winter right through until the New Year. But still Chris was back again.

Harriet rang Jimbo at the store. 'Don't express big surprise at this piece of news I'm about to tell you; keep a straight face, OK?'

'What on earth are you going to tell me? You're not pregnant, are you?'

She heard him chuckling at the other end of the phone.

'Don't be ridiculous. No I am not. Alice has just rung me and in an ultra-brief phone call told me that Chris is back. So if he comes in to buy something or asking to see Fran be careful, OK? I'm relying on you. I mean it, I'm serious. Home for lunch?'

'Definitely.' Before he put down the receiver Jimbo chuckled again, knowing it would amuse her. And it did. But what then stuck in her mind was the word 'pregnant'. She wished he hadn't said it. He didn't mean anything by it because she was way past that kind of jolly surprise, but Fran certainly wasn't. And so Harriet spent most of her morning off worrying about Fran.

By the time Jimbo came home at two o'clock she had relaxed though. After all, Fran knew all the rules, the two of them talked about it endlessly during her teen years, so Harriet was absolutely certain that Fran would have taken precautions every time. Every time? Said that way it sounded far too often for Harriet's peace of mind. They'd never spent a night away, nor a weekend, all those weeks he was here. So how could they? Should she ask Fran outright when she came home? Or assume she wasn't? Deep horror filled Harriet's head. She honestly couldn't imagine Chris not wanting sex – he looked that kind of a man. Had they been doing it at the Big House, under Johnny and Alice's roof? If they'd colluded with Chris to make it pos- sible, she and Jimbo would have an awful lot to say to Johnny and Alice, and a precious friendship would be in ruins.

Harriet and Jimbo had quiche and salad and some lovely bread rolls for lunch, finished off with one of Harriet's tasty fruit pies. She kept giving him looks full of meaning, and eventually he had to ask why she kept looking at him like that.

'Where's Fran?'

Jimbo said he'd asked Fran to go round collecting the food from their outworkers in the villages.

'Greta has declared she can't fulfil her orders as she's been so busy this week her shelves are almost empty; and we're right down on organic vegetables, and so Fran's calling on absolutely everyone she collects from. Lucky if she's back by three. I've given her the money for lunch at the Wise Man, as she's got to keep her strength up. They've started letting out rooms now, you know, apparently they're doing rather well. They've opened up four rooms, all en suite.'

'I didn't know that. How long have they been doing it?'

'Started in August. You've got to make use of every inch of your establishment if you're to succeed nowadays. Can I finish the fruit pie off?'

'Of course. I won't have any more.' Harriet couldn't have eaten a single piece of anything at all she felt so sick. So that was where it happened then. The Wise Man. He must have paid for a room when they had dinner there. She'd skin him alive if anything untoward had happened. Face a few facts, Harriet, she thought, speak it out loud in words of one syllable. 'Jimbo, you don't think Fran might be pregnant, do you? I mean, she isn't, is she?'

Jimbo's spoon clattered into his dish. 'She'd better not be. Believe me, I'll kill him if she is.'

'Takes two, you know.'

'No, it takes one when he's so much older and more experienced than she is. If you suspect she might be you'll need to have a word when she comes home. Tonight. Don't let another day go by. When did he go back to Rio?'

'I think it's about six weeks.'

'Six weeks. She'll know by now if she is. Where's my diary? He went back almost straight after that meeting where we had to bring Johnny up to speed on Bonfire Night and such. So ...' Jimbo flicked through the pages and worked out it was six and a half weeks since Chris left the village.

'So if she is she's at least six weeks.'

'She won't be, will she? She and I talked through it several times as she was growing up. Flick told her a few home truths too one night. I know, Fran told me. And even Fergus put his oar in.'

'Fergus? Heaven's above, he wouldn't spare her blushes. You know what he's like.'

Harriet felt failure flood all over her. 'I've done all I can to keep her safe, and what's more I don't agree with abortion.'

'I know you don't, I don't either,' Jimbo added. 'Nor do I agree with shotgun marriages. Nor with Fran in Brazil. No. Definitely not. They wouldn't be happy for long. I think he's a bit of a bully. Johnny isn't, but he is.'

'Pity Venetia isn't alive, she'd have been just right for Chris.'

'I always had a soft spot for her, you know. She longed to get married, she told me, but no one ever offered other than Jeremy, poor chap.'

Harriet grunted a mumbled response at the idea of anyone wanting to marry such secondhand goods as Venetia, and immediately went back to her more immediate problem. 'Frankly, I want Fran home here in this house right now.'

'Soon be three o'clock. Let's both go to the store and help her unload the Range Rover. Right now, this minute.'

'I'll clear up then we'll go.' With no pans to wash they soon tidied up the kitchen and reached the store at ten minutes to three to find Tom just starting to help Fran to unload. Between the four of them the organic vegetables were unloaded first, having been picked up the last, and then they unloaded the boxes of chutney and the preserves Greta Jones was waiting for, and the home-baked cakes for the freezer, in no time at all.

'Fran, have you had lunch, darling?'

'No.'

'In that case come straight home with me.'

'Dad needs me here, Mum.'

'You don't need her, do you, Jimbo?' This was an order rather than a question.

'No, I don't.' Jimbo was relieved that Harriet had taken it upon herself to find out. 'Off you go, Fran child, you've already done a day's work. Tom and me can manage, can't we, Tom?'

'We certainly can.'

Harriet threw together a salad with the rest of the quiche, found a lemon drizzle cake that needed finishing off, and shared a fresh pot of coffee with her daughter.

When Fran had wolfed down her meal and was emptying the last of the coffee into her mug, Harriet told her that Chris was back. Fran almost shuddered and then pulled herself together. 'Is he? He hasn't been here, has he?'

'No.'

'Why have you told me?'

'Thought you should know that's all, just in case.'

'In case of what, Mum?'

'I don't know, just thought I should tell you. You know, in case he came in the store and you weren't prepared. Or he rang you unexpectedly.'

'Prepared for what?'

'Well, the surprise of seeing him when you thought he was back home in Rio. Fran, why are you so touchy with me? I thought I was being helpful.'

Fran drank down the rest of her coffee and then stood up, saying, 'All right if I leave the clearing up to you, I'm tired, it's been hard work today, there was so much to collect. I'm going to lie on my bed for a while.'

'You are OK, aren't you, Fran, about Chris? He left the village so abruptly and I did feel that you were very hurt.'

'Well, I wasn't, so don't worry about me. If ... *if* ... he should ask about me I'm not going out with him. I don't even want to see him. I'm playing hard to get. Right?' Fran went to leave the kitchen, but she paused in the doorway as though debating whether she should stay and talk some more. Then she changed her mind and Harriet could hear her slowly climbing the stairs. Things weren't right with Fran. If she said that to Jimbo his answer would be, 'What do you mean? What's she said?'

But Harriet wouldn't have an answer for him. It was simply a mother's intuition.

Chapter 14

Fran didn't have long to wait to see Chris. He arrived at exactly three pm the following afternoon. She was sorting out the fresh fruit displays, making them look so tempting that the customers wouldn't be able to resist buying, a skill she had honed since she was about eleven and had been put in charge of keeping the greetings cards neat and tidy. She was concentrating so hard that she didn't hear Bel, who was on the till, say very softly to her, 'Fran, someone for you, love.' So Chris was beside her before she'd had time to prime herself for their encounter.

A split second before he gently tapped her on her shoulder she smelt his aftershave and immediately stopped piling the oranges into a pyramid and swung round to face him.

'Hi, Fran. I'm back.'

'So you are.'

Chris bent his head with the intention of kissing her on the mouth but she put her hand on his chest and pushed him away. 'Sorry, not when I'm working.'

He drew back, surprised by her response. Refusing a kiss from Chris Templeton simply wasn't allowed. 'Too busy with a few oranges to greet me?'

'They're Jaffas and worth sixty-five pence each and the very devil to stack.' Her hand trembled slightly. 'Oops!' The pyramid began tumbling to the floor.

Chris laughed. Fran almost wept.

Chris began picking up the oranges and handing them to her.

'You stack them again and I'll pick them up for you. No, no, don't, *I'll* pick them up.'

'Please, I can manage. Thank you.'

Bel, hearing the stress in Fran's voice, decided to intervene. 'We can't have customers helping doing the displays, now can we, Fran? I assume you are a customer? What can I get you?' Bel, normally the gentlest of people, had a sharp edge to her voice which brought Chris to a standstill.

'Right, I'll leave you to it. What time do you finish today?'

Fran never even turned to look at him, she simply said, concentrating again on stacking the oranges, 'I'm not free tonight. Got things planned. Sorry.'

'I thought perhaps the Wise Man might be an idea tonight.'

'Fortunately for me I have other things planned, as I have already said. Hope you enjoy your stay. There, Bel, I've finished the oranges. Do you fancy a cup of tea before the school mums all turn up?'

'I fancy a cup too.' But Chris's request was ignored. He half made up his mind to follow Fran into the store's kitchen, where hopefully they could talk more privately, but she shut the door behind her with a rather bigger bang than it needed. Chris decided to take the hint. Instead he chose the largest box of chocolates he could find on the shelves, paid Bel for it, and asked her for a piece of paper he could use to write a note. He tucked the note under the ribbon on the box, and said to Bel, 'Could you give her this when she brings your cup of tea?'

Bel, secretly loving being involved in their romantic affair which no one was supposed to know about but which they all did, accepted the box with feigned reluctance and promised she would do as he asked. Chris, rather puzzled by Fran's response to him, but at the same time wise enough to know the ways of women and to assume she was playing hard to get, quietly wandered out. He was disappointed that he would have to spend the evening with Johnny and Alice and their two demanding babies.

Still, tomorrow was another day. But it was a bit unexpected to be rejected in this way. He was unaccustomed to it.

Fran stayed behind to help in the mail-order office as Greta was fretting about getting behind with her orders. 'These will all have to be posted tomorrow because Tom'll have cashed up in the post office by now. I do hate not getting them off straight away.'

'Never mind. They'll all blame the delay on the post, not you.'

'Do you think so? Yes, I expect you're right. I heard that Chris talking to Bel a while ago. He's very handsome.'

'He is.'

'My Vince isn't handsome, never has been, but he is *very* irresistible.'

'Handsome is as handsome does, Greta.'

'Oh, my word, you sound very down about him. Isn't he all he's cracked up to be, then?'

Greta watched Fran's face for her reaction, but Fran had turned away and was leaving. 'I like it in your office, I'll miss you when you move to the Old Barn,' she said.

'I'll have a lot more room though, and at least something pleasant to look out on which I haven't got here, all I have here is dustbins and recycling bins to look at, and the light on for most of the day, even in summer. Still, you can always sneak away and come to visit me on some kind of trumped-up excuse. Parents aren't always the best people to confide in, you know, and though most people think I'm a gossip, I do know when to keep my mouth shut.' Greta smiled at Fran and patted her arm to illustrate her good intentions. 'I've known you since you were born, and wouldn't do anything to harm you. You can trust me. Right?'

'Thanks, Greta. I'll remember what you've said.'

Bel handed Fran the box of chocolates as she was leaving, expecting Fran would be delighted, but she accepted them without any enthusiasm. 'Goodnight, Fran, love. See you tomorrow.'

'Goodnight, Bel.' There was a big fancy waste bin outside the store and Fran was very tempted to put the chocolates in it, but decided that her mum, to say nothing of her dad, would be delighted to help her eat them. And why not? That's what chocolates were for. Was she wrong? Should she be more welcoming to Chris, when that was what she wanted to do more then anything? Was she throwing away something she would never have within her reach ever again?

Harriet fell on the chocolates with delight. 'I love these. If I was being hanged for murder and they asked me what I would like for my last meal I'd say these chocolates. There's only one centre I don't like and that's the coffee cream.'

'Find one and I'll eat it. In fact I'll eat all the coffee creams to make sure you don't get one by mistake,' said Jimbo.

'Oh, darling. What a sacrifice. That's devotion for you, isn't it, Fran?'

Whereupon Fran burst into tears and fled upstairs.

Harriet started up, intending to follow her, but Jimbo said, 'Leave her a while, Harriet, then go up.'

'But she needs me.'

'She needs time to cry too. Bel called and told me that Fran deliberately gave him the cold shoulder in the store this afternoon when he wanted to see her, and he had to leave without her really acknowledging him. Hence the chocolates.'

Harriet sat down again. 'Ah, right. How long shall I leave it?'

Jimbo sorted out another coffee cream, saying, 'You're right, these are a bit disgusting, aren't they? Give it ten minutes.'

'Right.' Harriet religiously watched the clock and when the ten minutes was up headed off upstairs calling out, 'I'm having a gin and tonic, Fran, would you like one?'

There was no reply.

Harriet rapped on Fran's door. 'Are you all right?'

When there was still no reply she opened the door and said, 'It's me, darling, can I come in?'

Fran was laid on the bed staring at the ceiling through tear-filled eyes. Harriet sat on the end of the bed and waited. Eventually Fran said, 'I'm being a fool. This person, who wants to be treated as an adult, is behaving like a twelve-year-old with a crush on the school's head boy.'

Harriet burst into laughter. 'Honestly, for heaven's sake, he bolts off back to his old stamping grounds, and then comes back here imagining he can carry on where he left off. The absolute gall of the man, who does he think he is? He really needs a kick up the backside.'

'Mum!'

'Well, he does, thinking you've gone into a state of suspended animation while he prances off into the night.'

'My trouble is I half-expected he would ask me to go back to Rio with him. I knew he wouldn't, but I was convinced, kind of, that he might, that he *would*.'

'I can understand that, he seemed so keen, didn't he?'

'He did to me. Then he went. He hasn't even emailed me while he's been away. Mind you, I haven't emailed him either.'

'Ask yourself why you haven't.'

'Mmm. I don't know the answer to that. I wonder why I didn't?'

'Some sixth sense telling you something? After all, he's almost an old man compared with you.'

'He isn't, honestly.' Fran drifted off into another world but then said, 'We did it, you know.'

'I guessed.'

'I wasn't going to tell you. Perhaps that shows I'm not old enough for him. Fancy, telling my mother, like a child in primary school wanting a gold star for good behaviour. I must be an idiot.'

'No, Fran, that you definitely are not.'

Fran sat up, swung her legs off the bed, saying at the same time, 'I'll have that gin and tonic now if it's still on offer.'

'It certainly is.'

Fran drank three and asked for a fourth, which made Jimbo say, 'Are you sure? You don't normally drink four gins.'

'Yes, I am sure, Dad. Here you are.' Fran offered her glass for a refill. 'I did when Chris and I went out. One night I had six. I don't know how I got home.'

Appalled by the prospect, Jimbo said, 'And then you drove home?'

'Yes. He followed me just in case.'

'Just in case! You still could have had an accident, whether he was there behind you or not. And it wasn't such a big deal on his part, he was on his way home himself seeing as he was living at Alice and Johnny's.'

'Dad. Honestly. He did care.'

Harriet, seeing they were on the brink of a full-scale argument, interrupted. 'Chris should never have let you drink *six* gins and then cheerfully let you drive home. That was irresponsible, Fran, whatever you say, it was downright irresponsible. He knows better than that. He's not a fool, just too blessed good-looking for his own good.'

'That's about the first true word you've said. He treated me like an adult—'

'Only because it suited him to,' Harriet snapped back.

'Mum! If you're going to speak of him like that I shall not mention him again in your presence. He deserves better than that from you. You're usually so fair-minded.'

'She isn't any more,' said Jimbo. 'She didn't want to welcome poor old Merc and Ford back to the village.'

'Why not? They've never done you any harm, now have they?'

'No, but he is an ex jail-bird, and there's no smoke without fire.'

'It was a miscarriage of justice, they said so.'

'"Not enough evidence to convict him" doesn't mean he was

125

completely innocent. They jailed him when perhaps, give or take a bit, they shouldn't have, I know. But there are no grey areas within the law. It's either yes or no.'

Jimbo declared he'd never known his dear wife to be so dead set with her ideas. 'It's not fair to Merc, who is lovely.'

'I don't like her going along with him being the innocent party. I think she knows more than she lets on.'

Turning to speak to Fran, Harriet said, 'However, you're well shot of Chris, darling. Be brave and don't let him persuade you otherwise.'

'That's for me to decide, not you. If he genuinely asks me to go to Rio when he goes back, I very well may go with him. It would be so exciting, so different, especially with him. Now I'm off to bed. Goodnight. Don't eat all the chocolates.'

After they had listened for her footsteps crossing the landing and the door to her room being shut, Jimbo said, 'Well, that was well handled, I must say. Very reassuring.'

'Oh, shut up, Jimbo. Just shut up.'

Upstairs Fran lay in bed thinking about crossing the world to be with Chris. She imagined herself meeting his mother, his friends, and how envious the old girlfriends would be that a slip of a thing from good old England had won him for herself. She had to admit she loved parties and when he'd talked about life back at home it appeared that the parties were super exciting, far more so than here in England; more daring, more dynamic. All Fran could think about was Chris and how he felt, and what he looked like, and his sense of humour, and his roars of laughter when she said something even only mildly funny. He really was well and truly the man for her. He wouldn't want babies one after the other like Alice and Johnny; he'd want life to be more fun than that. Alice once told her that Johnny wanted at least four children and wouldn't be satisfied with less. *Wouldn't be satisfied with less?* Huh! Not likely. For one brief second before she fell asleep Fran recollected what a happy childhood she'd had with two brothers and a sister all older than her, lavishing endless time and patience on her. She'd been so lucky. But now she had Chris to look after her.

But at three o'clock in the morning Fran woke with all her thoughts about Chris in a total jumble. Was he really as wonderful as she always imagined? If there was a major crisis of some sort in her life, would he be the man to stand alongside her, supporting her, caring for her, helping her to sort out her life, like her dad had always been there for her mum? After all, life isn't actually always full of parties and laughter. Sometimes there are bad times that have to be got through, like when Mum lost that baby when she, Fran, was about three. She was too young to understand about it all, and remembered wondering why they talked about a baby though she hadn't seen one anywhere; but she was aware of the complete sadness in the house, and how the others were so thoughtful to Mum and Dad, and how Grandmama Charter-Plackett had come to run the house and keep everyone well looked after because Mum was so depressed.

Fran remembered Dad shouldering the burden of managing everything to relieve Mum of her worries about them all. How he put Fran to bed, when it had always been Mum who did that, and how he had given her the wrong pyjamas to wear and she'd cried. How he even sewed a button on her cardigan because she definitely wanted to wear it to nursery and she wouldn't go if she couldn't wear it. How Mum cried and Dad was so patient and loving with her. That was the kind of man you needed when your life had crashed. Fran fell asleep at about half-past five, but the alarm rang at six because she was on early start and she crawled out of bed feeling like death.

She felt like that for most of the day, like death was just around the corner, and yet she rarely had such morbid grave thoughts. She was one of those people who felt as if she would live for ever; but today an early grave almost felt welcome. Chris had left a note for her. He must have pushed it under the door after closing time so it was there for her to find when she opened up. Love notes at that time in the morning for some strange reason didn't appeal today, and so she put it in her uniform pocket to deal with when she felt more in the mood.

The endless day dragged on and finally, about four o'clock, when she was due to finish, she decided that she'd go home, strip off, have a shower and go to bed to catch up on her sleep. Before she put her uniform in the wash as she was expected to do every day she took the note out of the pocket, along with the tissues that had gathered there, and opened it.

Dear Frances. If you are feeling like it I shall be at the Wise Man at eight tonight and would love to book our favourite table (!!) for the two of us. How about it? Yours, Chris.

She knew that (!!) really meant he'd book a room for them too. Well, not tonight, Chris. I'm in no fit state to bare my all for anyone, least of all for someone who thinks he can disappear off into the night and not communicate for weeks. So Fran tore the note into little pieces and put it in the waste bin in her bathroom. She showered and went to bed falling asleep almost before she'd pulled the duvet over her and got cosy.

When she woke about half-past nine she vaguely recollected her mother coming in at some stage to ask if she wanted dinner but she had no recollection of answering her, and at the same moment Fran realised the bed was wet. Horrified to think she could possibly have wet the bed she leapt out and went straight to her bathroom to find she was wrong, she was bleeding. Copiously. Frightened she shouted, 'Mum! Mum!' as loudly as she could.

Harriet didn't hear her at first, but Jimbo did. 'Harriet? Fran's shouting for you. Shall I go?'

'No, I'll go.' Harriet raced up the stairs and straight into Fran's bedroom, knowing in her heart of hearts that something was seriously wrong. 'It's me, Fran. Shall I come in?'

'Yes, please. Oh! Mum! This is awful. I can't move, I'm losing so much blood and stuff as well.'

'Blood?' Harriet opened the door and rushed to her daughter's side.

'Yes. Blood. A haemorrhage. You know, really bad. And I've got a lot of pain too. What can I do? I can't sit here on the loo for ever.'

'Oh, darling.' Harriet knew instantly what it was. It was an early miscarriage. That must be what it was. How to deal with it? She didn't know. But she'd better tell Fran outright, no messing. 'Do you think you might be having a miscarriage? I mean, it may not be, but perhaps it is. Have you missed a couple of times?'

Fran, already pale and delicate looking, went paler still. 'I'm always so irregular that I never know when. I suppose I might be, you know, like you said. I'm not on the pill. Chris took the precautions.'

'Mmm. Well, there's no doubt about it – we have to get you medical attention, Fran.' Harriet stroke her hair to calm her.

Fran grimaced. 'I'm not going to hospital, definitely not.'

'You are, because I say so. This isn't normal at all.'

'I really don't need to go to hospital. It'll stop in a bit.'

'Is it stopping?'

Fran shook her head.

'I'm sorry, darling, but you do, for whatever reason it turns out to be. Now I won't be long, but I have to talk to your dad about what to do.'

'Does he have to know?'

Harriet nodded. 'Absolutely. He does. Stay where you are till I get back.'

Jimbo, not realising the seriousness of the situation, was in his office working on the computer. When he saw that Harriet was as white as a sheet and trembling, he asked, 'She isn't alright, is she?'

'No, she is not. As far as I can tell she's,' Harriet took a deep breath, 'having an early miscarriage.' She cleared her throat. 'It's so bad she can't get off the loo.'

Jimbo shot to his feet. 'Right, let's go.'

'Where are we going?'

'Hospital, of course. After that I shall be up at the Big House tearing Chris Templeton to pieces. He won't be called good-looking after I've finished with him.'

'Right.'

They left Fran at the hospital looking more worried than they had ever seen her. Vulnerable and very desperate. Fran whispered to her dad, 'I'm so sorry. So very sorry. I'd no idea, though I have felt funny today, I thought ... anyway ... a miscarriage. Oh, God. Chris will be so upset.'

Harriet didn't think that he would be upset; just the opposite, more likely.

Jimbo answered her. 'Look here, darling child of mine, what you have to do is get on with being brave. Have this minor op if you need it in the morning to make sure there's no infection and that everything has come away as it should, and then you come home and you'll be loved and cherished and cared for, and you'll be better in no time. You'll have to get better. After all how will the store manage without you? The takings will plummet without you there. I know I certainly can't cope without you, and neither can your mum. We'll all be rooting for you, believe me. Good night, my darling.' Jimbo pressed a kiss on his daughter's forehead.

'Mum. I've never had an operation before. I don't want everyone to know. Mum, don't tell anyone, please. No one must know.'

'They won't if I've anything to do with it. Don't worry,

darling. We'll be back before you know it. Bye, bye, see you tomorrow. Oh no, it's today *now*, so it's not that far away, is it? Anyway, goodnight, sweetheart. You try to sleep for a while.'

Jimbo and Harriet left the hospital and arrived home about three in the morning, both of them feeling worried almost beyond endurance. They didn't sleep at all. Jimbo kept muttering loud oaths concerning Chris Templeton's integrity and what he would do to him when they met, while Harriet couldn't stop weeping at the thought of the pain of losing a child, and how distressing it was going to be for Fran. Damn that Chris. Damn him! It didn't seem to have occurred to Fran at the moment that it was a child she was losing, but it would, Harriet knew.

Chapter 15

News travels fast especially when you don't want it to and it was the same with Fran being in hospital. It couldn't be expected that a hospital so close to home as Culworth wouldn't have someone working there who knew someone who lived in one of the three villages, who knew exactly who Fran was and because of being on night duty had spotted her emergency operation on the schedule. So by eleven o'clock that morning a woman who lived in Penny Fawcett burst into the store full of the news.

'My neighbour works there, you see, she told me, I'm so sorry.' She leaned confidentially towards Bel. 'Did she take something to get rid of it then?'

'I'm afraid I don't know what you're talking about. I only work here.'

'You must know, Bel, of course you must. I mean where's Jimbo this morning? You must have had an explanation about him not being here. Where's Fran? Where's Harriet? Where's Tom? He'll know, being manager. Well?' The woman leaned her elbow on the till counter and waited for an explanation.

'Tom's making coffee for him and me, and we know nothing about anything. Are you shopping or just here to spread rumours?'

'It's the truth. Her name was down for whatever it's called when you've had a miscarriage, D and B, or something. No, that's not it. D and C, I think that's it. Must be that Chris's. They'll have given her something to get rid of it, I bet, them with their money and connections in high places. Is he here at the moment or back where he belongs?'

Bel pressed the emergency bell under the till and also shouted at the top of her voice. 'Tom! There's an emergency. Can you come please. Now!'

Tom arrived almost before Bel had finished speaking. Due to his years in the police force before he came to live in the village he was secretly held in awe by many of the people who lived in Penny Fawcett because on more than one occasion, as he frequented the pub in Penny Fawcett rather than the Royal Oak, he'd assisted the publican to tackle punters who were requiring instant removal, assistance he gave with steely efficiency.

He didn't inquire why, but simply said, 'I'm afraid I shall have to ask you to leave. Thank you for calling.' With a dramatic gesture he pulled the outside door wide open. 'Now, if you please.'

The woman debated if Tom had any legal right to be evicting her, but the harsh chilling stare he gave her from his usually warm, friendly eyes put an end to her deliberations.

'I shall tell everyone I've been turned out for speaking the truth. That's all I did. Speak the truth. On the list it was. In black and white.' With an angry flick of her head she stormed out, determined not to darken their door again, until she remembered she couldn't be going all the way to Culworth for every little thing she needed, not with the cost of petrol nowadays.

Tom went back into the kitchen to collect their mugs of coffee and he also brought back a biscuit or two each for their mutual comfort.

'We might have known this would happen. Honestly, I'd nothing I could say except we didn't know anything as we only worked here. It's going to be like this all morning.' Bel's eyes filled with tears. 'Poor Fran, I love her like a daughter, I really do, and she doesn't deserve this.'

'On the practical side, losing the baby has done her a good turn. Got rid of an almighty problem, let's be honest.'

'Yes, I expect you're right in one way. Is the baby the reason he's come back here, do you think?'

Tom pounced on Bel's explanation immediately. 'Of course that'll be it. But now it's all too late. Intending to make an honest woman of her, that'll be why.'

'I don't think that counts for anything now. It doesn't matter, you know, like it did. Maybe, though, he's brought the stuff she's taken to get rid of it.'

'No, no, Bel, that's not Fran at all, she wouldn't do a thing like that, now would she?'

A customer came in needing stamps and so Tom went into the post office cage and served him. The man didn't ask any questions about Fran at all. After he'd paid for the stamps he then decided to take a Mars Bar to keep him going until his lunch, and then he left without another word. Tom and Bel sighed with relief.

'Look, Tom,' said Bel, 'we'd better get our stories straight. What shall we say, do you think?'

'We know nothing. Absolutely blinking nothing. Not a word. It nearly killed Jimbo having to tell us, I felt so sorry for him. The most sorry I've ever felt in my life for him. We're in the front line of defence for them, you know, Bel, so it's up to us. We need a solid immovable wall around us so it can never be said we let the cat out of the bag.'

'Oh, you're so right, so right. As for Harriet, she looked terrible. They'd been up for most of the night from what they said. So mum's the word.'

The next three customers enjoyed shopping as everyone did who came into the store and they left without any awkward questioning, so Tom and Bel began to relax a little as they realised not everybody knew about Fran.

Bel was busy shelf-filling and Tom was doing his bookkeeping for the post office when the doorbell rang hysterically, and in walked the man of the moment. Chris appeared to have had a good night's sleep because he was smiling and apparently very happy indeed with the world.

'Good morning. Isn't it a wonderful day?' he said.

Bel was surprised by his jollity. Did he know? He must, she presumed, but didn't it matter to him? Wasn't he concerned? She hoped to avoid any difficult questions by endeavouring to match Chris Templeton's enthusiastic mood, and so she said with vigour, 'It most certainly is. Couldn't be better.'

'I've come in for one of my big shopping events for delivery on Friday. Here's my list. What do you think?'

Bel checked his shopping list and agreed they'd have everything in by Friday. 'The caviar might not come in time but we'll do our very best. How is everyone up at the Big House. Babies doing well?'

'Yes, they are. Ralph appears to be settling down, with not so much wind as he used to have, so that's a bonus. And Charles is very active and rushing about the house at great speed. Yes, they're all doing very nicely. Thanks.' Chris beamed at them both and then asked if Fran was in as he needed a word.

'Sorry, we're in today, just the two of us. Quiet day, you see.'

'Not like Jimbo, Fran and Harriet to be all off together.'

'They don't do it often but today they are,' Bel answered, pretending to be busy clearing an excess of small change from the till. She knew he was watching her and she knew it wouldn't take her long to sort out the change, so she braced herself.

'Do we have any idea when they'll be back?'

'No,' said Tom.

'I might drop back before closing time to see if they've got home.'

Bel shrugged. 'Just as you like. We close at seven but Tom and I will have gone by five o'clock. It's the casuals after that. They won't know anything either.' She immediately wished she hadn't said that. The solid wall Tom had spoken of had suddenly felt to be crumbling and she knew Chris was astute enough to have picked up on that. Blast, thought Bel.

'I see. A conspiracy of silence then.' Chris looked from one

135

to the other of them, turned away and left, but in a second he was back as though expecting to learn something more when he caught them unawares. But they'd not spoken at all. 'I'll have some jelly babies for Charles please, got to have something to tempt him into submission with.' He paid and then finally left, giving them a long penetrating look before he closed the door.

As it turned out, Jimbo had arrived at the Big House to see Chris, and Chris was in so he never got to the store when it was only the casuals in charge.

Both Johnny and Alice were in too. Alice told him that Chris was in his room reading, but Jimbo guessed maybe that was a cover and in reality Chris was more likely sleeping.

'Well, I need to see him rather urgently. Shall we disturb him or shall I sit here and wait?'

'It sounds serious, Jimbo.' Johnny got to his feet, aware Jimbo appeared to have something unpleasant to impart to Chris.

'Oh, it's serious, yes.'

'I'll go get him then. Would you like to use my study?'

'Yes, I would. Thanks.' Seated in Craddock Fitch's old study brought back lots of memories for Jimbo, and he allowed himself a wry smile as he remembered the challenges he and Craddock had often faced in here. But this challenge was the biggest ever.

He heard footsteps and then in came Chris. He went straight round to what was now Johnny's chair, seated himself comfortably, and said, 'Am I to be told the secret of the entire Charter-Plackett family avoiding me this last couple of days? I hope so, as it's all getting very mysterious.'

'There's no mystery at all. We've been otherwise occupied.'

'Right. It's still mysterious.' Chris lit a cigarette while he waited for Jimbo's explanation.

If ever there was a man in charge of himself, utterly confident that nothing he could be told would faze him, it was Christopher Templeton at this moment, and Jimbo felt an element of repugnance when he looked at Chris. Jimbo knew that if Chris was the last man on earth he would not allow him to marry his daughter, not even for the survival of the whole human race. 'Remember Frances?'

Chris smiled. 'Of course. How could I forget her? She's a lovely, fun-loving, exciting, charming, wonderful person, and you should be proud to have her as a daughter.'

Jimbo agreed. 'We are very proud of her. After what she's gone through this last twenty-four hours we know she's a strong, wonderful person.'

Not a flicker of curiosity crossed Chris's face.

'You see, Chris, she's suffered,' Jimbo paused to take a deep breath, 'a miscarriage. She's home now, from hospital, in bed resting. It's been a terrible shock for us and for her.' Jimbo waited for a reply.

Chris knocked some ash from his cigarette into his cupped hand. 'And?'

'And?' Jimbo leapt to his feet, placed his hands on the desk, leaned forwards and through gritted teeth, said, 'It's your baby, I thought you might be interested to know what's happened. We are deeply grieved for the loss of the baby and for what Fran has gone through.' Jimbo raised his voice to make sure Chris understood how he felt. 'Have you no conscience, man? She believed in you. What are you? *Twelve* years older than she is, an experienced man of the world and you have no conscience when you knew she was a virgin, knew she was all those years younger than you, when you swept her off her feet with the glamour of your position, your wealth, your charm, your good looks. You knew all of that, and still you didn't take enough care to make sure she didn't get pregnant?'

Chris stood up, stubbed out his cigarette, put his lighter back in his pocket, faced Jimbo with a face utterly under control, and said, 'She knows what makes the world tick and believe me she was willing. Very willing.'

Jimbo blanched.

Chris almost began to smile and in that split second Jimbo sensed this wasn't the first time Chris had faced an irate father.

'*C'est la vie*, Jimbo. *C'est la vie!*' Chris said

Perhaps if he hadn't said it in French, Jimbo might not have hit him quite so hard. But the fact that he dismissed the idea of Fran's vulnerability in French somehow made Fran appear cheap, and Jimbo wasn't having that.

He punched Chris on the chin with an almighty blow that much to Jimbo's surprise knocked Chris out cold. He fell between the desk chair and the fireplace, catching the side of his head on one of the brass spikes of the ornate Victorian fireguard as he collapsed.

'My God! I've killed him!' Jimbo prodded a toe at Chris's leg and Chris responded with a slight squirm. So he wasn't dead, just stunned. Wouldn't matter if he was, it was what he deserved, Jimbo felt.

Breathing heavily, Jimbo marched into the sitting room to tell Johnny what had happened. With a dead straight face he said slowly and deliberately, 'I've just knocked your brother unconscious. He may need hospital treatment. Sorry and all that. Why? You may well ask. He's made our daughter Frances pregnant, but last night she had a miscarriage, and he's not the slightest bit repentant in any way at all, and so I punched him. He's still breathing though. Good day to you both.'

Jimbo didn't start the car until he'd got his emotions under control. When he did he roared down the drive, swung right into Church Lane and then down Jacks Lane, Stocks Row, and home. Harriet found him sitting on a kitchen chair helpless with mirth. She asked him what had happened up at the Big House and he couldn't tell her for laughing.

Harriet was angry with him. 'I've been worried sick about what might have happened to you. It is neither the time nor the place for roaring with laughter. Nothing, absolutely *nothing*, that has happened since last night is funny, you know. Fran's asleep, that's *if* you're interested.'

Jimbo wiped his eyes, and said, 'I've locked the front door so no one can get in. If the doorbell goes, I'll answer it.'

Making no sense of what he said because she was so angry she ignored him, asking instead if he'd like to share her pot of tea.

'Yes, please. I knocked him out.'

Harriet sat down rather more heavily than she'd intended. 'What? Not Chris?'

Jimbo nodded. 'Everything was going fine until he told me twice that it was Fran who was more than willing, he said ...' Jimbo began laughing again. 'He said, "*C'est la vie,* Jimbo, *c'est la vie.*" And that did it. I saw red and punched him, right there on the jaw, and he fell down. He's not dead, well, he wasn't when I left, but you should have seen him. You should have seen him! He went down like someone pole-axed. I'd no idea I could do something like that any more.' Jimbo rubbed his knuckles and then picked up his tea and drank the whole cup down in one go. 'Can I have another one, I've got the most terrible thirst?'

'I didn't know you could either.'

'I was just so incensed. I found Johnny then, and told him what had happened.'

'What did he say?'

'Nothing at all. He just looked shocked.'

'And?'

'Then I left for home, as there was no point in hanging about because I wasn't sorry, just blazing mad. Chris isn't sorry, you know. I expect that for him the miscarriage has solved a very awkward problem.'

'No doubt it has. I'm sorry Fran's had to go through it, but in one way it's solved a problem for her too. But on the other hand, we've lost our first grandchild.'

Jimbo sobered up. 'I didn't think about it like that. Of course we have. Have you told the others?'

'I will when I've started feeling better about it all. What an experience! Never again, I hope.'

The other person who couldn't stop laughing was Alice.

Whether it was the shock of it or what, Alice couldn't decide, but the prospect of Jimbo walking calmly into their house needing as he said 'a word with Chris' and then knocking Johnny's fabulous brother out stone cold on the study floor, well, who wouldn't find it funny?

Chris had to be taken to hospital because, firstly he'd been knocked unconscious and was only just coming round when Johnny found him, and secondly he had this rather nasty-looking wound on his left temple with a lot of blood about, so obviously that needed looking at too.

Between Johnny and Alice they managed to manhandle Chris into the 4×4. And then Alice was left to smother her smile as best she could and, as Chris had once so pointedly reminded her, to look after the children.

She knew, though Johnny hadn't said anything, that he was steaming with temper. All the effort he'd made to renew relationships with the people in the village, people who were already beginning to accept him as their rightful Lord of the Manor, had possibly been thrown away by his own brother. Johnny was never openly critical of Chris and his wild ways, but Alice knew his attitude to life seriously disappointed Johnny.

Johnny waited at the hospital until some decisions had been made about Chris's care. The powers that be decided he needed to stay in for at least one night as they were none too happy about the wound on his temple and so Johnny went home, collected some overnight things for the invalid, went back to the hospital to find Chris still in emergency, waiting until they found a ward bed for him.

He had a steadily swelling lump on his jaw where Jimbo's fist had landed that not even Chris would be able to find a believable excuse for, and a dressing on his temple over the cut made by the spike of the fireguard, and now around the edges of the dressing, a rapidly spreading bruise was becoming more obvious.

'Right. Here's your stuff. I'll ring the hospital later on to see how you are. If you can come home, you can ring for a taxi. We'll talk when you get home. Other than that I have nothing to say. Bye, Chris.'

'He told you, did he?'

Johnny nodded.

'You've brought my cigarettes?'

'No. They won't allow you to smoke.'

Chris gave Johnny a lop-sided grin. 'I'd get round them somehow.'

Finally Johnny could take no more from him. 'How could you have been so careless? Have you no conscience?'

'I was careless once, that's all. Just once when she caught me by surprise.'

'You do know the very first moment I feel you are on the mend, you're going home. If I have to handcuff you and drag you there all the way, so be it. I just regret I didn't send you straight back home. Why did you come back? Really?'

'To see Fran, of course. I kept thinking about her such a lot, and so I thought I'd come to see if the old magic was still there. And I did briefly toy with the idea of taking her back to live in Rio ...'

'And have you?'

Chris grinned. 'Have I what?'

'Seen Fran?'

'No. Well, I did, yes, in the store briefly. But she refused to have anything to do with me. I sent her a note telling her I'd see her in the Wise Man that evening, but she never turned up. Other than that ...' Chris tried to settle himself more comfortably, but found the effort too much. 'God, my head. Aaah!'

Johnny said, 'I'll be off then. I shan't visit tonight. I've lost such a lot of time today.'

'Would Alice come? I'm in need of some tender loving care.'

'That's up to Alice, I doubt it though, as she hasn't stopped laughing since Jimbo left.'

'Alice! *Laughing* at *me*?'

'Yes. Bye.'

Johnny pulled up outside the Big House, switched off the engine and sat thinking about what to do next. He wasn't going to Jimbo's to apologise; that was for Chris to do, although Johnny guessed he wouldn't do it without pressure. Poor Fran. She was a lovely girl, good looking, sweet natured, hard-working. She didn't deserve Chris tempting her. Well, it hadn't happened in his house, that was for certain. The trouble was that Chris was so hard for women to resist; he had such charm, he was so handsome. Well, the moment he was well enough to travel he was going home.

Johnny thumped the steering wheel with the heel of his hand. Damn him. So careless with other people's emotions was Chris. Since he was fourteen he'd ridden roughshod over people, caring only for his own physical satisfaction, and nothing for them. But for it to be Fran, that was the worst part of this mess. Everyone who knew Fran was fond of her, and she was genuinely very likeable. But for Jimbo to knock Chris out, it must have been an almighty punch. Suddenly Johnny's amusement tipped the scales and he was laughing like Alice had. Alice had always had a much more frank assessment of Chris's character than everyone else, not being quite so bowled over by his good looks.

Johnny leapt out of the car and went into his house, his happiness rising as he entered. The Big House always had that effect on him, partly because he loved the house so much, and also because inside were the three people he adored more than anyone else in the whole world. Charles came running to meet him. 'Dada. Dada.' His arms spread wide, ready to clutch his

142

daddy's legs. Johnny caught hold of him and swung him up on to his shoulders, and the two of them went to find Alice and Ralph.

Chapter 16

They knew there was some connection, Bel had almost let it slip to Dottie that there was a very serious connection between Chris and Fran. But the fact that Chris had gone back after only five days in Turnham Malpas and most of that had been spent in hospital, and the fact Fran was nowhere to be seen, gave everyone something to speculate about.

So on the following Monday afternoon when the embroidery class met as usual there was no need to scratch their heads for something to talk about. It was there waiting to be discussed, the most interesting part was that none of them had any answers. But Evie needed to speak first.

'Good news, everyone. It's settled, they've accepted the new design. I've brought all the materials we need and so we can begin at last. Here we are, look.' Evie unrolled a detailed plan of what the congregation had decided upon, and was delighted by the admiring silence while they studied it.

Eventually Sylvia said, 'Well, you've done some brilliant designs in the past but this, well, it's the best ever. It's wonderful, Evie, and we're all so very lucky to have you in charge. Fantastic.'

Some of them were speechless, so captivated were they by what she showed them.

'We're privileged, totally privileged to work on this. I'm gobsmacked. They'll come from far and wide to see it. It's marvellous,' said Barbara the weekender.

Merc, who felt humbled by Evie's spectacular talent, said

softly, 'Amazing! Absolutely amazing! Thank you, thank you so much for giving me the opportunity to work on such a splendid hanging. I love the colours. I love the face of the saint, so strong, yet compassionate, and the background, by Jove, Dottie, that'll keep you busy.'

Dottie was overawed. 'It will, it will. I shall be proud too, yes, proud to work on that.'

'I like that gold thread, Evie,' said Sheila, wondering if she, Sheila Bissett, with her humble origins, was clever enough to do justice to Evie's design. 'I wish I had talent like this. You are lucky, so lucky, Evie.'

'They took a while to decide they'd accept it. It was the new vicar who persuaded them, he gasped when he saw it.'

'And so he should. Well, let's get cracking,' said Barbara. 'I can't wait to start.'

It took a while to sort everyone out but none of them could leave until they'd actually made a start on their part of the hanging. 'Let's stay another hour, shall we? It's already quarter-past three and we've done nothing yet,' Evie suggested.

They all nodded their agreement and it was silent for a while until Evie had made the tea and as they always did – tea and embroidery not being good bedfellows – they'd moved away from the big table they used to work at to a couple of the tables reserved for the coffee mornings. It was then that Dottie asked if anyone had any more news about Fran and better still about why Jimbo was suffering with a painful hand.

'When I was in there this morning choosing a card for my gran's birthday—' began Barbara.

'She must be a big age, how old is she now?' someone asked

Barbara answered, 'One hundred and three on Thursday.'

'No!'

'Well, anyway, he moaned a bit about his hand hurting and said he'd sprained it. But I don't think you get bruises on each knuckle when you sprain your hand; it didn't look right somehow. Harriet said how painful it was and quickly changed the subject. Grandmama Charter-Plackett came in to say she was going to their house and did she need to take anything with her for lunch? Harriet said no and almost pushed her out before she could say any more. So Harriet's working in the store instead of Fran, and the old lady's making lunch. So they can deny it as much as they like, but things aren't right, whatever they say.'

Sylvia, who wished she still worked at the rectory because then she might have got to know a bit more, said, 'Bel and Tom know nothing, they say, and instead of a big laugh when you go in it's more like the reception at MI6, blank expressions and mum's the word, with a bit of avoiding-looking-you-straight-in-the-eye thrown in. They'll be asking us for identification soon, us that's known them for years.'

It was Dottie who contributed the most mind-blowing piece of information. 'Well, I clean Thursday afternoons for Harriet, as you know, but I've been told this week I don't need to go, but they'll pay me double next week when I go, because they know I rely on the money.'

This information from Dottie shocked them all. 'Pay you for doing *nothing*! That doesn't sound like Jimbo at all, he must have had a nervous breakdown. There must be something very serious going on. But what?' said Sheila, intrigued by this piece of extremely worthwhile gossip.

Grandmama went straight round from the store to Jimbo's house, glad to be of use. She'd been given a key and as she let herself in she called out, 'Fran. It's me, dear. Ready for your morning coffee? Because I am.' She got no reply. 'I'll make it, then.'

Though Katherine Charter-Plackett sounded cheerful, she didn't feel it. First she was horrified to find that the lovely Chris, whom she'd met a couple of times and who had impressed her with his charm and good looks, had been, as they said now, 'having it off' with her granddaughter. First she'd been livid, then she'd accepted it happened nowadays (and had frequently in the past for that matter, except then it was all swept under the carpet), but for her Frances to undergo all that ... If Johnny hadn't despatched Chris off to Rio, she'd have personally gone up to the Big House and told Chris what she thought of him. As she filled the kettle, she laughed at the thought of Jimbo punching him. Served him right. If she'd been twenty – well, perhaps thirty – years younger she'd have done the same.

Grandmama, tray in hand, cautiously climbed the stairs calling out, 'Sit up, I'm nearly there. Now, darling, how are you this morning? I've brought a lovely steak pie for tonight for supper, made by my own fair hand. Here's your coffee. Have a sip and tell me if I've got it right.'

Fran looked a better colour this morning but she obviously wasn't up to scratch. There was not a remnant of a smile yet.

'Gran.'

Well, at least she'd spoken. 'Yes, dear, I'm all ears.'

'I've been such a fool.'

'No, Fran, you haven't. You fell for a perfectly gorgeous man. I know I did myself, except I was much too old for him.' She grinned wickedly at Fran. 'Because he is, or rather was, ut-terly wonderful and so good-looking, though not so much now perhaps, now your Dad's sorted him out. Men like Chris, who are so very tempting, are very rare. But he is, or rather was, just a mite too unscrupulous for such a lovely girl as you.'

'But Dad knocked him out cold.'

'Don't feel sorry for him, it was just what he deserved. Have you had a shower today? I've brought you a new shower gel of mine. I think it's wonderful, and so would you like to try it? If you like it, I might be persuaded to leave it with you.'

Fran ignored the offer, but she did say, 'He sent me some lovely flowers.'

'That was kind.' Frankly Grandmama rather thought it might be Johnny who'd done that, but he'd put Chris's name on them;

it seemed more a Johnny gesture than a Chris one. 'We mustn't let that naughty man put us off for the rest of our lives must we, you and I? I'm certainly not going to. I know it's been hard but remember the good times.' She wished she hadn't said that. 'The times when you laughed and when you thought about how lovely and exciting he was. Those are the times to cling to, not the time when he forgot you were a human being and left you feeling desolate, because that's what he's done. This new shower gel, it's not old lady's lavender. Have a smell.'

Fran showed some interest but then Grandmama changed tack and said, 'There's lots of reasons why babies abort you know, because they're not—'

'I don't want to hear. I'm going to stop thinking about the baby and think it's perhaps the best thing that could have happened. I didn't do anything to make me lose it so there must have been something wrong with it, and nature took its course.'

'Well, I must say that sounds like a very intelligent way of thinking about it.'

But Fran burst into tears and thrashed about on the bed. Grandmama invaded her en suite, found a box of tissues and mopped her face, gradually calming her down.

'You can't stay in bed for the rest of your life, can you, Fran?'

'I can't, can I? I might get up today.'

'That sounds very sensible. I approve of that. I'm not staying in bed for the rest of mine either. We both lost someone we thought was terrific, didn't we? I've always loved Peter, you know, with his charisma and his good looks and his compassion for even the most wicked of us, but that clerical collar is a barrier, Chris was much more fun.'

Fran managed to snigger at the idea of Gran being in love with Peter.

'I'm off down now. Have a shower and use that gel I've brought you. I'll be in the kitchen making lunch. The store, you know, is more dead than alive without you.'

'But what will they all say to me if I go back?'

'Stuff them.'

'Gran!'

'I mean it. You don't have to explain anything; it's your life, isn't it?'

As she headed for the kitchen Grandmama punched the air with triumph. The best place for Fran was in the store facing up to it. OK, she'd have bad days – anyone would with what she'd had to face – but it was the only solution.

The scent of Grandmama's shower gel wafted down into the kitchen even before Fran had arrived in there. 'My word, Fran, you smell lovely. It's not ready yet; I'm slower than I used to be. Your mum's joining us for lunch, she says, that'll be nice. Your dad's having his usual pork pie and a mug of tea made for him by Greta, as if he isn't capable of making his own tea. That Greta worships him, even though she finds fault with him at every turn.' Grandmama turned to look at Fran and felt heartened by the improvement in her face. She almost looked quite chirpy. 'You look, and smell, lovely. What do you think of that gel?'

'Magnificent and I'll keep it, if that's all right. Thanks. Chris would have loved it.'

'Don't look back, darling Fran. That does no good at all, believe me. There'll be some other very worthwhile young man who'll appreciate it just as much as Chris would have done, if he'd had the guts to stay.'

'Dad told him, you know.' Fran stared out of the window. 'About what happened. But he never mentioned it, not even in an email. But it was his baby as much as mine. No regrets at all, apparently.'

'So as well as no guts, he'd no feelings either.'

'Except for those beautiful flowers.'

Best leave her with the comfort of the flowers coming from Chris. 'Well, of course, yes. Except for the flowers. So I suppose he had some feelings, but he didn't know how to express them.

149

Lunch is ready, come and eat. Harriet won't be long, she says.'

A week later Fran put in a full day in the store and found the customers more than willing to forget they'd not seen her for a fortnight. They all treated her as though they'd seen her only yesterday.

Chapter 17

That same day Grandmama got Fran out of bed, over their lunch in Ralph and Muriel's old house, Kate and Craddock were discussing what to do. 'You see, Craddock, your two sons will be astounded to hear from you, and they may well feel very resentful that you've never been in touch.'

'How could I when I didn't know where they were?'

'Exactly, but at the age they were when your wife ran off with them they weren't old enough to understand. One day they had a dad and the next day they didn't, nor the next day, and the next day they still didn't. Birthdays, Christmases; nothing from Dad. Perhaps every birthday and every single Christmas since Stella ran off, they thought surely this time you would get in touch. But, through no fault of your own, you didn't. That is neglect in big capital letters as far as children are concerned. You must see it from their point of view.'

'I've tried, but it is hard.'

'Do you know anything about this Cosmo fellow?'

'Only what I've found in the *Yorkshire Post* in the newspaper section of the reference library. He's been a councillor for years. He seems to specialise in children, their safety, their education, protecting them from paedophiles, speeding up adoption processes, things like that. He's a loudmouth, even so. Had a lot to say when the Queen went to visit Yorkshire about the expense of the Royal family and such, which annoyed me when I read it. I bet he has a beard and mumbles into it when he talks.'

'More coffee, darling? Did you ever see him then, when it happened?'

'No, never. She just went. Came home from work to find the door locked, and no wife or children. Yes, please to coffee. Well, they never will hear from me if I don't write will they, but what the hell I can say I do not know. I've been thinking about it for days. Or would it be better if I go up there and knock on their doors?'

'If it was you in their situation, what would you prefer?'

Craddock deliberated for a minute and then said, 'I think I would like to have a letter first as then I can throw it in the bin and ignore it completely if that's how I feel, or I could reply and tell me to get stuffed, or write to ask when can we meet?'

'Seeing as they are your flesh and blood, maybe they would feel exactly like that. So do it today, write something straight from the heart.' Kate paused for moment and then asked him, 'It has occurred to me, why, if you've had that letter from that solicitor all these years, have you never written before? Made contact like you are going to do now?'

This straight from the shoulder question silenced Craddock. He'd no answer. None at all. Why hadn't he? He didn't know. 'Too busy. Too angry.'

'In forty years, too busy? Come on, darling, that's no answer.'

'Too scared.'

'You?'

'Yes, me. Never bothered me before. I did used to comfort myself when Ralph was alive that no matter how much better he was at getting his own gentlemanly way as opposed to my big fat brown envelopes, my only advantage was I'd fathered two sons, and he would never have any. It gave me a lot of pleasure, comforting myself with that.'

'Really, my darling, that's rather sad.'

'I know that now, but not then. But now I will do something

about these two boys of mine. If I don't get replies, well so be it. I can only blame myself.'

An hour later he said, 'This is the one I'm sending to Michael. Read it, please, and tell me what you think.'

Dear Michael,

This is a letter from your father, a father who has been a hectically busy businessman for years and neglected living an honourable life. If I had led that kind of life I would have somehow found a way of finding you. But my heart trembled with fear at the thought. Although I would love to become part of your life, it is entirely up to you to decide. I can only ask. I was a wealthy man but am no longer. I am married again to a lovely woman called Kate who would be delighted to welcome you to our home, along with your possible wife and children.

It was 23rd October when we last saw each other. You were too small to know that though, and neither did I know. And amazingly that is the date at the top of this letter. Coincidence or a good omen?

I know it is years and years ago since we saw each other, but it would please an old man and his wife if you could find the time to fit us in to your life, even if it's for only one day. We live in a wonderful part of the country with trees and hills and lovely views by the score. Give us a try!

Henry Craddock Fitch.

'Well?'

Kate studied the letter for a short while and then beamed her approval. 'It's nicely matter of fact, with just the right touch of sentiment, and it's not too mushy. Was it really the 23rd? Because you must have it right, he'll ask, I'm sure he will, and if you've got it wrong this letter will be in the bin, immediately.'

'Engraved on my heart.'

'Do a similar one for Graham. No, do a different one for him as they'll be sure to compare.'

It took even longer to write the second letter and Craddock was out of patience by the time he was satisfied with it. 'There that's the best I can do. I deserve a whisky.'

Kate read it through twice and then said, 'This is excellent, the same but different. I like the bit where you've said about his hair always being unruly, just enough to make a contact but not forced. Yes. Copy it out again because of your spelling mistakes, and then I'll walk down to the post box with them.'

'Thank you, Mrs Fitch.' Craddock tugged his forelock. 'Can I go out to play now?'

'When you've copied it out, yes, you can.'

They both burst out laughing.

It was almost three weeks before he got his answer. It felt more like two hundred weeks, but the calendar said three.

Dear Craddock Fitch.

Thank you for your letter. It arrived while I was away at a conference so I've only just opened it. What a wonderful surprise. Of course I would like to meet you. Choose two weekends when you would be free to come and I will fit in with one of them. My dad, Cosmo, will probably want to meet you at some point too. Looking forward to hearing from you,

Sincerely,

Michael Patterson.

Craddock almost, but not quite, danced round the sitting room with delight. OK, there wasn't much information in the letter, but at least he'd been invited for the weekend. A whole weekend.

Two weeks later when he'd decided Graham must have thrown his letter in the bin he heard from Graham. This was a very different letter.

Dear Craddock, Dad,

I have never forgotten you, and missed you tremendously at first, but time heals, you know, and gradually I settled here in Leeds. Cosmo has helped and supported us throughout our lives and been like a real dad to us both. I have a lovely wife called Anita and five children. Two girls and three boys. I am a GP and love my work. Anita is an orthopaedic surgeon and works part time. At half term we are coming your way on holiday as it happens. What luck! We have a minibus so there is room for Michael who will be holidaying with us, can we all come at the same time? We would be able to call to see you on our way down to the house we have rented, so you won't need to provide accommodation. So glad you found us.

Looking forward to seeing you,

Yours, Graham.

'Now that is very encouraging, very encouraging.' Kate said as soon as she read it. 'Graham sounds a lovely man. I think perhaps that Michael has either never married or has married and is now divorced or she's dead. What do you think?'

Craddock, filled to the brim with delight, said, 'Well, by the sound of it we shall soon find out. This is excellent. Five grandchildren. I say! Shall we have room for them all?'

'Well, they are obviously not staying the night, so we don't have to find beds so that's a relief. I'm looking forward to this. Now, darling, aren't you glad you plucked up your courage? I know I am.'

'I am. Shall we send them a photo of us?'

'Yes, let's do that. And ask them exactly when they are coming down this way on their holiday.'

'I wonder how old the children are. A doctor. I say! That's one in the eye for Ralph.'

Kate was ashamed of Craddock for an instant, but still she didn't want to spoil his pleasure. 'Craddock, don't reply for a day or so, just take it slowly.'

'I wonder what Michael does for a living.'

'They don't mention their mother do they, either of them? It'll all come out in the wash I expect. Perhaps they think it will only annoy you if they do, considering the trick she played on you.'

'I've no resentment about her, you know, none at all, I wouldn't mind finding out she's done well for herself or had a cracking job, I was so wrapped up in my work, you see, building the business, you know, I left the children to her. I feel rejuvenated after this news, though. A grandfather, and I didn't know it. Isn't it wonderful?'

Kate hugged him. 'Of course it is. It's wonderful. I have five ready-made grandchildren, and I'll be able to tell the children at school all about them and they'll think they're mine.'

Craddock detected a hint of wistfulness in her voice. 'I'm sorry we haven't any of our own.'

'As much my fault as anyone's. I didn't want any children and I was fulfilled enough with the children at school. But maybe right now, for a little while, I wish I had children of my own. It'll soon pass.'

Craddock went to stand beside her and, putting his arm around her shoulders, he said, 'They'd have been lovely children if you'd had some, with you for a mother.' He kissed her temple and hugged her again. 'I love you, Kate, so much, and I shall love seeing you with the grandchildren. They'll like you more than me as I'm no good with children.'

'Give yourself a chance, darling. I suspect you'll do better than anyone I know.'

They had exactly a week in which to prepare themselves. In her own mind Kate decided that for at least one part of their visit she'd take the children to the new play area the council had recently provided down by Turnham Beck, and leave Michael and Graham to talk with Craddock. She so longed for them all to get on well.

★

They were a whole hour late arriving but Graham had rung and explained about the traffic holding them up. So the minibus pulled up outside the house and the children flooded out of it and were ringing the doorbell before Craddock could get organised. He was almost trembling with apprehension and fear that he wouldn't do well, and he desperately wanted Kate beside him, but she'd decided he had to greet them himself.

The older girl, judging by her height, introduced herself. 'I'm Sarah, this is my sister Gemma, and here are the three boys. Stand up tall, boys, please, this is your new grandad. Grandad, this is Judd, this is Max, and this little one is Ross. They are six, four and two. I'm twelve and Gemma is ten. And here's my dad Graham getting out of the driving seat. This is our mum; you can call her Anita. And this is Uncle Michael. And Ross needs the toilet immediately. I'll take him. Where is it?'

Totally confused by the size of the family and the confidence of this little girl, Craddock was speechless. He waved an arm vaguely in the direction of the downstairs loo and all the children formed a queue outside the toilet to await their turn. Craddock took this moment to look at his daughter-in-law and his two sons. She was stunning; a model, but a surgeon? She kissed his cheek and hugged him and apologised for her family. 'I do hope they're not too overwhelming, Craddock, they are well behaved.'

Michael stepped forward. 'Craddock.' And they shook hands.

Graham took one look at him, smiled warmly and before he knew it Craddock was wrapped in a bear hug the like of which he couldn't remember having experienced before. Graham stood back to appraise him. 'Sorry we're late, the traffic was horrendous. But we're here and glad to be. Your wife? Where is she?'

'In the kitchen checking the soup.'

'Which way?'

'Right through to the back.'

Graham marched past the toilet queue and straight into the kitchen where they could hear him greeting Kate. 'Anita! Come and meet Kate.'

The soup was ready so Kate decided with Graham's approval that they should sit down immediately as the children had declared themselves starving hungry. Craddock had imagined chaos with so many children at the table, but they all made conversation, had beautiful table manners, apart from Ross who was too young to have beautiful manners although he tried hard. Conversation flowed easily, although Michael remained a little withdrawn, but it was scarcely noticeable with so many squeezed round the table. Kate's salad and especially her puddings were greatly appreciated by everyone.

'Now, look, you haven't got long I know, but shall I take the children to our very new playground here in the village so the grown-ups can have a talk. It'll do them good when they've another long journey to face.'

Anita wholeheartedly agreed but with reservations. 'It's rather a crowd. Will you be able to manage?'

Kate smiled. 'I'm the head of the primary school here in the village, so, yes, I shall be able to manage.'

'Oh, sorry! You will be able to cope then. I didn't know.'

So Kate left them to talk and she marched round to the playground with the children, much to Grandmama Charter-Plackett's surprise who was heading off for a very late lunch at the Royal Oak with a friend from her schooldays.

Kate had left Craddock and his guests with a huge pot of coffee and they sat together in front of the fire in the sitting room with Anita playing hostess.

Michael decided to speak. 'Strange this, sitting here together, when I've resented you all these years for letting mother take us away like she did.'

'I didn't *let* her, Michael. Without any warning, she simply

158

wasn't there when I got home from work, and neither were you and Graham. I was working on a building site about five miles away, and I came home in my van expecting you all to be at home, and you weren't. There wasn't even a note to explain.'

'But why?'

'I honestly don't know. You all went in the old banger we used. I had the van; it was mucky and had no proper seats for anyone other than the driver and one passenger. Where did you go?'

Graham said, 'We don't know. We were too young to understand. We thought, I suppose, we'd gone out for the day. But we just never went home. She did it again when I was about twelve and Michael ten. She palmed us off on a neighbour for the morning, she said. But we never saw her again. We still haven't.'

'Again? Dumped you on a neighbour? I can't believe it. What about Cosmo?'

'The neighbour took us round when he came home from the office and that was that. We'd been dumped again.'

Michael spoke up. 'You've no idea what it feels like. Your whole world destroyed. You never feel safe again. It's as if you don't count any more. There's no security, no safe haven.' He clammed up after this sudden outburst.

'I can't believe it. Do you know where she is now?'

Graham replied because Michael obviously found the situation too difficult. 'We have no idea. She has never communicated. If it hadn't been for Cosmo, I don't know what we would have done. Been put in a children's home, I suppose.' The pain in Graham's face as he remembered was unbearable for Craddock to see.

'He cared for you then, even though your mother had disappeared?'

'Yes. They never married, you know, but he told us he thought of us as his own and so he brought us up. School fees, the lot. We couldn't have had a better dad.'

Craddock had to do a rapid on-site revision of his opinion of Cosmo. 'Three cheers for Cosmo then.'

'Absolutely.' Michael smiled properly for the first time and Craddock saw in that smile that he would have an uphill battle to make a real friend of Michael, never mind a son.

'You've never married then, Michael.'

'Couldn't take the risk after the example our so-called mother set us. Makes you feel like rubbish, complete and utter rubbish. Might as well be thrown in the bin for all she cared. It's extremely hard to trust anyone at all. Without Cosmo ...' Michael lapsed into a reverie and stayed that way, leaving Graham to enlighten Craddock about their lives when Cosmo took over.

Eventually Kate came back with the children, and after a while of desultory conversation everyone was toileted again and then moves were made to leave.

While Kate sorted out drinks and treats for the children to have on the next part of the journey, Anita went in to the kitchen to talk to her. 'Would you be willing to come to stay with us later in the winter? In the New Year perhaps? We'd be delighted if you would. I'm sorry about Michael; he's one of those who has never got over losing his dad, and then his mother abandoning him. I don't think he ever will. Cosmo would like to meet you both, I'm sure, and that would be a chance, wouldn't it?'

'It would, and we'd be pleased to come to visit. Cosmo must be a very special man.'

Anita agreed he was special. 'He certainly has been to Graham and Michael, very special. He'd no need to do what he did, school fees, school trips, paying for Graham to go to university, and that's a big commitment as medicine is eight years. It's a long time. He cared for them as if they were his own. They called him Dad too.'

Kate packed the children's treats into a bag and handed it to Anita. 'It's meant so much to Craddock you all coming. There you are, will that be enough?'

'More than enough, thank you so much. It could all have been very awkward this meeting, but instead it's been lovely. I'm just sorry about Michael; he may not ever get over it, you know.' Anita reached forward to kiss Kate and Kate kissed her back.

The children came to find their mother and say their goodbyes. Sarah spoke for them all. 'Thank you so much for having us for lunch, it's been great. Say goodbye, children, to Granny Kate.'

Unaccustomed to her newly acquired role, Granny Kate blushed bright red with surprise, said her goodbyes and went with Craddock to wave them off.

The two of them collapsed in the biggest armchairs and breathed a sigh of relief, not because they were disappointed in the success or otherwise of their day, but from the sheer exhaustion of having all those young children in their home.

'I was a little disappointed with Michael. He could have made more of an effort.'

'Anita says he has never got over losing his dad and then his mother just disappearing. That's why I assume he's never married; he just can't trust people any more.'

'I hope he isn't blaming me. I didn't make her go. She went, it was her choice.'

'Craddock, take it easy. Anita didn't lay blame on anyone, and neither should you. It was your Stella who did the departing.'

'If Cosmo was the kind of man who paid the school fees and looked after those two boys even though he and Stella weren't married and he'd never adopted them, I'm sure he would have been reasonably easy to live with. What is the matter with the woman? She must be unbalanced.'

'I'm looking forward to meeting Cosmo.'

'Are we? Meeting him I mean?'

'Anita has invited us to go and stay sometime in the New Year.'

Craddock sat bolt upright. 'She has?'

'Yes, in front of the children, so I expect she'll keep her word.'

'That's better than I had ever hoped. What were the children like in the new playground?'

Kate smiled at her memories. 'Lovely. Little Ross needs a lot of attention but then he is the youngest of five and he's only two. I suppose he feels left out sometimes and he has to make sure everyone knows he's there. He's a very dear little boy.'

'They are all lovely. Gemma is very quiet, Sarah has a lot to say for herself, and I can't separate the two older boys as they're so alike.'

'Be honest, aren't you pleased you found them all, Craddock? You do realise they've come more than sixty miles out of their way to visit you, remember that.'

'No. I didn't realise. I'm so chuffed and so glad it went off all right. I'm sorry about Michael. But underneath it all I think he's quite a nice person. He's a computer programmer, you know, he told me but only when I asked.'

Kate smiled. 'Well, that explains a lot. They get very introverted, computer programmers, he needs a good woman.'

'All I have to do now is find out where that damned stupid inconsiderate woman is.'

'Who do you mean?'

'My ex-wife Stella, and find her I shall. Stella Fitch, presumably, if she never married Cosmo. She was definitely married to me, although she was more than fifteen minutes late getting to the registry office and we nearly missed our slot.'

'Why bother? You've got what you want, contact with your two sons and a positive heap of grandchildren. Isn't that enough?'

A vicious sneer crossed Craddock's face which he quickly changed to a smile, but not before Kate had caught sight of the sneer. 'She's responsible for a lot of heartache, Kate. I'd like to see how the years have treated her after the tricks she's played on me and Cosmo and those two boys of mine.'

Kate heard the pride in his voice when he said 'those two boys of mine' and rejoiced for him.

Chapter 18

Zack Hooper in his position as verger at the church was still upset about the theft of lead from the roof. Though several weeks had passed, the police had no news about any arrests, and Zack had decided to pay Ford a visit to see if he could help, considering he'd once been a scrap metal merchant.

Marie was horrified. 'You simply mustn't. I know exactly what will happen. You'll lose your temper, he'll think you're accusing him of stealing it himself, and before we know where we are you'll be in hospital with a broken jaw.'

'For goodness sake, woman, you're letting your imagination run away with you. I'll do no such thing. I'm going to get him to help me find out who did it that's all. After all he won't have forgotten who is and who isn't in the business nowadays; they haven't all dropped dead since he was here last.'

'Please, Zack, please don't do it.'

'I have to, Marie, it's my duty. I've no alternative, we've waited long enough. I'm sure our Kitty would make a better job of it. Makes my heart bleed every time I look up and see it missing. And as for the insurance, we might as well not have bothered to pay the premiums; they're twisting and turning about paying.'

'You are right about the cat making a better job of it. She's very bright is our Kitty. Won't they pay up, the insurance, I mean.'

'All I can say about that is the rector's been to see 'em, and you know how persuasive he can be in his lovely way; but it's

164

had no effect. All sorts of loopholes they've discovered. So after I've done my jobs in the church, I'm off to see Ford.'

'Zack, please keep your cool, we don't want any trouble.' Marie laid a gentle hand on his arm and squeezed it, adding, 'Think about your mum. At her age I don't know how she'd take it if anything happened to you.'

'I shall be very careful, I promise. In any case she's so far gone is my mum she'd probably say "who's Zack, do I know him?" See yer later.'

All his tasks completed to his satisfaction, Zack put a comb through his hair, checked the body of the church to make sure nothing was amiss and went out before the tourists, at the moment reading the inscriptions on the gravestones, went inside. Past experience had taught him they'd question him about anything and everything, and take hours of his precious time. Today he had more important matters on his mind, and why he hadn't thought of taking such dynamic action before, he couldn't imagine.

The front garden of Glebe House was immaculate as usual thanks to Merc's tender loving care. Everyone knew she loved flowers and made sure something or other was flowering in every possible corner of her beloved garden. Zack rang the bell and tried the doorknob, but the door was locked. This was unusual in Turnham Malpas, as hardly anyone bothered with door locking unless they were out for the day or something.

Zack went round to the back door and found Ford painting it a vivid orange, a positively eye-stabbing colour, necessitating sunglasses to prevent going blind if you stared at it for too long.

'Morning, Ford, how's things?'

'I'm painting, as you can see. Nearly done. Come to see me about something, Zack?'

'I need your help.'

'Here I am. Ready and waiting.'

'Well, Ford, when I ask you this question I'm not inferring you've done anything wrong, you must understand that, nothing meant by it. But I'm wanting information and you're the man to give it.' Zack paused a moment waiting for reassurance from Ford, but he didn't get it so he stumbled on. 'You see, we've never solved the problem of who stole the lead off the church roof, if you remember? Well, you don't remember because you didn't steal it, I didn't mean it that way, but you know what I mean.' Zack stopped speaking, he couldn't find any more words to explain and he was certainly not getting any help at all from Ford who was solemnly putting the final brush strokes on the back door.

Zack tried opening his mouth but when he did no words came out so he shut it again.

Ford carefully hammered the lid back on the tin of paint, having already placed the brush in an old jug kept specially for that purpose, judging by the multi-coloured streaks of paint they had never managed to wash off it.

He straightened up and looked Zack straight in the eye. 'And?'

Zack cleared his throat. 'Well, it occurred to me that because of your past, I mean, when you were in the scrap metal business, you would likely be able to tell me who *might* be guilty of stealing our lead round here. After all we've no main road through the village so no one sees the church as they're passing by, so it must be someone local, don't you think?'

Ford remained silent.

Zack said, 'I intend to find them myself as the police have made no progress at all in that direction.'

Ford mulled over what Zack had said. Well, at least it appeared that was what he was doing, but he still didn't reply.

'Anyway, if you can't help, I'll be on my way.' After a moment's hesitation Zack decided to go home. If the chap wouldn't even speak . . .

'Come in. Merc's making coffee.'

Zack's spirits rose. He slipped off his shoes as Ford did and followed him into the house.

Seating himself at the kitchen table Ford pulled a pad of paper towards him and took a pen out of his shirt pocket. 'In a twenty-mile radius of Turnham Malpas there are four scrap metal merchants. I shall write them down on this paper in the order of the likelihood, in my opinion, of them being guilty. So the one at the top is the most likely, the least likely is at the bottom. Right?'

Zack nodded. He'd always been able to read upsidedown writing and he watched with interest. As the list lengthened his eyebrows rose up his forehead. Them? Surely not? Never. Couldn't be, not them.

Ford tore the sheet off the pad and passed it to Zack. 'That is as far as I am prepared to go. You don't know me and I don't know you. You do not mention my name because I could possibly be a goner if you do. But, for the sake of the village, which I love, I am prepared to point you in the right direction. If you fail, don't feel disappointed. Everyone on that list will tell you nothing but lies, they don't know what truth is, believe me.'

'You mean they're all ...' Zack didn't know how to say guilty without inferring. But Ford said it for him.

'All guilty. Yes.'

Zack raised questioning eyebrows, asking Ford if he knew more than he was letting on, but Ford avoided his eyes, and instead of answering his unspoken question, asked Merc if the coffee was ready.

'It is. Here we are. Sugar, Zack?'

'Just one, please.'

Merc began telling Zack about the hanging they were stitching for the new church the other side of Culworth, and the atmosphere changed completely. Ford appeared to drink his coffee in peace, while Zack seethed in turmoil. Had Ford confessed to him or not?

Ford suddenly interrupted their conversation. 'Zack, you do know you won't actually find the lead. There are no names on pieces of lead, and the turnover at the moment is so fast after perhaps three weeks it will have been sold on. You do realise though that his own workmen could be stealing for the business with the owner's connivance?' Ford winked, excused himself because he had some more painting to do, he said, and left Zack with Merc to finish his coffee.

'Does he mean that?'

'What?'

'That sometimes the workers in the scrap metal yards steal lead, and the owners buy it from them?'

'Ford doesn't lie.'

'I see.'

'Don't ask me any more. Ford's said more than he should. Finished your coffee? I have to press on. Housework, you know. That list you have in your pocket, you don't tell a living soul where it's come from, right?'

'OK.'

'In fact, I'd like it a lot better if you wrote it out in your own hand and I burned his original list. Here, another piece of paper.'

So Zack copied the list out on to a sheet of writing paper Merc found in the kitchen-table drawer, and she got the matches and burned the original.

It was only when he was walking down Shepherd's Hill on his way home that Zack realised that Ford and Merc were actually scared, really scared, and a shiver ran down his spine. Maybe he wouldn't use this list; it all appeared far too dangerous to him. Anyway, he'd think about it.

But soon a curious incident took place which lead Zack further down the path of finding out who'd stolen the lead.

Marie needed another wardrobe for one of their B&B bedrooms. 'I can't ask people to pay to sleep in that bedroom any longer because the wardrobe is falling to bits.' She'd said this several times over the summer, but Zack had put off doing anything about it. However, by chance she'd caught sight of an advert in the *Culworth Gazette*. *Smart French style single wardrobe for sale. Good condition, coloured ivory. £25 Buyer takes away.* The phone number was a Little Derehams one.

'It sounds ideal, very stylish too, I should imagine. Better than that awful dark-brown thing of ours. Shall I ring up and we'll go and have a look? What do you think? After all, we're not obliged to buy it, are we?'

With nothing better to do, Zack agreed; he liked the price tag of twenty-five pounds. So they rang up and found the address was the one that had been the old pub that had been bought and converted into a house.

The lady with the wardrobe for sale was very well dressed, much more so than anyone Marie thought they would be dealing with. She took them upstairs to see the wardrobe, and on the landing they came across the man who purported to be her husband.

Marie was delighted by the French wardrobe. It was ivory in colour, like it said in the advert, and it would brighten up that bedroom no end. It was in good condition too, stylish and, best of all, it didn't need anything doing to it. 'I'm having all new built-in wardrobes fitted and they're coming Monday to start work so I want this out of the way as soon as possible.' So they paid the money over and agreed that at the weekend they'd come with some transport and collect it.

The husband, who smelled as though he hadn't had a wash, let alone a shower, for days, volunteered to help get the wardrobe down the stairs and out of the door when they came.

'Well,' said Zack, 'that would be very kind indeed. See you Saturday morning about eleven, will that be convenient?' It was. So that was agreed.

'Funny that,' said Marie on the way home, who'd learned a lot about people since they'd started doing the B&B, 'The house is beautiful, the furniture and all that, and so's she; but he's too scruffy for words. He just doesn't fit in, does he, how he looks? He's too well-spoken to be in such scruffy clothes. It's almost as if he's playing a part in a play. Looking unkempt on purpose, kind of. I mean they've got money somewhere, taking into consideration the house and the furniture and all that, and her. But you wouldn't think so to look at him. There's a reason, believe me.'

Zack scoffed at her theory. 'For heaven's sake, Marie, you do get some daft ideas.'

'It's true. I'm pleased with the wardrobe though. I'm taking a hammer to our blinking wardrobe when I get home. It's all it's fit for. We'll save the wood for Bonfire Night up at the big house. Sir Johnny says it's definitely on.'

Marie didn't go with Zack to collect the wardrobe as she'd promised to do a turn helping at the Saturday coffee morning in the church hall. She couldn't believe it when Zack wasn't home at one o'clock when she got back. It was two-thirty before he finally appeared with the wardrobe, and he was drunk like he hadn't been in years. So was Barry Jones who'd agreed to give him a hand seeing as Zack had no van, but the lady had generously given them the bedside table that matched the wardrobe, and so Marie really couldn't complain. The old brown bedside table joined the smashed-up wardrobe on the pile waiting for Bonfire Night, and the B&B bedroom looked stunning.

When Zack finally became coherent round about six o'clock, he explained what had happened. 'The minute we walked in he offered us a drink. Barry thought he meant a cup of tea but he didn't, he meant *drink* as in alcohol. You should have seen his cocktail cabinet, stuffed it was, *stuffed* with quality drink. We could have whatever we wanted and more. Barry said no he wouldn't because he was driving, but Baz insisted.'

'Baz?'

'That's her husband's name. Baz. We got talking, a right talker he is. He's had a very interesting life, he has: market trader like Del Boy on the telly. He's dabbled in just about everything, and you won't believe this, but he asked us if ever we wanted some extra money to let him know and he could make good use of us and Barry's van. Just the right size, he said. Well, of course, Barry's saving up for a big holiday for Pat and 'im next year, and he jumped at the chance. I wasn't too sure, but Barry gave me a nudge and so I said, yes, OK. By the way, Pat doesn't know yet about the holiday, it's a big surprise for her, so don't say a word.'

'All right. All right. But what are you doing, and when? Barry's not so free as you are, you know, he has a five-day week to put in.'

'Evenings it'll be, and weekends. I said not Sundays as I'm needed at the church, and Baz agreed. Not Sundays, he said. So it might not come off, but it could. Anything to eat tonight? I'm starving.'

'So he didn't say what it was?'

'No.'

'Is he just as scruffy as when we saw him?'

'Yes, he is. Now where's my food? I've had no lunch, yer know.'

Further than that Zack was not prepared to go. If he revealed to Marie that him and Barry with his van, helping Baz, were to be rewarded for a few hours' work with more money than Zach earned in a month as verger, then she definitely would put a stop to it and he wasn't having that. Because, let's be honest, it must be something illegal to be paying that kind of money for a few hours' labour. Somewhere right at the back of Zach's mind he remembered a casual mention of scrap metal and lead, but he couldn't quite remember if he was right, being drunk at the time. He should never have agreed to drinking that special whisky as he lost count after three; it went straight to his head. Nor could he remember giving Baz his phone number, but he must have done because one week to the day of collecting the wardrobe the phone rang halfway through the morning. Marie had three B&B guests and had just finished clearing up after their late breakfast when Zack told her he'd had a call from Baz.

'When?'

'When what?'

'When does he want you?'

'Ten o'clock.' Zack neglected to mention he meant 10 p.m.

'Oh. I wanted to go to the market this morning and the bus will have already gone.' She glanced at the clock. 'You'll be late, does Barry know?'

'Ten tonight.' Zack girded himself for Marie's response.

Marie instantly knew it was something illegal. '*Tonight?* Oh, Zack. Please don't go. I told you he was a wrong 'un. I knew it. Please, I'll ring Pat and tell her, then you won't have the van.'

Zack sprang to life. 'You won't, you've not to. And for once in your life you do as I say.'

'Well, I never have before, so I don't see why I should start now.'

'If I have to tie you to the bed before I go, I am *going*.'

'Oh, Zack!'

'I am. Not another word. You know nothing, and that's the way it will stay. I'm not a complete fool, you know. Just leave it with me.'

They spent a stormy Saturday, kind of speaking but not speaking all day, and Marie was glad when it was half-past nine and she heard Barry tap softly on the back door. That was significant in itself coming to the back door as everyone used the front door because that was the easiest, seeing the way round the house was built.

Marie asked Barry, 'Will you need a torch?'

'Good idea.'

Marie went back to watching TV, but she couldn't settle and decided she'd read in bed for a bit. She dropped asleep about midnight with the light on and the book still in her hand, and never even heard Zack creep gently into bed about half-past two. If she'd been awake she'd have seen the big grin on his face, a weary grin but full of satisfaction. He smiled at the thought that Marie had been right about Baz; he was playing a part. Zack would have a great tale to tell the rector. Zack, exhausted, fell asleep in seconds.

'You see, rector, it's complicated to explain. It all began when Marie and me went to buy a secondhand wardrobe for one of our B and B bedrooms.'

Peter could tell immediately this story was going to take a long time to tell so he settled himself on his study sofa and awaited enlightenment. By the time Zack was explaining about Baz and his need for new clothes and a very essential bath, Peter was intrigued.

'They sat on the floor of the van in the back 'cos Barry's van only has three seats and Baz and me and Barry were sitting in those. When we picked 'em up they had a huge collapsible ladder with 'em, and Baz gave them a hand to put it in the back of the van so they had to squeeze in the back with it, and there wasn't much room for 'em. Baz talked to 'em as though they were bosom pals; but Baz had told Barry and me not to speak, so we didn't join in.'

'Did you know any of them? Were they from round here?'

'I thought I knew one of them. I think he's the chap who helps out sometimes in the petrol station on the by-pass, stacking shelves and that. But I could be wrong. Anyway we trundled on till we arrived in Compton Tester of all places. A more dead-alive place you are unlikely to find anywhere in the world. We pulled up, pitch black it was 'cos there was no moon, no street lighting like we haven't got, and sat waiting. There wasn't a leaf stirring, never mind any people; they've no pub, yer see. We sat and sat, not right outside the church like, more to one side but with the church in view. No one spoke 'cos Baz had said

173

don't. The bedroom lights started going out, one by one till all the light we had was the eyes of a white cat crossing the road, dead spit of our Kitty.

'Then he said "Right!" and slipped out quiet as quiet, and stood in the road listening. We opened the van doors and took out Baz's huge ladder. Barry helped him like, and the other two men got out and we all walked over to the church and believe it or believe it not they put the ladder up against the church wall and the two chaps we'd picked up started climbing up onto the roof, and then Baz he went up, but he told us to wait at the bottom of the ladder and watch for them coming back down with the *lead*. Well, I couldn't believe it, there I was taking part in a theft. I've got it all wrong I thought.

'Then I heard some heavy breathing like someone had been running and were getting their breath back so they could speak, and then suddenly there were two men standing beside Barry and me with a finger to their lips to warn us not to speak. By this time Barry and me was shaking, believe me, caught red-handed I thought, caught red-handed, I should have listened to Marie. We seemed to wait a long while but then Baz whispered from up on top "Right!" and we could see their shadows and they were holding something that I guessed, obviously, was a big length of lead roofing. It was then I realised that the two chaps who'd sneaked up on us were each holding a pair of handcuffs, and I still couldn't work out what was happening.'

'So what did happen?' Peter asked, just as puzzled as Zack had been at the time.

'The three of them started coming down the ladder slowly, 'cos it's very heavy; they handed it to us and the two chaps who'd put their fingers to their lips to warn us to keep quiet, clapped the handcuffs on them as soon as their feet hit the ground. "Got yer!" Baz shouted, and followed on with that bit where they say, "I am arresting you …"'

'Sweat was pouring out of me, I was so het up. Barry, in the light of the torches the policemen had switched on, was white and shaking like a leaf, and so was I. The two men in handcuffs were put in a police car that was parked behind a derelict barn bottom end of the village, and on the way to the police station Baz explained.'

Peter waited for the explanation but Zack didn't continue. 'Yes? What then?'

'Ah, well, it was Baz was the undercover policeman, yer see. Barry's van was just right for him, no advertising slogans on it, just a plain dark-red van that nobody would take no notice of. All this because of my Marie seeing the advert about the wardrobe. We're going to be called as witnesses at the trial.'

Peter was delighted. 'So they have confessed to stealing our lead?'

'Yes, and so would you have done if you'd been held in an arm lock like they were, by that Baz. He's tough and not half; he must work out every day, muscles like steel he must have. They were in agony when they confessed. One of 'em tried to escape when we got to the police station, but he'd only gone about five steps when Baz, quick as lightning, grabbed him and held him in an arm lock, and the chap was sweating with the pain and he confessed all. I began to feel sorry for the chap, honestly I did, till I thought about our lead being stolen, and then I decided it was all he deserved.'

'Well, at least that's been sorted out. You were very brave, Zack, to do what you did, very brave indeed, especially when you thought Baz was the real thief.'

Zack began to laugh. 'He, Baz that is, put Barry's van registration number on the police scanning thing to check ownership before he conscripted us and found Barry'd forgotten to renew his road fund licence on his van, three months out of date it was. "See to it Barry," he said. "I don't want attention being drawn to your van when I've used it for police surveillance." So, rector, what do you think?'

Peter stood up. 'I am so proud of you, Zack. So proud. And such a string of coincidences. You see, Marie was right, wasn't she? Sometimes we men need to take notice of a woman's intuition.'

'Except she thought he was the thief, not the police. I did too. Never thought about these undercover police needing to be so real, if you get me, unkempt, mucky clothes. You'd never have thought he was police if you'd seen him; he looked as if he hadn't two ha'penny to rub together, just like the men he arrested. Still he did the trick, didn't he?'

'You'll have a good tale to tell in the pub!'

'I will indeed.' Zack paused for a moment as he made to leave. 'Should I say anything though, me being an unofficial policeman like?'

'Don't mention where he lives, then they can't identify Baz.'

'Of course, yes, that's important. I'll remember that. I'll be off then. Bye, rector.'

It wasn't often that Merc and Ford joined those who felt they owned the table with the ancient settle down one side, but that night they did. And by the time Zack arrived, with his mind primed for the telling of his adventures, accompanied by Marie for their usual Monday night indulgence, the others were already ensconced with a drink in front of them, listening to some story about a race meeting Merc and Ford had been to on Saturday and what an uproarious time they'd had, and Ford had won £157.50 betting on a horse that hadn't a cat in hell's chance of winning.

'How did you know to put a bet on it when it was so hopeless?' asked Dottie, who'd always done well out of taking Ford's advice and was forever mystified by his good luck.

'Something about the way she flirted herself all the way round the ring; as far as she was concerned no other filly in the race had a look in, and so I took a chance on her and won.'

'I told him. I said, she won't win, how can she, she's come nowhere near winning all season.'

Ford laughed. 'But she did. The bookies were laughing all the way to the bank, believe me.'

'And so were you, Ford. Brilliant.' Dottie was completely absorbed by his story, and never noticed that Marie and Zack were adding chairs to the group so they could join in the fun. 'Oh, sorry. Here, look, I'll move up this way. OK now?' Dottie shuffled her chair closer to Merc, so Marie and Zack managed to squeeze in.

'I don't understand why you always win, Ford,' Dottie said.

Ford laughed. 'I don't. Ask Merc, she knows.'

'No, he doesn't,' said Merc tapping the table with a well-manicured fingernail. 'He only tells you about winning, never about when he loses three race meetings on the trot.'

'Tonight,' said Ford, 'I shall buy one round for all of us out of my winnings, OK? A celebratory drink on me for all of us round this table. Right!'

'You're more than generous, Ford, thanks,' said Zack bursting to tell his adventures but not knowing how to make it sound like a casual episode and not the peak excitement of the year, which it was to him. Words of thanks for Ford's generosity said by everyone at the table were followed by a silence, and so Zack chose to speak up. 'I've solved the problem of who stole the lead from our church roof.'

He took a long drink of his home brew to give time for his news to sink in.

'You have? How?' asked Merc.

'You? How've you done that when the police are baffled as they say?' added Sylvia, incredulous.

'Go on then, tell us,' Willie said eagerly, feeling he had a vested interest in Zack's statement, seeing as he'd been the verger before him for more years than he cared to count. 'Get on with it.'

And so Zack related the events of Saturday night to a rapt audience. Within moments of beginning his story, other people in the bar had come to stand around the old table to listen in, and a burst of applause greeted the conclusion of Zack's adventures.

'The strange thing is while we were waiting a cat the spitting image of our Kitty stalked across the road from the direction of the church. Gave me a bit of a funny turn.'

Marie startled, said, 'No, I don't believe you. You never told me.'

'I forgot. But it did. Snow white except for that one black ear and a slightly longer tail than most cats have, just like our Kitty. I swear.'

Someone with their feet firmly planted in real life said, 'Get on. How can your cat have got from here to Compton Tester? It's miles.'

A woman from Penny Fawcett protested, 'Not across the fields it isn't. Over the by-pass and then across the fields it wouldn't take a determined cat all that long. There's not many cats all white with one black ear.'

Someone else who was sceptical of all mysteries involving animals asked, 'Which ear has your Kitty got that's black?'

Marie and Zack both spoke at once.

Marie said, 'Her right ear.'

Zack said, 'Left ear.'

Spontaneous applause broke out.

Zack, disgruntled by their mockery, said, 'Just depends where you're standing when you say it.'

'In any case what's the cat got to do with stealing lead?'

Zack wasn't too sure about that. But then he remembered Marie saying that their Kitty would do a better job finding the thieves than the police were doing. So he explained that, and then he added, 'And I agree with Marie she could; she's bright, is our cat.'

Unfortunately that night Kitty was killed crossing over the

by-pass, presumably on her way home to Turnham Malpas, which, sad though it was, appeared to prove she really was involved seeking out lead thieves. And this was how Kitty joined Jimmy's legendary Sykes the Jack Russell in the mystical animal stories of Turnham Malpas.

Chapter 19

Fran had begun receiving regular texts from Chris. At first she read them minutely, savouring every single word. But after a week of receiving texts at least once a day, she began to bin them the moment she knew they were from Chris. He began by asking how she was, then he moved on to telling her she was always in the forefront of his mind, and the seventh one asked her to visit him in Brazil.

Fran was tempted, very tempted. But he still hadn't mentioned the distress of her miscarriage. There was no mention at all of what she had gone through; no sympathy, no regret, no sadness at his loss either. She stopped reading his messages. Damn him. Damn him.

She worked in the store, harder than ever if that were possible. And gradually she began to rediscover her enthusiasm, so that some days she loved what she did, while on others she simply tolerated the work but had to struggle to be interested. But the texts still kept coming, and occasionally she read them. Finally he was begging her to reply. So she did: NOT COMING. STOP TEXTING.

But he didn't stop, except now they were longer messages sent less frequently. Inside Fran was desperately grieving for Chris, but mostly for the baby.

She still enjoyed the gossip just like her Dad did, and she overheard Marie one day, sitting in the corner by the coffee machine enjoying her free coffee, while talking to Jimbo. 'It broke my heart when our Kitty got killed, you know, Jimbo.

She was such an interesting cat. So Zack and I went to the animal rescue yesterday and we've chosen a four-month-old kitten someone abandoned in that old quarry where they found ... what was her name? I'm blessed if I can remember. I know! Jenny Sweetapple, her that was murdered. Anyway, this kitten's beautiful. She's a tabby with streaks of ginger, and we're calling her Tilly, don't ask me why, and we're collecting her tomorrow. I can't wait.'

Jimbo said, 'I'm not that keen on cats.'

Marie looked up at him in surprise. 'Your Flick had two.'

'I know she did but I never liked them.'

Suddenly out of the blue their conversation was interrupted by Fran. 'I'd like a cat.'

There was such longing in her voice that Jimbo recognised it and tempered his reply accordingly. 'Well, I'm not that keen, but their plus is you don't have to exercise them like when you have a dog.'

Their conversation was interrupted by a rep arriving to see Jimbo and a customer wanting a frozen coffee gateau that required Fran going into the back to the main freezer and picking one out for her. In fact the conversation about cats never picked up again because Marie left, Jimbo went home to sort out some problem with the Inland Revenue that Jimbo described as the Inland Revenue getting far too greedy, while Fran took over in the post office because Tom had to dash home to rescue Evie from a flood in the kitchen.

But later that night, her head having been full of wanting a kitten all day, Fran tackled her dad about it when he'd finished his evening meal. 'I still want a kitten.'

'Kittens grow up into cats, Fran.'

'Obviously.'

'So I'm not too sure. Have you asked Mum?'

'No. But she won't mind.'

'What if you decided to go to university? What then? We'd be left with it.'

'Mum wouldn't mind, and you never know, you might take to it straightaway.'

'And I might not. Why did you throw your mobile on the floor in such a temper, just before we sat down? Are you getting unpleasant calls from someone?'

Fran finished the last mouthful of her marmalade sponge, placed her spoon tidily in her empty dish and finally said, 'If you want to know, I've started getting a lot of texts from Chris. Mostly I don't read them, but sometimes I do. This time he's wanting me to go to Brazil for a holiday, and he'll buy the plane ticket and pay for it. First-class, believe it or not; that's because I once said I'd never be well enough off to fly first-class.'

'Tempting.'

'Yes.'

'Are you going to accept his generous offer?'

'No.'

'Good.'

'He thinks money can buy everything, but it can't. Certainly not me anyway.'

They heard the front door open. It was Harriet back from a meeting she'd been speaking at, and Jimbo went to greet her. Harriet came to sit down at the table while Jimbo supervised the microwave.

'The talk go all right?' asked Fran.

'As well as can be expected, in the circumstances, thank you. They were all teenagers wanting to know how to become chefs overnight. What sort of a day have you had?'

'All right, thanks. I want a cat. Dad says he's not keen, but please say you are. Please.'

'What's brought this on?'

Fran was silent for a moment and then said, 'I just need something to love.' Suddenly tears crept into her eyes.

'Another bad day? I'm so sorry. I'll see what I can do. Where from though?'

'The cat rescue where Marie Hooper's getting hers from tomorrow.'

'Dry your tears before Dad ...'

Jimbo came in, placed a fresh pot of coffee on the table and put Harriet's warmed-up supper in front of her. He sat down to enjoy another coffee with Harriet.

'I'd really like a ginger cat. Ginger all over, no white feet or tummy, just ginger every bit, and I'd call him Tiger. What do you think, Mum?'

'They are quite rare, ginger all over; they normally have some white.'

'I know, but that's what I want, otherwise I can't call it Tiger. Please.'

Jimbo kept his own counsel and waited to see the turn of events. He knew Fran was attempting to find something to fill the vast black hole left by Chris. He just wished the damned man would go away, preferably for ever. It might be a good thing for Fran to focus on a kitten instead of Chris and certainly a lot less painful; in fact he might just say yes.

That night before they put out the light Jimbo told Harriet that Chris was pestering Fran with text messages.

'Oh, no. The man is obsessive.'

'I wonder maybe whether concentrating on training the kitten might be a good thing for her. Take her mind off him. He's now offered for her to go for a holiday in Brazil, and he'll pay the first-class fare.'

'No! He hasn't. Damn it. That's where too much money becomes evil. Trouble is a kitten is a poor substitute for a good man, isn't it? Although, I don't know. Perhaps not.' She smothered her laughter in her pillow.

'Harriet. No, but if it helps her ... And anyway Chris isn't a good man.'

'We still have the basket that Flick's cats used, just needs new bedding, and it wouldn't be on its own a lot because there's three of us in and out of the house, and I love the dear little dishes and things they sell for cats now.'

'Might be a good idea then. Shall we say yes, but kind of reluctantly, don't give in too easily.'

'Why not be enthusiastic, just this once? She does need help to recover. Chris is a total cad, as my mother would have said.'

Jimbo propped himself up on his elbow and leaned over to kiss Harriet. 'You're right, she does. Goodnight, my darling, goodnight.'

'I'm going right now to tell her.'

'No, leave it till morning and then say you can go with her to the cat sanctuary or whatever it's called straightaway tomorrow. More than likely they won't have what she wants and so it'll give us some breathing space to acclimatise ourselves to the idea. That way she can't feel we've rejected her.'

'There is one thing that I am determined on. We get a cat, no messing. She is desperate and that fool in Brazil hasn't as much compassion in the whole of his body as she has in her little finger; she feels things very deeply. Remember that. She thinks the bouquet came from Chris, but it didn't.'

'It said so.'

'It was the florist who wrote the card, as it always is when you do it over the phone; and I know that the florist acted according to Johnny's instructions.'

'Just a minute, I didn't know you were a confidante of Johnny Templeton.'

'I'm not, Alice told me.'

'Ah, right. It makes Chris even more of a pig of a man than I thought. I should have hit him twice as hard.'

'Considering the damage you did in the first round, I rather think not. Goodnight. I can't wait for tomorrow.'

★

The following morning Harriet did her yoga as usual but cut her programme short because she couldn't wait any longer to tell Fran of their decision.

'Fran, I know it's your day off—'

'It isn't, that's tomorrow.'

'Well, it's been changed. You have to have today off.'

'Why?'

'Well, you see I'm going to the cat rescue to look for a kitten or a young cat, whichever. Ginger, I thought. Come with me?'

Fran sat up in bed, her face aglow. 'You mean for me, a kitten for me? Is it all right with Dad?'

'Of course. You can use Flick's old cat basket and we'll find some old blanket and cut it up, and I have a cushion I've no use for, so it can have that in the bottom. What do you think?'

Fran was out of bed and heading for her bathroom. 'I'm coming!'

On the way to the cat rescue, Fran said, 'We'd better not go, they'll think I'm an idiot wanting a kitten at my age. Turn round, and we'll go home.'

'Certainly not. We'll say the house feels empty now the other cat has died.'

'Which other cat? We haven't got one.'

'I know but we can always say we have, mention Flick's cat basket, you know, as if it's only just been vacated. In fact I have a tear coming to my eye right now just thinking about it. Remember it was called Muffet. Kidney problems and old age, it died of.'

'Honestly, Mum. OK then. It's a family cat and not just mine. But it's mine when we get home.'

'That's right. And no tears if they haven't got one to adopt. We may have to wait for a while.'

'I know. No tears, promise.'

Fran leapt out of the car when they arrived in the cat rescue car park, then recollected she was twenty-one now although she felt eleven, straightened her face, and followed her mother into reception.

There were regiments of cats of all colours and all sizes. Fran had never seen so many. Cage after cage. Black, white, tabby, part Siamese, part this, part that, and overwhelmingly adult. Some were cruelty cases brought back to full health; one had only three legs, another only one proper ear, one was totally deaf, another had only one eye. But while Fran felt incredibly compassionate about the damaged ones, she knew she had to have one in perfect health because at the moment she felt quite enough damaged without having a cat that was damaged too. She almost went back to take a second look at the damaged ones though, but she hardened her heart.

Fran was standing watching three kittens playing together, obviously from the same family as they were all black with white markings in differing degrees of intensity. While she watched she felt something pulling at her jeans round about her ankle.

She turned to see what it was. It was a tiny cream-coloured kitten in the next cage trying to get her attention because it wanted to play and couldn't quite reach her. 'Oh, Mum! Just look at that.' Around its ears it tended to be chocolate coloured, but the chocolate was haphazard as though it had made an attempt to be Siamese but it hadn't quite worked. 'Oh, isn't it beautiful.'

Harriet wouldn't allow herself to become captivated. 'That's not ginger and it's never going to be either.'

'I know. It's like a Siamese misfit, just like I feel I am. A misfit, ever since ...'

'Fran. Stop it. I won't have you talk like that. It's not you who is the misfit, believe me. Go ask about this kitten's history then, and perhaps they'll let you hold it for a while. I think it looks too young to be going to a new home just yet, so don't get upset if we can't take it with us.'

Half an hour later after both of them had played with it and completely fallen in love, they left. It had been agreed they could take the kitten home two weeks from today.

'Oh, Mum, thanks for agreeing. Dad will like her, I'm sure. She is so sweet.'

'She is. She looks naughty to me.'

Fran looked delighted. 'Really? Do you think so? Good. I'll be pleased if she is. I can't call her Tiger, can I? I'll have to have a good think.'

'She needs a distinguished name, if she'd been a boy Orlando would have been a good name.'

'Orlando? For heaven's sake, Mum!'

Two weeks seemed to take an age to pass, but inevitably it did and Harriet deliberately pretended she'd too much to do to spare the time to go for the kitten, so reluctantly Fran went on her own with a brand new travelling cage in the back of her estate.

She signed for it and became its official owner, and she drove home in her new role as little Bonnie's owner. Fran couldn't explain the feelings she had about Bonnie; they were so powerful that she almost couldn't cope with them. Just how she'd been about Chris, but in a very different way. Overwhelmed, passionate, deeply possessive, deeply ... she ran out of words, although Fran knew whatever the words were she was searching for, Bonnie was hers to be loved.

She parked the car and got out full of excitement. But there was no Bonnie in the travelling cage. The door was open and she'd gone. Eventually Fran discovered her hiding amongst the collection of belongings Fran couldn't travel without, curled in a ball under the plastic raincoat Fran had flung in the back of her estate one wet day when the raincoat was too sodden to take inside to dry. With relief she scooped up Bonnie, secured her in the cage and rushed her inside. Very, very gently, and with as little fuss as possible so as not to alarm Bonnie, Fran opened the cage and sat waiting. But Bonnie wasn't for coming out, and so

Fran went into the kitchen to get the bowl already filled with water before she left and put it on the carpet in front of the cage. Very slowly Bonnie took her first steps in her new home, stood on the edge of the water bowl, turned the bowl almost upside down, the water soaked her through before it soaked the carpet and the shock made her cry out.

Bonnie shot back into the safety of the travelling cage and refused to come out ever again. Until, that is, Fran put a bowl of very tempting food in front of the cage, and when hunger got the better of her Bonnie dared to come out. Her new owner sat on the carpet to watch her eat. When Bonnie finished her food she glanced up at Fran. They looked at each other for a long moment and a bond developed between the two of them in that moment, which Fran knew could never be broken. Stuff Chris and his first-class travel. This was far, far better than that. This was loving on a grand scale, every minute of every day. All the same a feeling of desolation crept into Fran's heart that she resolutely pushed away.

Chapter 20

Craddock Fitch had several cards sent to him by his newly discovered grandchildren, and he had been thrilled to receive them.
He immediately sent cards by return. But the biggest surprise
of all was answering the front door one lunchtime, just when
he was wishing that Kate would be home for lunch soon, and
finding his son Michael on the doorstep. This strange oddball
of a son said, 'Hallo, Craddock Dad. Are you too busy to talk?'

'I'm never busy nowadays. Come in. Please.'

Michael came in and stood looking at his father. 'You know
I was too young to have a memory of you, but I'm glad ... you
know ... glad we've met.'

'So am I. I was just about to make my lunch. Have you time
to have some with me?'

'If it's not too much trouble.'

Craddock was intensely aware of this tall skinny man following him into the kitchen. Michael had done all that growing
and he, his father, had never seen it happen, and now Craddock
felt shattered by the thought. 'You were coming this way on
business?'

'Truth to tell, I've taken a day off to come to see you. I never
take days off, never take holidays, except if Graham and Anita
ask me to go with them. Nowhere to go and no one to go with.
A sad state of affairs. So I thought about you and decided that I
did have somewhere to go now, so I've come if that's all right
with you. But I'll go immediately if that's what you want.'

Craddock was overcome with sorrow. This was what a

ruinous family life had done to Michael. Craddock turned to face him and, meaning every word he uttered, he said, 'While ever I am alive, you'll always have somewhere to come. Don't forget that.'

'Thank you, thank you for saying that. Graham's different from me, you see. He's got a different kind of confidence, he can take hold of life in both hands, and he has so much belief in himself he can go right ahead, find a lovely wife and have five children with her. But me, when my mother left us I was ten and Graham was twelve, and it nearly finished me. I turned into the school bully, a thoroughly unpleasant son to Cosmo; he must have despaired of me, until I discovered this talent I had for computers, where everything was certain, permanent and secure. And I made it my life.'

'The soup won't be long. I've got quite good at cooking since I retired ... well to be honest ... since my business collapsed. Mind if we eat in the kitchen as it saves me having a lot of clearing up to do?'

Michael stood looking out of the window at the garden. 'Nice garden.'

'The previous owners created it; I just keep it looking smart. Not much of a gardener, me; more a deck chair and the *Financial Times* sort of chap.'

Michael managed a smile. 'Who did it then? It's very lovely.'

'A lady, a lady with a capital "L", a very dear lady whom I admired.'

'Ah! Of course you rent this house, I'd forgotten.'

'Sit down, it's ready. Who told you that?'

'Young Sarah.'

'A very sharp young lady is Sarah. Bread roll? With your soup?'

Michael picked up his spoon and for no reason burst out with, 'I found out where Stella went, you know.'

'Your mother, you mean?'

190

'I can't call her that. Stella is as far as I go. She's in Liverpool in a home that specialises in dealing with elderly people who've gone crackers. Not dementia, not Alzheimer's, just plain crackers.'

Craddock was horrified. 'You've been to see her?'

Michael nodded. 'It's one of those places where every door into every room is kept locked so none of the inmates are able to escape because they are categorised as possibly dangerous. So as far as I am concerned, she's in the right place.'

'Did she know who you were?'

'I never asked her. Just said I was Michael. But it meant nothing to her, which when you think about it, is par for the course anyway with her, isn't it?'

'I think you were brave to go see her. When she was married to me she was very beautiful. What does she look like now?'

'A barmy old bat with nothing to recommend her.'

'Does Cosmo know?'

'No, I haven't told him I've seen her. He adored her apparently, so when she dumped us on him and disappeared without a word, he was distraught. But he never let us see that, he was always his kind loving self to us, nothing changed. He carried on being our dad, yet he must have been missing her dreadfully. Brave of him really. It would have been so easy for him to stick us in a home, but he didn't, so Graham and I owe him a lot.'

Michael turned his head away from looking directly at Craddock and remained silent. Craddock knew what it must have cost such a reserved quiet man like Michael to talk so openly to someone like himself who was almost a total stranger.

'Thank you for telling me that. It must have been a shock for you seeing her.'

'Not for me, because I don't care enough to be shocked. What good turn has she ever done me?'

'Given birth to you?' Craddock suggested.

'Well, there is that. She never married Cosmo, but she did

marry again after she left him, except of course it wasn't really married, just like it wasn't for you. '

Craddock put down his roll. 'We got married, I mean I was there, I know.'

'According to the records I have researched, she was already married when you went through a marriage ceremony with her, and there's no record of a divorce. I've checked.'

'My God! Are you sure? I mean, heavens above!'

'I have been very thorough. That's my way.'

'But we went through a ceremony together, I remember it distinctly.'

'But then she was already married when she went through the marriage ceremony with you. It wasn't legal. So you have never been married, until you married Kate, that is. So to add to the fun, Graham and I are also illegitimate.'

'God! Is there no end to the woman's treachery? Best try to forget her, leave her be, it's nothing less than she deserves. You and Graham have Cosmo, and now me, so forget her. I can't believe it.' Craddock looked away into the distance, as though seeing someone Michael couldn't. 'She was so beautiful, physically so beautiful ... I'd no hint she was going to leave, you know, none at all. I was frantic. I rang the police, asked the neighbours, went to the school next day to ask what they knew, did everything I could, but no one knew anything. I was devastated.'

With a wry smile on his face, Michael asked, 'Well, you were the one who said she wasn't worth bothering about.' He raised his eyebrows at Craddock.

Craddock took possession of himself again saying, 'Yes. She isn't. Now Kate suggested I had cake to finish off with today. Are you a cake man?'

'I am indeed.'

So together father and son enjoyed the cake made with love by Kate. It tasted delightful and the atmosphere brightened.

Afterwards, the two of them went for a drink in the Royal Oak, Craddock almost bursting with pride to be entering with his son. He was disappointed to find most of the clientele were still in the dining room finishing lunch. But Craddock did have the pleasure of introducing Michael to Georgie, Dicky and Mary-Lee, who greeted him with great enthusiasm which gratified Craddock enormously.

He and Michael had a quiet drink sitting companionably at the table beside the inglenook fireplace, discussing business and computers and Graham's family. Michael opened up enough to tell Craddock about the house he'd just bought and the work it had entailed, and Craddock talked about the heyday of his business enterprises and how much he'd enjoyed it all.

They went round then to the store where Michael was introduced to Jimbo and then over to the school when the children were leaving for home. Kate was standing at the main door talking to them as they left. Her mind was so preoccupied with the children that it took her a moment to recognise Michael, but when she did she gave him a gentle hug and a peck on his cheek, which embarrassed him to death but delighted Craddock.

'Why, Michael! What a wonderful surprise.'

'Hello, Kate. Just thought I'd come down to see ... Craddock.'

'And why not? Has he looked after you, have you had lunch?' Kate turned to speak to one of her boys. 'Shane, you've forgotten your painting.'

'Oops,' said Shane, and immediately turned back into school.

'Yes, he's given me lunch, we've been to the pub for a drink and I've been introduced to Jimbo at the store, then we came to see you. Graham and Anita send you their best wishes, Kate.'

'Well, now that is lovely. Thank you. Are you able to stay overnight? I'd love it if you could.'

Michael shook his head. 'No. I have to be back to work first thing tomorrow. It's just a flying visit.'

Three of the school children were playing football on their

way out of the playground, and for some unimaginable reason, and totally out of character, Craddock Fitch went to join them. Kate and Michael watched in silence. Then Kate said, 'Thank you for coming. I do appreciate it; he's so pleased.'

'I wanted to. I don't think he minds, does he?'

'Of course he doesn't mind; he's delighted. He's so glad to have found you.'

'Must be off now.' Michael made to go but Kate stopped him.

'Please, don't go without saying goodbye to him. You're welcome to come back any time, to stay for the weekend if you can.'

Michael joined in the football for a few minutes and then after speaking to Craddock for a moment he left. The football game came to an end, Kate went back inside the school and Craddock followed her. He sat in the visitor's chair in her office while she tidied her desk.

When he'd caught his breath back he said softly, 'That was nice. Just as if he'd been at school all day and I'd come to take him home. His face relaxed, you know, as if he'd lost a lot of years and was a boy again. Nice that. He's been doing some research and found out about his mother. He has told me that what I thought was a marriage ceremony for Stella and I, wasn't, because she was already married to someone else. And so we were never married, she and I, but this means that you and I *are* married. Which makes me feel much better, and I'm glad. I shan't bother to go look for her, it's all far too late for that. Ready now, Kate?'

Chapter 21

Johnny Templeton favoured walking young Charles by the lake this particular Saturday morning and the two of them were making great progress. They often came this way as the walk was the exact length that Charles could manage without having to ask for a ride on his father's shoulders, and mostly he preferred the freedom of walking. Johnny talked a lot about what they saw, squirrels and birds, ducks and coots, flowers and trees, and Charles did his best but at thirteen months he didn't have much conversation. Though he could say 'Chris' very clearly now. Why this was so when he'd not seen him very much during his short life no one knew, but he could say it, and could even recognise him in a photograph. This Saturday morning he began to shout out, 'Chris! Chris!'

'No, Charles, Chris isn't here, he's gone home.'

But still he kept saying it. Johnny took his attention from making sure Charles didn't accidentally fall into the water and looked up. There he was. Chris. Standing close to the boat house, watching them.

'Chris! What are you doing here?'

'Hoping I can beg breakfast.' They clasped each other briefly, as Johnny said, 'Of course you can.'

'Slept in here last night.' Chris banged his fist on the boat-house wall.

'Why didn't you knock us up? What time did you get here?'

'Plane got delayed due to bad weather, and I didn't get here until about two a.m. But I found the boat house unlocked and kipped down on that battered sofa in there, covered myself up with an old sail.'

'Good thing you did, it was cold last night. Come on, we'll turn back and get you some breakfast.'

'How's Alice, and Ralph?'

'Alice is fine, absolutely fine. You won't recognise Ralph; he's almost three months old and I'm certain he's going to be a boxer. Why are you here, Chris?'

'No reason, felt like a change.'

'You're a liar, Chris. I've known you too long, I can always tell. So don't do it.'

'Do you need anything from the store? I'll go if you like.'

'It's Fran you've come to see, isn't it?'

'No.'

'Please don't. Not to me. Tell me the truth. Right now, where no one can hear you.'

There was a silence. Charles asked to be picked up by Chris, Johnny asked the question again, and by the time they'd reached the gravel in front of Turnham House, Chris decided to tell Johnny the truth.

'Don't tell anyone, especially Alice, but I've been texting Fran, begging her, well, no, not quite begging, rather *asking* her to come to Brazil for a holiday, and I'll pay the fare, first class knowing that would tempt her, but she won't say yes. So I've come and I intend taking her back with me.'

'Oh, Chris. If she won't, she won't. You can't make her.'

'She must. I've decided. What is there to keep her here? A shop worth nothing, and some shows and parties in that Old Barn thing in the grounds of Turnham House that you own. If she won't come, you could always give him notice on the barn and that would finish him. He needs the money the barn earns, not that it's much by our standards.'

'What the blazes are you on about? The Old Barn gives work to lots of people in these villages, and it gives me a sound regular rent every quarter, never late. And thanks very much but I don't intend giving Jimbo notice, not for you, nor anyone else.'

'The rent is peanuts to you. Here, take this little monstrosity of yours and get me some breakfast.' Chris strode into the house without even a backward glance. Charles cried at the roughness of his rejection, and Johnny was left appalled. He'd never known Chris to be so ... he couldn't find words to describe his mood.

Alice was feeding Ralph so Johnny got Chris's breakfast and sat with him after he'd put Charles to bed for his morning nap. 'You know you can't get your own way just because you're who you are. Round here, being well connected, wealthy, and having more than enough charm for five men doesn't work, as you've to *earn* their good will. And I for one won't put up with you trying to persuade Fran against her wishes. After what happened to her, due entirely to your arrogance I might add, why should she do as you say, for heaven's sake?'

Chris glared at Johnny and then deliberately avoided his eye.

'Taken your bat home then? OK. You clear the table as I've a load of emails to answer. Alice says usual room. Sorry for losing my temper, but I'm trying to build good relations with the people round here, and you seem determined to undermine my efforts. The further away you stay the better I shall like it, believe me. If Dad were alive he'd say the same.'

'They're such ... such piffling little people, I don't know why you bother.' Chris stormed off, leaving the table littered with the remains of his breakfast. Johnny heard him showering and despaired of Chris ever doing the honourable thing if it didn't suit his purposes.

Alice came across Chris as he marched through the hall on his way out. 'Hi, Alice. I'll borrow Johnny's car, as I'm just going into the village.' He dangled Johnny's car keys for Alice to see. 'Are you well?'

'Yes, thanks, and you?'

'Better when I've got over the jet-lag. Won't need lunch.' He charged off without another word.

That man is arrogant beyond belief, thought Alice. To get her own back she quickly phoned the store. It was Tom who answered. 'Good morning, Tom. It's Alice Templeton speaking. Is there a Charter-Plackett in today?'

'Will Fran do?'

'Yes. Hello. It's Alice, Fran ... Just to let you know Chris arrived during the night, and he's just shot out in Johnny's car heading for the village. Thought I'd let you know ... You can count on Johnny's and my support. Take care ... Bye.'

Alice stood in the bay window of their sitting room staring out over towards Home Farm and wishing passionately that Chris hadn't come. She wondered if her own two sons would be as different from each other as Johnny and Chris were. You just didn't know, did you, how they would turn out. Well, she'd see to it there was no room in her own family for jealousy and arrogance of the kind she recognised in Chris. She decided to check on Charles and Ralph, although she'd checked Ralph twice since she'd laid him down to sleep. She slipped her hand under the blankets to make sure his feet were warm and they were. Charles, upstairs in his cot, had flung his blankets off but was snug even so. She'd found motherhood suited her and intended to eventually have four. But she'd leave a gap for now, and then in a few years have two more.

Alice went to play the piano which always brought solace to her soul, but somehow Chris and the Charter-Placketts kept intruding into her peace of mind.

No wonder. For there was no peace there whatsoever. Bel had left to do her lunchtime stint in the Royal Oak, Tom was doing the till and the post office, and Fran, after speaking to Alice, had simply vanished.

'Good morning. Bill, isn't it?' said Chris as he stormed in

through the door, amused to find the entire store empty of customers.

'No, it's Tom, actually.'

'Right. Fran in?'

'She was a moment ago, but she's just gone for a spot of lunch.' Tom smiled though he felt more like socking this chap right the way round the green for what he did to Fran. *Is Fran in?* Huh!

'I'll have a coffee while I wait. It's early for lunch, isn't it?'

Tom shrugged. 'Well, we have to fit it in when we can when we're short-handed.'

'Short-handed. You're not that busy; I could run this place single-handed. Where's Jimbo?'

'Where Jimbo is, is his affair, not mine, nor yours.'

'Oh, I see. That's how it is. I'll get my own coffee then, shall I?'

'Customers usually do. It's freshly made.'

'OK.'

Chris sat himself down to drink his coffee, on the chairs allocated for the purpose. When he'd finished his drink, ignoring the carefully placed rubbish bin intended for empty cups and discarded sugar wrappers, he left the empty paper cup beside the machine, and the wrappers and the two little cream cartons he'd emptied on the other chair, and he stood up. 'I'll call at the house, see if anyone's in. Bye, Bill.'

He tried the knob on the Charter-Plackett front door and found the door was unlocked. 'Fran, sweetheart, it's me, Chris. Bit jet-lagged but feeling on top of the world at the prospect of seeing you. Where are you?'

He got no reply even though he called her name three times.

He found her sitting cross-legged on the rush mat in the kitchen playing with ... a kitten? A very charming kitten, but kittens were not part of his life. Chris almost shuddered at the thought of touching it.

'Who's this then?'

'She's mine. She's called Bonnie. Don't you think she's beautiful?' He noticed she didn't even show any surprise, nor did she look up at him when she spoke. Who had told her he was in Turnham Malpas? Alice?

'Not especially, no. It's me, darling Fran. Chris. Look at me, please.'

The kitten, with Fran's attention focused on it, ignored him and, much to his annoyance and despite his request, so did Fran.

'I've come a long way to see you. How about a kiss?'

'No.'

'No? Why not, Fran?'

She didn't reply, just carried on tickling the kitten behind its ear which it obviously found delightfully pleasurable.

'I will not be ignored, Fran. For goodness sake, stop playing with that little monster and at least *look* at me.'

'Chris, I have told you repeatedly I do not want to holiday in Brazil. I have asked you, repeatedly, not to text me. But you will not do as I ask. Once and for all ... *no*. Now please leave my house. Right now.' Fran got to her feet but daren't step any closer to him because she could sense the feelings she'd had when he was here before already beginning to surface. She thought about the tenderness of his beautiful hands, so sensitive, and it almost killed her to say what she knew she must, 'Just go away and forget all about me.'

Bonnie took her attention again as she tried to climb up onto a kitchen chair and fell off halfway up.

'You pay more attention to that blasted kitten than you do to me. Can't you see it's you I want? That's why I'm here. Despite all the work piling up at the office, I've come to take you back with me to Rio. Wherever I look, wherever I go, you are always there. I have only to look at a photo of you and I hear your voice, feel you beside me, smell your perfume, hear your laughter. Please, Fran, at the very least give me some of your time.'

'Chris.' Fran paused while she threw a little ball across the floor for Bonnie to chase. 'I have told you, like I said before, I am not interested, I am not going to Brazil, no matter how many times you ask me. You've left the front door open, so please just go through it and shut it after you. I don't want Bonnie out in the road.'

Being determined wasn't succeeding apparently, so Chris decided to change tack. His last effort must have been too flowery, too passionate for a practical village girl like Fran, though there was less determination in her voice than when he'd first walked in. Maybe rather more charm was required. And so he tried speaking to her more gently. 'Let's go to the Wise Man pub like we used to, let's recapture some of that lovely warmth we had, still have in fact. We were made for each other, we truly were, my darling Fran, please.' Chris reached out his hand to touch her, but she stepped away from his touch. He took a step closer. 'What do you say?'

'What is there to talk about? We can't talk about how much we love each other can we? We don't.'

'We don't? Why do you think I am here again. Of course I love you. I love every bit of you.'

Fran looked directly into his face for the very first time since he'd walked in. 'If so, why do you never mention the baby I lost. I didn't take any drastic steps to get rid of it, it just happened, but I was frightened, scared to death, in fact. I needed you, your support, but it wasn't there. If my parents hadn't—'

'Well,' he interrupted with a shrug, 'I mean it wasn't a baby as such, was it? Just a few cells really, it was so early, barely eight weeks, if that.'

Chris's callous, thoughtless words shocked Fran to the core. How could he? How could he speak like that about *their* baby. Her silence following this statement made not the slightest impression on Chris. He felt that all he'd done was make a statement of fact, and he couldn't understand her hurt.

'You obviously don't appreciate what the loss of the baby has meant to me. You've no compassion, no sorrow, no nothing. Just leave this house, right now, and never come back. Never *ever* come back.' Fran's eyes brimmed with unshed tears.

Chris held out his hands to her. 'I can't leave you when you're so upset.'

'Oh yes, you can. I'm upset, you're right there. I know you find it hard to talk about painful things. That was why you sent me the flowers instead of saying—'

'Flowers? Ah, yes, the flowers.'

He'd looked startled and then tried to look as though he remembered what she meant. And immediately Fran knew it wasn't him who'd sent them, more likely it had been Johnny. Yes, it wasn't a Chris Templeton kind of thing to do. So the one redeeming act she thought he'd done, he hadn't in fact done.

This was the moment when Chris Templeton finally lost the battle.

To prevent Bonnie running out of the front door Fran scooped her up, flung the door wide and waited for Chris to leave. She stood there trying so hard not to break down in tears, endeavouring to ignore his pretence of sympathy. Chris stood in the hall working out the right approach to her. He wanted her, and what he wanted he was used to getting. He'd try another angle. Too late. Beyond his beautiful Fran a shadow appeared which materialised into Grandmama Charter-Plackett.

Grandmama eyed him from head to foot, slowly and deliberately. 'Hmm. By the looks of it you've had your marching orders, young man. So why are you still here?'

Tight-lipped, Chris did his best to appear the suave confident man about town, but he was so angered at his rejection by Fran that he could only stutter, 'G-good morning, Mrs Charter-Plackett.'

Grandmama looked up at him, totally at ease. 'Well? I'm waiting. Get out before I send for the police.'

Chris turned to say goodbye to Fran. 'I shan't give up. You're mine, and I'll be back.'

Grandmama answered on Fran's behalf. 'You might be back, but Fran has finally seen the light. You are the very worst of a low-life kind of man: shallow, thoughtless, a user of women for your own gratification as though you've a right because you're good-looking, a fine figure of a man ...' She held up her hand. 'No, don't even attempt to justify what you have done. There is no excuse for it, none. You say you won't give up. "I'll be back", you said. Well, this granddaughter of mine is as tough and uncompromising as her grandmother, and you can get yourself a season ticket for flying between Rio and London if you wish, you can certainly afford it, but it won't do you any good because what Fran has said she has said, and that's an end to it. Well? Is it the police?' Grandmama began to fumble in her bag for her mobile.

Chris, prior to departing, wagged a finger at Fran, obviously intending to fire a final salvo at her, but Grandmama said loudly, 'Don't you dare!'

The two of them watched him roar away in Johnny's 4×4. Then Grandmama went inside and sharply closed the door. 'Tom told me, so I came to see that you were all right.'

Tears rolled down Fran's cheeks. 'He wants me to go back to Rio with him, but I know I mustn't. He'll only break my heart again.'

'How right you are.'

'Those flowers we thought he'd sent, he didn't.'

'Ah. Give little Bonnie her lunch, the dear little thing, and we'll go to the Royal Oak and have lunch together. Dry those tears, he's not worth it, and put it all down to the whole episode being one of life's challenges. You've been so brave, and I admire you very much indeed. Turning him out was exactly the right thing to do. Just get yourself done up, and we'll be off. I'll play with Bonnie while I wait. She really is gorgeous, I'm thinking I might get one for myself. Were there any more like her?'

'Yes, but they were boys. Anyway, I must get back to the store, as there's only Tom.'

'No, there isn't; Jimbo's back. I have his permission.'

'What about Bonnie?'

'Like I said, get her lunch ready but don't put her lunch down till we're ready to go, then she'll eat it and fall asleep while we're out. She'll be fine. Believe me. Go on, go up and get ready.'

Privately Grandmama was proud of the way Fran had been firm with Chris. She saw something of herself in the girl, and she was thrilled. Fancy Chris threatening Fran like that. Grandmama got out her mobile and reported to Jimbo what had happened, at the same time as trying to stop Bonnie from plundering her handbag.

The moment Bel got back from lunch duty in the pub dining room Jimbo, in his role as outraged father, headed for the Big House and Chris Templeton. This time he would flatten him; it wouldn't be five days in the hospital, more like five weeks. He'd reached the end of his tether with the man. Halfway up the drive to Turnham House Jimbo pulled up and turned off the engine. Perhaps it would be better if Johnny dealt with Chris. On the other hand ... no, it was for the best. Jimbo rubbed his knuckles which were still slightly tender from their previous encounter with Chris's chin and decided he'd do a three-point turn and park instead outside the Old Barn. He would visit Harriet in her new kitchen.

Best to leave the whole matter in the Templetons' hands.

Chapter 22

When Chris got back to the Big House after his altercation with Grandmama Charter-Plackett he was in two minds. Uppermost was his disappointment at Fran's strength of mind and her rejection of him; and his fury that he hadn't got his own way. He always got his own way with women, and he could not recall a single one who had not been charmed by him to the extent they would do exactly as he wanted. There had been the odd angry one that he had decided he was bored with, but mostly he even got his own way about that because they finished up accepting the huge bouquet of flowers he sent them to appease their fury, and the added bonus of making sure there was a piece in the Rio papers – with a superb picture – about the wonderful prize they'd won in some obscure beauty contest or other, or a magnificent picture of the injured party swanning around a fashionable race course on the arm of a handsome beau, sworn to secrecy naturally, especially recruited by Chris from an escort agency.

But this . . .

Fran was so stubborn, and then of all things, being defeated by that old grandma of hers. He had never been defeated before, and most definitely not by a grandma, with or without an acid tongue.

The first person he encountered in the hall was Alice with the two little boys, Ralph in her arms and Charles trotting beside her.

'It was you, wasn't it?'

'Hello, Chris. Everything all right?'

'No, it isn't. You rang her didn't you? Told her I was coming.'

Alice debated her reply and eventually decided the truth was what he needed. 'Yes.'

'She's told me what to do with my first-class fare and what was worse, her granny turned up and did the same. Out of good manners I had to leave.'

'Of course. Ever the thoughtful chap.'

Chris cast a sceptical glance at Alice and then turned to stare out of the window. 'The damned weather doesn't help.'

Alice shifted Ralph across to the other arm. 'You'll be going home then?'

She got no reply. 'I suppose,' she said.

'Might as well, there's nothing happening here.'

'So, the all-powerful, all-charismatic Chris has been rejected.'

Chris swung round to face her. 'It's not funny.'

'But it is laughable.' And Alice began to laugh, knowing she shouldn't. But she couldn't help it. 'You've learned a lesson at last, Chris, and not before time.'

'Hasn't it ever occurred to you that I'm a good catch? Good looks, loads of money. What more can a girl want?'

'Kindness, understanding, compassion when life is doing the dirty on you? Have you told her how sorry you are about ...'

'No, I have not. Heavens above, it was just a few cells coming together; nothing recognisable as a baby for a long while.'

'It was your baby, Chris, and hers. Just because it wasn't growing inside *you* doesn't mean it had no value. You should have gone straight to her and comforted her.'

'The flowers. Who sent her them pretending they'd come from me?'

'Johnny.'

'At your suggestion?'

Alice shook her head. 'I knew nothing about it. That's the difference, you see, between you and Johnny. He cares for others, you care only for Chris.'

206

'That's not fair.'

'That's how it looks, how it *is*. I'll just put the baby in his pram, and we'll sit down and talk. OK?'

The first thing Chris said when they'd settled themselves in the sitting room and Charles was busy digging deep in his box of toys, was, 'Is that what you think of me, that I care only for myself?'

'Think about it, Chris. Charles cares only for himself but he's only one and a bit years old, that's how he survives; making sure those who care for him do a good job by putting himself at the forefront. At thirty-two you should have grown up, learned how to put other people first without thinking about yourself and how putting them first affects you.'

'I can't understand why Johnny likes the idea of everyone in the village having employment. What the blazes does it matter to him? Everyone should get up off their own backsides and find work and make money and then more money. They shouldn't expect some benign father-figure to give them a job without striving for it.'

'Chris! Not everyone has the ability to climb to the very top of the ladder. Lots of people have to do what is within their capabilities, like serving in shops, or cleaning the street, or driving a train, or attending to the sewers, or milking the cows, or whatever. The world would fold if they didn't, and so they've got to be respected for what they do.'

'Mmm.'

'We all have our part to play. You've taken all Fran had to give, and so it's no wonder she wants nothing more to do with you.'

'It doesn't happen in Rio, me being rejected.'

'That's because the women you have in Rio aren't real people. They're selfish and greedy and think only of your money and what it can do for them; and if you marry someone like that you deserve all you get.'

'Well, thanks very much. You managed to marry money. Are you selfish and greedy then?'

'To some extent we all are, every one of us. But lovely human beings keep a sense of proportion about love, and money, and greed. Johnny and I married because we loved each other so much, we couldn't not get married as nothing less would do for us, if you see what I mean. If anything dreadful happened to Johnny I'd be devastated for the rest of my life.'

Chris stood up and went to look out of the window. The view he had was of the fields, and in the far distance were Home Farm and the lovely old buildings still standing strong after four hundred years. After a short silence, he said, 'I've never been able to understand why Johnny so gladly came here and took all this on. And I never will.'

Alice smiled. 'Give yourself time and you will. It's in his bones.'

'Is it in yours?'

'I'm getting there. You're a worthwhile person, Chris, if only you would give yourself a chance.'

'Me? After what I've done to Fran?'

At last, thought Alice, he's starting to behave like a grown-up human being. She left a silence and then suggested that, as Charles had fallen asleep beside his toy box and Ralph was still asleep in his pram, she was free to go make coffee for them both.

'I'll make it, point me in the right direction.' By the time Chris had had two goes at making a decent cup of coffee the kitchen looked as though a maniac had been let loose in it. But Alice didn't care because she recognised this was his first effort as a member of the human race. When he offered to clear their cups and to take the coffee pot into the kitchen, she smiled to herself. Maybe. Just maybe.

'Alice. Where's Johnny this morning?'

'He set off to Home Farm to look at some young bull calves he bought for this veal project he and Jimbo are starting up. They've arrived this morning.'

Chris, exhausted by his efforts to become a normal human being, decided he'd go and find Johnny and see what he was doing, because staying in the house with two babies wasn't his idea of a fun day. Briefly, his thoughts went to Fran and what he might have been doing if she hadn't given him his marching orders. What was it about her that attracted him so much? She was so completely different from the women he usually favoured. In his right mind he wouldn't have given her a second glance. Did he do what he did to her because he was bored? Chris felt momentarily ashamed that that might indeed be the truth.

Chris strode off towards Home Farm in Johnny's spare pair of wellington boots and a rubbishy anorak of his that Alice had found in the boot-room cupboard. He caught sight of himself in a mirror on his way out of the house and ruefully admitted that perhaps he might have to buy himself a proper weather-proof country outfit to wear when he came next time. Next time? What was he thinking of? There'd be no next time.

Chris and Johnny got home for lunch about one. The two of them were obviously excited by Johnny's purchase. 'They look too young to leave their mothers to me, Johnny, is it right?'

'They'll get well looked after. Other than coming here, they'd have been shot.'

Chris was appalled. 'Shot?'

'What use is there for young bulls? The heifers will grow to become milking cows, but who wants a field filled with bulls?'

'I see your point. Do people in England eat veal?'

'Didn't used to, but they will when Jimbo's done his job; you heard how enthusiastic he is? If they know they've been cared for properly, that's the main factor with veal; and in this diet-dominated world today, the fact that it is very lean helps.'

'I see.'

When Alice went off to feed the ever-hungry Ralph, and the two brothers were sitting comfortably in the study, Johnny asked Chris, 'Are you going home straightaway?'

'Of course. I've made a real mess of this business with Fran, haven't I?'

'You have.' Johnny waited for Chris to speak again, but he didn't. 'She deserves better than this.'

'All right, all right. I expect you'll tell me the same as Alice. I shouldn't have treated her like the tarts I find in Rio.'

'Exactly.'

'But I do have such fun with them all.'

'But they are not marriage material, Chris. That's if you want to marry. Maybe you prefer to be a lonely, ageing bachelor all your life, with loads of so-called friends so long as the money keeps flowing. But that's not a fulfilling life for a man. However, if that's how you want it, so be it.'

'Unlike you, I'm not into nappies and howling babies depriving me of my well-earned sleep; I can't think of anything worse. I want a life full of fun, not responsibilities and commitments that eat up all my time.'

'Like I said, it's up to you. But whatever you decide you do not go anywhere near Fran again, right? Not for any reason at all. You leave her to get on with her life, and that's an order. She's beginning to look livelier than she was and so I'm glad about that.'

'You sent her those flowers, didn't you, with my name on them?' Chris got a nod from Johnny, affirming he'd guessed right. 'Anyone would think you were some kind of father-figure for the whole village. The idea makes me want to throw up.'

Johnny ignored him. 'Saturday is Bonfire Night. You saw the size of the bonfire Barry Jones has constructed? There's even old furniture on there. It'll be some fire, believe me. You could stay on and light it with me and Charles if you like. Apparently it's tradition for the owner of Turnham House to light the fire, and so I'm definitely committed.' Johnny smiled invitingly at Chris. 'After the bonfire and the burning of Guy Fawkes, we'll have a big firework display. Jimbo used to do spectacular ones but he's too busy nowadays, so I'm getting professionals in. There's a beer tent, baked potatoes to eat round the bonfire, a refreshment tent with hot food, that's run by Jimbo and so the food'll be good.'

Very cautiously, Chris nodded in agreement. 'I might just do that, and go home the next day. This is Thursday, so there's only Friday and then Saturday, and then home. I might just tolerate that.'

'Don't overdo it on the enthusiasm side; it might indicate a change of lifestyle, and that would never do.'

'OK. OK. I get the message.'

Chapter 23

'So, they say he's staying until Sunday so that he can help Johnny light the bonfire, which is a bit surprising when you think about it, 'im being in everyone's bad books,' said Dottie.

Sylvia eyed Dottie, unconvinced that the last piece of gossip was correct. 'Well, that's a big turn around considering how he's behaved. He thinks we're all country bumpkins, but we're not, are we?'

'Absolutely not. By the way, you know Fran's got that little kitten from the cat rescue and it looks like a Siamese but it isn't. Well, you'll never guess who's gone and bought its brother ...'

'Who?' But Sylvia never got her reply because at that very moment in walked Johnny, followed a moment later by Chris. Johnny headed straight for their table, and asked if they could join them.

Embarrassed to death, Dottie and Sylvia both agreed and said of course they could. But they felt as if their evening was in splinters. Now what on earth could they talk about? Not kittens and definitely not Fran Charter-Plackett, and they certainly couldn't ask Chris if he was enjoying his stay because they knew he wouldn't be.

'Now,' said Chris, using all his charm as only he could, 'what are you two ladies drinking because I'd like to get you another drink if you'll allow me.'

'Well, thanks,' said Dottie, 'I'll have a white wine now. Georgie knows which one I like the best, and Sylvia here, you prefer vodka and tonic at the moment, don't you?'

'In that case then that's what I'll get for you.' Chris went across to join Johnny at the bar, and Sylvia and Dottie covertly observed him chatting to Georgie as though they were old friends. Out of the corner of her mouth, Dottie said, 'There's been a big change in 'im. You don't suppose he's back with Fran, do you?'

'I hope not, he's not right for her. Oops!' Sylvia was mortified because Johnny had come to sit down with them and she hadn't realised, being too busy watching Chris. But Johnny was too much of a gentleman to make a comment and so she got away with it.

He did, however, ask Sylvia where everyone else was.

'It's the blessed World Cup or something, and they couldn't come out till they'd got a result, and so Barry, Ford, Willie and Zack are all over at our house watching telly, and there's another half an hour before it finishes. Georgie won't have a telly in the pub, you see, which I'm glad about.'

Chris arrived with the drinks and was duly thanked. A small silence fell until it occurred to Sylvia to mention the kitten's name. 'About the only interesting news we've got to impart is that Mrs Charter-Plackett has bought a kitten. It's a boy and the brother of Bonnie that belongs to Fran.' In her head she wished she could cut her tongue out, what a blinking stupid subject to bring up again. 'Anyway, you'll never guess what she's calling it.'

No one, not even Dottie, offered the right name and in the end she had to say it. 'Clyde, of course.'

'Clyde? Where did she get that from?' asked Dottie hurriedly filling the silence.

Sylvia nudged Dottie saying, 'That film, you know, *Bonnie and Clyde*. Apparently Fran thinks it's hysterical.'

'That's just the sort of idea that would make Fran laugh.' Chris said this, and smiled at the thought. 'You'll have known Fran since she was born?'

Together they both said, 'Yes.' And Dottie decided that a complete change of subject was required because she certainly wasn't going down that road again, not likely. 'Did you know that Beth Harris has gone back to university at last.'

'Why did she leave?' Chris asked.

'Not happy. Decided she needed a year off to grow up. Well, she's been back there must be two months now, and she's absolutely fine. Thank goodness.'

'She's a twin, isn't she?' Chris asked.

'Yes, she is.' Under the table Dottie felt Sylvia give her a warning nudge with her knee.

'I don't think I've ever met her twin.'

'Alex his name is. Tall like his dad and a lovely young man, same as his dad. Very clever; he's at Cambridge too.'

Chris recollected a conversation he'd had with ... he couldn't remember who but they'd hinted ... 'Isn't there something odd about them? Didn't the rector adopt them?'

Johnny tried twice to divert the flak from Dottie and Sylvia, but twice Chris pursued his suspicions. 'I'm sure I'm right, aren't they his, but not ...'

Dottie said firmly, 'I'm sorry, but I've got to leave. Things to do. Sorry. Thanks for the drink.'

'So have I,' added Sylvia, and the two of them stood abruptly and tried hard not to look conspicuous by rushing out, which was what they both would have preferred.

Outside they halted for a moment. Dottie dabbed at her face to cool herself down. 'We couldn't tell him, could we, not him. He wouldn't belong if he lived here fifty years.'

'Not a patch on his brother. If you belonged here, you could tell Johnny you'd done a murder and he wouldn't let on.' Sylvia debated what to do next. 'I tell you what, come to our house. The football will be nearly finished; they can go to the pub, and we'll have a quiet drink on our own, eh? What do you say? See if there's a good film on.'

'Lovely. Just the ticket.'

Johnny and Chris had moved to a smaller table after the two of them left, and Chris still felt annoyed that he'd been denied his answer to the Alex and Beth Harris question, and so he asked Johnny, 'Have I offended them in some way?'

'Not offended, no, but you've stumbled on a big secret that only the villagers know about, and they tell no one who they consider does not belong to the village.'

'You know though; why not me?'

'Because you don't belong.'

'I belong to you.'

Johnny agreed he did.

'Well, are you going to tell me?'

'No.'

Chris took umbrage at this. 'So how many years do I have to live in the village to be allowed to know their secrets?'

Johnny grinned at him. 'Something like fifty years.'

Chris couldn't believe it. 'Fifty years. My God! The sooner I get home, the better.'

'Yes.'

'You really want me to go, don't you?'

'Yes.'

'You mean it, seriously?'

'Yes, at least until you learn how to behave in a place like this.'

Chris leaned across the table and asked softly, 'Go on, give me a hint what that much admired, beyond reproach, well beloved rector did? More importantly, to whom?'

'No. It's his secret. Ask him, and if he wants you to know, he'll tell you.'

'Damn it, Johnny, I am your brother.'

Johnny grinned at him. 'You daren't ask him because you know one look from his candid all-penetrating eyes will be your undoing. All the sins you've committed in the last twenty years will be revealed to him in one long look. He's well known for it.'

'He won't find out my past, believe me. Right. I'll ask him. I'll go round to the church tomorrow morning and I'll ask him, if he's there.'

Chris did as he promised he would. Chris caught Peter playing the organ which he had to admit he did very well indeed, and so he sat to listen for a while out of sight from the organ behind a stone monument. And when Peter switched the organ off and headed for the vestry Chris followed him, knocked on the vestry door and pushed it open.

'Good morning, rector. May I have a word?'

Peter was searching through some files in a cupboard and turned to see who was asking to have a word. 'Ah, I thought it might be you.'

'You did?'

'The accent, it's just something a bit different from an English one. How can I help?'

The compassionate understanding smile on Peter's face, no different despite the passing years, almost made Chris decide not to ask him the heavily weighted question on his lips. But he did. After all, he didn't belong in the village, a fact he was never allowed to forget, and he didn't want to either, so it didn't matter to him if he offended. 'There's always this mystery about you that no one is ever willing to explain, not even my own brother will tell me, and so I'm asking it now. The entire village has it as its secret but not me.'

Peter turned away to pick up a file from the table behind him. 'Yes?'

'I'll come right out with it. Who is the father of your children? Alex and Beth?'

'Me.' Peter turned to face him.

Wow! Chris thought, those eyes of his such a bright blue, but somehow ... Then he became frighteningly aware of Peter's penetrating glance, the deeply thoughtful look, and somehow wished he'd never ... 'So, it's not you it's your wife, she was the unfaithful one.' He hesitated as he caught a change in Peter's attitude. 'No, I've got it completely wrong, haven't I?'

Peter's facial expression changed to one of cold anger. 'Yes, you have. I am disinclined to discuss this any further. It is an entirely private matter, and you can go back to Rio with the problem unresolved because it is no longer a matter for discussion between you and me.'

'Look here, are the children your wife's? I understand you prefer honesty, so let's have all our cards on the table.'

'She adopted them.'

'When you and she married I assume?'

He didn't get an answer from Peter, so Chris, who was struggling to get the matter straight in his mind, asked, 'So, it isn't she who is the guilty one?'

'That's absolutely right, Chris. There's a very apt sentence I can quote you from the Bible. *Let he who is without sin amongst you, cast the first stone.* You might do well to remember that. Unless it is, of course, that you are entirely without sin, in which case you are a very exceptional person and worthy of great praise, and I for one am very envious of you.'

Chris, tough and self congratulating as he was and always had been, fought to subdue the guilty shudder that began crawling relentlessly up his spine.

Peter looked Chris in the eye with a steady but compassionate expression that challenged his very existence. 'But somehow I think not. I think you are as guilty of sin as the rest of us, and have been all your adult years.' Peter sustained the challenge in his voice by adding, 'But it is never too late to change. Never ever too late to treat others as you would like to be treated, to be honest and truthful, to put a stop to the unkind rumours, to give generously of your time, to think of others first and yourself last. Never too late.'

For once in his life Chris was speechless, for he recognised that Peter had very astutely described Christopher Templeton's own shortcomings; and that feeling of guilt he'd sensed crawling up his spine finally exploded into his brain and with it, it seemed, the whole of his past life lay exposed to the world.

Peter collected the files he needed, and said, 'I must press on, unless there's something else you have to say?' Peter waited but getting no response he suggested that they left.

As they walked down the aisle together Peter asked Chris how long he was staying, and what was Rio like because he'd never been there, and how was the hotel business nowadays. And then they were out in the sun shaking hands, with Peter wishing Chris a good journey home, and then Chris was on his own walking back up the drive to the Big House and everything was so normal, as though their conversation about sin had never taken place.

But it had, and try as he might, he knew that today the deepest truth about him, Christopher Templeton, had been declared out loud by a very perceptive man. And he didn't like the sound of it.

Chapter 24

The notices about Bonfire Night had been put through every letterbox in Turnham Malpas, posters were nailed to trees, there was a full page advert in the church magazine that announced all the fringe activities, and as Bonfire Night was conveniently this year on a Saturday no one bothered to have a fire in their own garden. Fireworks provided by Johnny promised a spectacular show, and all they had to pay for was food and drinks if they wished.

Jimbo was delighted. At last the village was becoming the centre of everyone's lives once more, and he loved it. His Fran was getting better as each week passed, the Old Barn was firing on all cylinders, sometimes there'd be three or even four events each week, and although it was hard work keeping up with all the catering and the fringe requirements for the very varied happenings, Jimbo thrived on it. Now he'd got a wedding licence, people could both marry and have the reception in the Old Barn and so his calendar for weddings was rapidly filling up to capacity. And it all meant more money in the coffers.

He stood, in the early morning of Bonfire Night, on the doorstep of the store looking out over the village green. Cold, yes, but not so cold that he couldn't stand there for no more than a minute; it was a bracing, uplifting kind of cold, and the skies were bright blue with the promise of a brilliant day. Not a cloud in the sky, thank goodness. He had a wedding at 11 a.m. today so the whole thing would be over well before the bonfire was due to be lit.

Next week he and Harriet would be off to South Africa for ten days and goodness didn't they deserve it? He couldn't wait. Leaving, of course, Fran in charge. Fran. He dwelt on her for a few moments. His darling Fran, the youngest of his flock. How could he have been so careless as to allow her to go out with that Chris Templeton? He should have put his foot down right at the start. But he knew he couldn't, shouldn't, mustn't, because that was the way to drive her away. The outcome would have been the same though, with her pregnant, and Chris careless and fancy free. Which he was. Damn the man. How could a lovely gracious man like Johnny have a brother like Chris? They were as different as cheese and chalk. Johnny thoughtful and already more like Ralph than anyone had ever thought possible. Chris hard-faced, selfish, thoughtless, although he was off back to Rio tomorrow, thank heaven. The sooner the better.

Jimbo felt rather than heard Fran come to stand beside him. 'You're just like me, Dad. I like to have a moment here first thing, sniff the air, see how the world's doing today.'

'It's doing rather well, methinks. How about you, love? Are you doing rather well?'

'Just about, but it's not easy to put it all to one side and bash on. It's all certainly taught me a lesson.'

'What kind of a lesson?'

'To take a long deep breath before commitment, to pace myself, to be more certain. To assess people better, hold back till I'm certain.'

'That sounds like common sense to me.'

'I was too young for him, and if I met him now I'd know better how to deal with him. The bigger the distance between us though at the moment, the better it will be for me.'

'The world is full of wonderful people, as well as the charlatans, Fran. Before long there'll be someone else who will really love you, believe me.'

Fran slipped her hand into the crook of her father's arm. 'He'll have to be very much like you, Dad. Kindly and strong ... and round and bald.'

The two of them laughed uproariously, and Willie Biggs coming in for his morning paper enjoyed their happiness. 'Good morning, you two. Come for my paper, as if after all these years I have to tell you that.'

Willie stood beside the till, fumbling in his pocket for the right change as he always did, on the principle that at that time in the morning he couldn't expect them to have any change when all he was buying was his newspaper; but they'd never let on that before they opened up they filled the till with a fresh supply of change every single day. 'You know, Willie, you could always have your paper delivered. The boys set out at seven-fifteen on their rounds so you wouldn't have to come out in the cold and the rain,' said Jimbo.

But Willie straightened his back and marched out as best he could, saying just before he closed the door, 'The day I can't pick up my own newspaper is the day I shall be put in my box. See you at the bonfire, I'm right looking forward to it, same as always. We're lucky to have that Johnny inherit.'

The two of them watched Willie make his way home and the exact same thought was in both their minds, that Willie Biggs, the very last of a long line of the Biggs family living in the village, was running out of time. Fran thought about life in the village of Turnham Malpas and how much she loved it; but at the same time there remained in her mind a very strong interest in the gorgeous man she knew really belonged in Brazil, and she decided she wasn't going to avoid him like she'd first intended, because she felt strong enough to make a point of saying goodbye to him tonight at the bonfire. After all, it wouldn't be the last time she'd see him because he'd certainly be back to see Johnny and Alice and the little boys, and so she might as well get used to it. She simply would not allow him to *hurt* her any more, that was the thing. No more allowing him to draw close, no more meeting at the Wise Man, no more ...

Jimbo suddenly remarked, 'Do you know, Fran, although in one way I'm glad I haven't the responsibility of the firework display, at the same time I shall miss doing it. What will I do all evening without the responsibility for it?'

'How about *enjoy* yourself for a change?'

'I suppose so.'

'We never used to see you on Bonfire Night, this time we will and that will be lovely. I wish the other three were coming though, we never see enough of them, do we?'

'They'll have to know about, you know, the baby ... Your mum's not told them yet.'

Fran gripped hard on his elbow. 'Don't tell them, I don't want them to know. I feel such a fool. Flick will be sad for me, but Felix and Finlay will laugh.'

'They most certainly won't, Fran, they're not that hard-boiled; they'll be sorry just like Flick, I know they will. But *we* won't tell them, we'll leave it to you.'

'Thanks, Dad. I'm sorry to have caused you trouble like I did, you don't deserve it.'

Jimbo placed a kiss on her forehead. 'Must press on, work to do.'

They were busy all day in the store, people came into shop whom they didn't see very often, and Fran made sure they all got an enthusiastic greeting to encourage them to come again. Of Chris they saw nothing and for that Fran was grateful. Johnny came in for bananas as young Charles had decided that bananas were the food of the day. Merc and Ford came in full of the holiday they'd just booked to the States in the New Year, and Craddock Fitch came in, not on his own, but with his newly acquired family. Immediately the store felt too small to accommodate them all. 'Can I introduce everyone?' asked Craddock, beaming with gratification at having his whole family with him.

Jimbo and Fran said together, 'Of course. Please do!'

During the hubbub of sorting out who was who and shaking their hands, in came four more customers, and as Craddock was armed with a shopping list as long as his arm, and the four who'd just come in equally charged with lists, Harriet was called from home to help, and eventually the backlog went away well satisfied with their shopping.

The Fitch family, however, lingered, enjoying the atmosphere of a village store, comparing it favourably with the huge impersonal supermarkets they had at home. Jimbo and Graham were sitting in the coffee corner engrossed in conversation, the children were admiring the gateaux in the dessert freezer, and Michael, ever the loner, was studying the selection of computer magazines on the newspaper stands and choosing which of them might have something in them that was new to him.

When the Fitch family had eventually decided to leave with their purchases, Harriet said, 'Aren't they a lovely family? Who'd have thought that Mr Fitch would have relatives as nice as them? The grandchildren are a delight, and his sons. Except maybe the computer wizard. He's a bit odd.'

'They're coming to the bonfire tonight, Mum,' said Fran.

'Really?' said Harriet. 'The children will enjoy that. Just a pity they live so far away.'

Jimbo suggested that the family were making a much nicer man of old Fitch than he used to be. 'It's done him good, being able to count them as his own. Graham thinks he's lovely, and the children are glad to have a granddad because Anita's parents are long gone.'

'I wonder if he knows they think he's lovely? Still, why shouldn't he have a family; there's nothing better for rounding off the corners and warming the heart,' Harriet declared. 'Five o'clock! It's Saturday. Bonfire Night. Let's pack up. Six-thirty is lift-off time. Apparently the Guy Fawkes that Evie's made is perfectly wonderful, I can't wait to see it. Greta Jones says it's a crying shame to burn it.'

Soon the entire population of Turnham Malpas were streaming up the drive, full of eager anticipation as this was what made living in a village worthwhile. There was Pat, and Barry the master-builder of the bonfire, which was truly the largest they had ever seen, along with Grandad Stubbs, who only needed to walk from the head gardener's cottage and down the well-worn path past the glass houses, which were still Greenwood Stubbs' pride and joy, and over the field and he'd be right by the refreshment marquee in minutes. Others, such as Craddock Fitch and his family, had further to walk, but Craddock took them the secret way through the churchyard to the wall at the back where he made use of the little gate that had featured in Muriel and Ralph's romance all those years ago, past the Plague Pit, which was now not so threatening since the bodies had been removed and buried in the graveyard. The eager chatter of the children soon joined with the chatter of other children making their way up the drive.

Some, of course, like Sheila and Ron Bissett – sorry, Sir Ronald and Lady Sheila Bissett – went by car and parked in the car park at the Old Barn. Jimbo and Harriet, along with Fran, walked up from their house due to Jimbo's newly pledged decision to get more exercise. Dottie Foskett, who had stayed behind to help clear up from the wedding they'd had earlier in the day, had only to comb her hair, dig out her anorak, thick gloves and a warm scarf, and she was ready for the fray, walking only yards to reach the refreshment marquee and a much longed-for tea and bun. Sylvia and Willie got a lift from Tom and Evie, and so it went on. Villagers making their way up to the Big House as they had been doing for centuries. This time for the bonfire in celebration of that reprobate Guy Fawkes who had wanted to put an end to democracy.

Baby Ralph Templeton, cocooned in his pram and little Charles in his one-piece winter suit, warm socks and Wellingtons, trudging across the well-cut grass with their parents towards the site of the bonfire, were too young to know why they were doing it; but Charles was old enough to catch the atmosphere of excitement of the people who greeted him. With them was Uncle Chris, who was well wrapped-up against an English winter evening. He had resolved to speak to Fran if she was there, perhaps even buy her a drink in the marquee with the pub sign, the Royal Oak, flapping in the breeze above the entrance. Inside for the first time ever were Georgie and Dicky Tutt, who were loving the whole idea of closing the pub for the evening and instead serving here, at Johnny's special invitation, in the marquee. They intended to make a real go of it and as six-thirty struck on the church clock the crowds began to file in. Georgie grinned at Dicky, and he grinned back, and Alan Crimble and Mary-Lee squeezed hands and grinned at each other too, delighted to be in each other's company for the whole evening, each glancing over their shoulders to confirm Linda Crimble hadn't seen them. Poor Linda, thought Mary-Lee, but it was her own fault for not making a go of her marriage. If Alan was finding contentment with someone else it was all her own fault. She squeezed Alan's hand more tightly and enjoyed the feeling of passion she saw in his eyes as he glanced at her. Yes. She was glad, in fact, very glad, that he fancied her.

The punters flooded to the bar counter they'd set up earlier in the day and the evening began. Mary-Lee checked she had a bit of cleavage showing and then served her first pint of the evening.

The scout band played rousing tunes, Barry Jones prepared the torches for lighting the fire, Pat Jones settled Grandad in a chair with a rug over his knees, and everyone, excepting those too infirm to make it, braced themselves for the lighting of the enormous pile of furniture that included the old wardrobe and bedside table that had belonged in the B&B, the old floorboards that had been lingering in Dottie's garden ever since her house had been renovated all those years ago, the tree branches that had come down in the storm last January, and even two big dangerously rotten branches that had been sawn off the oak tree on the village green.

Johnny had provided a loudspeaker system, and he stood with the microphone in his hand, and having tapped it to reassure himself it was working properly, he began his opening speech.

'Ladies and gentlemen, boys and girls. Welcome on this, the first Bonfire Night with which I have been involved. Tonight is the night for enjoying yourselves, grown-ups, children and even our own baby Ralph. Chris, my brother, and I are about to light the bonfire that has been so wonderfully built by Barry Jones; let's have a cheer for Barry and all his hard work. Hip hip hurrah! Wonderful. There will be baked potatoes for everyone, delivered to you by the scouts as a thank you for all the support the village provides the scout troop throughout the year. There's a refreshment tent, a beer tent, or there is wine or soft drinks if that's your preference. And when the bonfire is beginning to burn down there will be fireworks. This year Jimbo has had to decline organising those due to the pressure of business, but we couldn't have a bonfire without fireworks and so a professional company is doing the display, and I know you will love it just as much as I shall. Which I will, because I love fireworks. Enjoy, everyone! Enjoy!'

There was a breath-taking moment when everyone feared that perhaps the fire would not take hold. But Johnny and Chris persisted, and gradually the fire began to burn assisted, unknown to everyone except Barry, by petrol he'd sprayed on the lower layers of wood earlier that morning, and within minutes the flames were beginning to flare right up to the topmost point of the pile. It made a glorious sight, and everyone clapped. Barry, whose heart felt to have stopped altogether while he waited for that moment, sighed with relief. The petrol and the dozens of firelighters he'd placed near the bottom had done the trick, and he stood back thrilled at the success of his efforts. The heat was so fierce that the people standing nearest the fire had to retreat.

Chris, having done his job with credit and with a kind of rising appreciation of what all this meant to these well-intentioned people, decided it wasn't for him. Certainly not. So the main feature of the evening accomplished, now he went in search of Fran. He'd searched every inch of the field around the bonfire, and eventually he found her in the queue in the food tent. When he appeared right there in front of her without any prior warning she wanted to make a run for it. A run to escape this man who'd come close to ruining her life. She looked up at him, and he took hold of her elbow as though intending to guide her away from the queue, but she stubbornly refused to move.

He looked down at her, and a slow smile began at the corner of his lips, the lips she'd loved and adored but did no longer, or so she thought. Her hands began trembling first, then it spread to her body and then she was trembling all over. Chris reached out a hand to steady her, but she wouldn't allow it. 'No, please leave me alone. I'm needing a hot drink and something to eat.'

'So am I. I'll pay for it.'

'You think money solves every problem, don't you?'

'Usually it does.'

'Not this time, it doesn't. Just leave me alone. Please. It's not much to ask.'

When he didn't leave, she turned to go. But Chris stopped her by gripping her elbows. 'You pay for the two of us then if it makes you feel any better.' He handed her a five pound note. 'Ham sandwich and tea, seeing as we're in England.'

She looked at the note and knew it wouldn't be enough for two of her Dad's super ham sandwiches and a pot of glorious tea.

Chris twigged, and asked, 'Not enough?'

'No.'

So he got a twenty pound note from his wallet and swapped it for the fiver. 'You should get it free.'

'Not allowed.'

Chris went to sit well away from the queue though he knew wherever he sat, him sharing a table with Fran would not go unnoticed.

As Fran approached carrying the loaded tray he was almost overwhelmed by disappointment in himself that he'd treated her so badly. Pull yourself together, man, Chris said to himself. Just pull yourself together; you're getting soft.

He stood up and took the tray from her, and clumsily played at being mother.

Fran shook her head when he asked if she wanted sugar in her tea. 'No sugar for me, thanks. I brought it for you, as I didn't know if you took it in tea or not. We don't know much about each other, do we? Still, it doesn't matter, does it, not any more?'

His ego forced him to win her back. Very softly and with a slight pleading tone to his voice, he asked, 'Doesn't it?' He reached out to clasp her hand. But she snatched it away.

'No. It doesn't. It occurred to me the other day that I never want to see you ever again. You've hurt me more than you will ever acknowledge, and our relationship can't be stitched back together again, because I won't allow it.'

There was a wheedling note in his voice when he replied, 'You don't sound *completely* certain.'

'Oh, believe me I am. More tea?'

'Yes, please. This sandwich, considering we're in a marquee and not a restaurant, is very tasty.'

'Well, of course it is. It's one of ours.'

She said it with such conviction that the two of them laughed. When Fran sobered up she said very forthrightly, 'I was determined to say goodbye to you properly tonight, face up to all that's happened, and say what I have to say.'

Chris asked her what she had to say to him, anticipating her approval, and lo and behold she began in just the way he wanted.

'You are a very handsome man, Chris, and very attractive.

I'm glad we ... had a relationship ... because I've learned a lot from you in all sorts of ways, but most of all I've learned to recognise ...' While she paused to put her thoughts into order, Chris imagined she would be choosing more flattering things to say of him which would make him feel better about being rejected by a woman for the first time in his life. 'What a pig ignorant, self-centred, thoughtless, egotistical, vain, inconsiderate, self-congratulatory man you truly are. God's gift to women you may be in Rio, but as far as English women are concerned, you are the lowest of the low. Rio is welcome to you. There. I've said what needed to be said. That's it. Goodnight, Chris. Safe journey home tomorrow.'

'Fran. Fran. Surely you don't mean all that.'

'Oh, I do. I can't believe how naive I was. I honestly thought you meant what you said.'

'I did mean what I said.'

'At the time, maybe you did. But not really. You knew I was totally inexperienced, and you took advantage of that. You expected me to behave in exactly the way *you* wanted me to; and there was no room for *me* and my opinions in our relationship. Despicable, that's what you were, absolutely without any moral code whatsoever. You should be ashamed.'

'I'm ashamed of nothing at all. There's nothing I said or did to be ashamed of.' As though justifying his attitude, Chris added, 'Anyway, you were very grateful for the experience; you know you were.'

So now he expected her to be *grateful*! Angered beyond belief, she could find no more words to say, and Fran wished she could stop herself from being childish, but she couldn't. She picked up her now luke-warm cup of tea, stood up and tipped the whole lot over Chris's head before he could stop her. She watched the tea soaking into his sweater, cashmere too by the looks of it, which made her rash move even more satisfying.

Fran picked up the other half of her sandwich and walked

off, threading her way between the tables, nodding and greeting everyone she knew, which was almost all of them, as she progressed. All those who witnessed her performance longed to applaud, but they refrained in case they might trivialise her magnificent exit. Not liking to look directly at Chris, they squeezed sneaky looks at him between their eyelashes and saw a man sitting completely still, deep in thought, with rapidly cooling tea trickling through his sun-streaked blond hair and all the way down the front of him.

Fran recommenced eating her sandwich once she was outside in the dark where no one could see the effect her speech had on her. She'd never meant to say all those things and she certainly never intended to pour the tea over him, but his last remark made her finally realise the true worth of the man. She meant it, and she was glad she'd said and done what she did, because it had cleared the air for her. Now she could think more positively about her situation and realise that for whatever reason she had lost the baby, and really it was the best thing, despite her sadness, because she was too young for motherhood and Chris was far too immature to take any kind of parental responsibility at the moment. If ever.

Fran dumped the wrapping from the sandwich and the tissue she'd wiped her hands on in the nearest waste bin, and marched off to collect her jacket potato from one of the scouts. She met Alex Harris, unusually for him he was by himself, and the two of them chose a potato each and wandered away, talking together enthusiastically. This was how life should be lived, thought Fran: on equal terms with good friends one could rely on.

In the light from the bonfire Harriet happened to see her from a distance chatting away to Alex as though Chris had never existed, and she felt uplifted. Maybe at last ... Entering the refreshment tent, anticipating buying something as she hadn't found time for an evening meal, Harriet was surprised by the amused greetings she got from many of the people, both in the queue and sitting at the tables. While she waited she spotted Chris far over the other side of the tent looking dejected. When she arrived at his table, she said, 'Not much space, mind if I join you?'

'Of course.' Chris looked surprised, but pulled himself together, intending to disappear as soon as he could comfortably do so.

Harriet, between consuming her pizza and chatting to him about the bonfire, remarked, 'It is the biggest I think we've ever had.' And then she noticed his dishevelled appearance. 'You look awfully damp. Are you all right?'

'Your daughter is responsible for this. She poured her tea over me.'

So, thought Harriet, that's why everyone's smiling at me. Suppressing her own amusement, she said, 'Is it well-deserved, do you think?'

'She certainly thinks so.'

'Well, if she does, so do I.'

'No sympathy from you then.'

'Definitely not. Fran survived the miscarriage because she was looked after by people who *cared* for her. You consider that none of it – the pain she suffered, the on-going distress, the unbelievable disappointment – was your fault. *A few cells* you described the baby as; it was very early on, I know, but the potential was there, and you contributed half.' Harriet paused for a moment, and when she realised he had no feelings about the baby at all she exploded, 'I can tell you don't care at all. It has nothing to do with you, you appear to be saying.'

'I didn't know, so how could I care? It was all over when I heard. However, thank God, I'm leaving tomorrow. I can't take any more of this very upright caring for each other, etc., etc.'

'Well, I expect they'll all be glad to see you back in Rio, though heaven knows why. Have a good journey.'

Chris got to his feet, saying, 'I'm going into the house to

mingle with Johnny's guests. Goodnight. See you some time, perhaps. *If* I come back on a visit, that is.'

'Oh, that's bad luck for me. In that case I may see you later because we're invited too. You'd better change your sweater or someone might ask you for an explanation. If they ask me, I shall be delighted to tell them.'

Later, Harriet glanced at her watch in the light of the lamp over the front door of the Big House and saw she still had about an hour to enjoy the pleasurable atmosphere and especially the warmth before the firework display began. There was a motley collection of boots just inside the door and so she kicked off her own boots and went to enjoy the fray. Jimbo found her almost immediately.

'There you are, darling. We've had a crisis in the refreshment tent. One of the microwaves has packed up, but I've brought ours across from home in case you wonder where it's gone. You OK? Enjoying yourself?'

Harriet kissed him, and her cold nose touching his cheek made him jump. 'By Jove, you're cold. Let's go to the bar and get you a drink. There's mulled wine if you prefer it?'

'Sounds just right, does mulled wine.'

Harriet, standing to one side sipping her mulled wine and loving every scented mouthful, caught sight of Chris over the heads of the other guests, in a bright scarlet sweater now, chatting to some people she didn't recognise. He looked fully restored, and Harriet had to admit he looked very striking and that it was no wonder Fran had fallen for him. At the same time she was glad Chris was leaving tomorrow, just as glad as he was, apparently. Harriet decided she would avoid him, believing the Charter-Plackett family en masse had had enough of the man. Then she saw her mother-in-law approach him, and her heart sank. Please, please, Katherine, not a scene in here. Please.

Grandmama apologised very firmly to the guests he was speaking to, saying, 'Excuse me, I need a word with this young man. You don't mind, do you, it's important.' She smiled her sweetest smile and whoever they were, they reluctantly moved away, leaving the field clear for Grandmama.

'I think, Chris, I may have been very badly behaved towards you the last time we met and I owe you an apology for it.'

'Not at all. You only said what you thought was fitting.'

'You speak like a gentleman. That's very kind of you. Thank you. You have so much going for you, you know. You're a very impressive, good-looking man, wealthy way beyond normal mortals, but you do need a touch of your brother's graciousness. Then, believe me, you would be perfect. This idea you have of getting whatever you want as some kind of right, well, that side of you needs curbing. Then, believe me, you'd be terrific. If I were many years younger I'd marry you myself.' Grandmama burst into laughter and so did Chris. The two of them propped each other up while they laughed, and Harriet rejoiced at the sight.

She kept her eyes on them as Chris guided Grandmama towards the free bar and watched them toast each other with their glasses, still smiling broadly. Then Grandmama reached up to kiss his cheek; she patted his arm and left him with a big grin on her face. She walked straight towards Harriet and as she reached her she said, 'Lovely man, really, you know, he just needs to grow up. Great crowd here tonight, although I can't decide if I can last out till the fireworks, though I do love them. Always have.'

'Well, I've been on my feet all day, so shall we both sit down for a while to recover?'

'What a good idea. Over there, look, just two chairs in that corner and then no one will join us; and we can gossip together about all the guests. I love a good gossip. Did the wedding go well today, by the way?'

'Yes, we did have a hitch though. The bridegroom's parents' car broke down on that horrendous roundabout with all the traffic signs that caused all the confusion they were put up to avoid; and they couldn't explain exactly where they were so Jimbo had to go out and rescue them seeing as he knows that roundabout like the back of his hand. They were in a terrible state by the time he got them to the church.'

'Was that all?'

'It was enough, believe me. Other than that it was a success, and the bride looked beautiful, the groom even more so, and the three tiny girls they had as bridesmaids tried hard to be good. Oh, look, there's Craddock Fitch with his family. They do look nice. Have you met them?'

'No. Have you?'

'Briefly. They came into the store the other day. When they've got their drinks we'll go across. Craddock looks delighted with himself. I suppose when you have no family it must be very lonely, but now he has, good for him.'

'Harriet. You never have a good word to say for him; what's changed?'

'Him. He's much more kindly. I don't know if it's losing all his money or getting a family, but whichever it is, he's so much nicer to know. Kinder, you know. More approachable.'

They sat together alternately criticising the guests and praising them as they saw fit because, as Harriet remarked, that's what living in a village is all about. Then they watched as Chris made a valiant but discreet attempt to avoid Peter and Caroline. He'd been speaking to someone Johnny had invited who was a complete unknown as far as the village was concerned, and he was turning away to escape when Harriet and Grandmama saw Chris swerve to avoid walking straight into Peter and Caroline as they moved towards the bar.

Chris promptly headed for Harriet and Grandmama as though they were his target.

'Hello, Chris, enjoying yourself?' Harriet asked for want of something to say.

'Yes, thank you, I didn't think I would, but I am. You ladies look as though you could do with a refill. Can I get you something more to drink?'

Harriet held out her empty glass. 'Yes, please. A G and T for me, and a whisky for my mother-in-law.'

Unfortunately for Chris, Peter and Caroline headed their way. Chris rapidly moved off towards the bar, leaving the four others to talk.

They chatted generally about the evening, with Grandmama casually saying in the midst of their chat, 'Chris moved off quickly just now. Have you had a fall out?' She looked at Peter rather pointedly so he felt compelled to answer. 'He came to see me to talk about something, and I think maybe I was too outspoken.'

Grandmama chuckled. 'That's how he is, outspoken, and he doesn't care who knows it. You did right, Peter, to be forthright. He needs it.'

'I only spoke the truth.'

'Of course you did, as only you can.' Grandmama grinned up at him and the two of them agreed without another word that Peter was right to speak his mind. 'I'm glad he's going back to Brazil tomorrow. Best place for him.'

'Fran OK, is she now?' Caroline asked.

There was a slight hesitation before Harriet replied. 'Yes, thank you. She is. Much improved.'

'Good, I'm glad.'

They talked for a while until Grandmama decided she would go outside and get a good position from which to watch the fireworks. 'Coming, Harriet?'

'Of course.'

Caroline and Peter watched them push their way through Johnny's many guests enjoying their free drinks. Caroline said, 'I'm going to watch, you are too, surely?'

'I am. Ah. Here comes Chris.'

'Are the two of you not speaking?"

'I don't know. Let's see.'

Chris felt foolish for once in his life and decided to offer the drinks to Caroline and Peter. 'I'm too late,' said Chris, 'obviously they've gone outside. Ah, well. Drink anyone?'

'I'll have the G and T, thank you,' said Caroline.

'I'll drink the whisky. Thanks.'

The drinks were on a small tray and alongside them was a large glass of ale for Chris. 'Good. I don't like drinking alone.' But before Chris had a chance to drink from his glass the cry went up from Johnny. 'Fireworks! Don't miss the show! Come along everyone! Firework show. Outside. Chop, chop. Enjoy!' Johnny led the way out through the front door. His guests streamed across the gravel past the bonfire which by now was a large heap of wood smoking and smouldering away into nothingness, and joined the others patiently waiting for the first rocket to go up. Jimbo had always begun the fireworks with a single stupendous rocket that went up and up into the night sky, but tonight the show began with *six* rockets going up: two red, two blue and two silver. They went up and up, and everyone was watching them going higher and higher till they couldn't tilt their heads any further back. Suddenly they all exploded in a shower of lights.

The whole show was lavish beyond everyone's imaginings, and after ten minutes it finally concluded with six enormous Catherine wheels spinning and spinning as though they would never stop. But eventually they did, and then the cheers of appreciation filled the sky.

'My word! What a show!' Jimbo felt envious. He'd thought the shows he'd put on were brilliant, but this ... well ... it had exceeded anything he'd ever attempted.

Harriet nudged him. 'That must have cost a fortune, and I mean a *fortune*.'

Peter, standing close behind them, agreed. 'That is real money, that is.'

'Exactly. I knew they were rich, but ...' Caroline was lost for words.

'Best ever,' said Dottie. 'Best ever.' And she knew as she said it that Johnny Templeton was absolutely loaded with money to have afforded the show she'd just watched.

From the youngest to the oldest, everyone there clapped long and loud to show their appreciation. Jimbo decided to ask for three cheers for Johnny. He climbed up on the low wall beside him and called for three cheers, which were willingly and loudly given. What an ending to a wonderful night, they all thought!

Fran was still keeping Alex company, and she thought that she had never spent a whole evening with someone she found so compatible. They were equals in a way she never had been with Chris, but at the same time her heart lurched a little at the thought of Chris. But Alex insisted on seeing her back home, and as he'd never met Bonnie Fran decided to invite him in to meet her.

So, when Jimbo and Harriet arrived home, they found the two of them playing with Bonnie as though they were children and not both in their twenties. It felt an awful lot better than when they'd had Chris for lunch that Sunday.

Craddock Fitch took all his new family back home. The children were exhausted. Ross in particular, being the youngest, was already fast asleep in his father's arms. Craddock had walked home hand in hand with the other two boys, enjoying their comments on the fireworks and the size of the bonfire, and how high the rockets had gone. He remembered the days when he'd financed it all and he realised that Johnny was in a very different league to himself, even when he was at the height of his success. Craddock squeezed the boys' hands and was grateful that instead of money he had grandchildren.

'Grandad! Are you tired?' asked Judd.

'I am indeed. Are you?'

Judd nodded. 'I am. It was the best night ever though. Can we come next year?'

'Definitely.'

Judd squeezed his Grandad's hand and replied, 'Good. Here we are, home at last.'

Craddock's heart swelled with joy.

When the children were all tucked up in their makeshift beds the grown-ups sat in front of a roaring fire with drinks and slices of sumptuous chocolate cake before they went to bed; and Craddock might have felt thrilled when Judd asked if they could come next year to the Bonfire Night celebrations, but it was nothing to how he felt when Graham broke his own news out of the hearing of the children.

'We haven't told the children yet until we feel convinced we're doing the right thing, but,' he took a deep breath, 'we are hoping to come to live right here in the village.'

Craddock thought he must be tired because obviously he'd misheard what Graham had said.

'We decided that our children are missing out not living in a village, and as this village has a good school ...' Graham nodded and smiled briefly at Kate. 'And there is a big hospital in Culworth where eventually Anita may find work, and there's a general practice in Culworth that I've been in touch with and there's a strong possibility there'll be a job available in another month or two. But mainly it's because of our quality of life. Where we live we hardly dare let the children out on their own, whereas here they'd be safe if they wanted to go to that vastly superior playground they never stop talking about and ...'

Delighted though Craddock was at Graham's news, he couldn't see how it would work out. 'But you'd need a big house, having all the children to accommodate and there's none for sale that would be big enough. Thatched roofs and roses round the door almost always mean small rooms and even smaller bedrooms.'

'Well, yes, but you know Nightingale Farm? Well, the family have in fact put their farmhouse on the market so ...'

Craddock strongly protested. 'You can't. No. No. You're not

a farmer, you're a doctor, surely. That's what you want to do, not farming. There's no money in it, and with all these children to feed and clothe ...'

'I know, I know, we're not going to be farming, believe me. That's why the Nightingales are leaving as they just can't make money being dairy farmers nowadays. All their children except the youngest one have left school and are working or at university, and so they are down-sizing. They've already sold most of their land to a farmer nearby, and when I got the brochure from the estate agent both Anita and I fell in love with the farmhouse. We haven't been to see it yet, but fingers crossed we shall be living at Nightingale Farm in a few months.'

Graham smiled triumphantly at Craddock and Kate, and she couldn't stop herself hugging Anita and kissing Graham's cheek and patting his shoulder. 'That's wonderful news, you've no idea how delighted we are.'

Graham added very firmly, 'We don't need to live in each other's pockets, and we're not anticipating the children making nuisances of themselves coming over to see you on some flimsy excuse or another. It's just that we love the idea of a country life for the family, and this seemed to be the most sensible direction to go. Michael, of course, isn't coming, but maybe he'll be a regular visitor.'

'Good,' said Craddock, more delighted now than he could possibly find words to explain. 'Good. I'm delighted. We are, aren't we, Kate?'

'Of course we are, absolutely delighted. So I'll have three new children in school, perhaps as early as Easter. Gemma, Judd, and Max. Sarah will need to go by bus into Culworth to the secondary school, and little Ross can go to the nursery class we have for the under-fives. Another drink to toast this wonderful new venture of yours?'

★

That night everyone in the village went to bed weary but elated by the wonderful celebration the entire village had enjoyed. Contentment was rife, and a good night's sleep was had by all.

It felt like the good old days for everyone, which they all put down to having the rightful person sleeping under the roof of Turnham House, with two small boys to carry on the Templeton name when the time came.

The contentment was especially rich in the house where Grandad and Granny Fitch slept along with their new found family. For the very first time the attic had been put to use and it felt deeply pleasurable to have the house filled to capacity with them all.

Fran Charter-Plackett slept deeply too, having spent a long evening with someone as kind and friendly as Alex Harris, who allowed her to be herself and have opinions, and did not make demands on her.

On November 21st the following paragraph appeared in a major United Kingdom newspaper.

A private jet owned by the Brazilian-based Templeton Hotel Group has gone missing over the Amazon jungle. It is three days since the pilot, Christopher Templeton, a director of the company, has been in contact. He took off from their company aerodrome intending to take an extended excursion lasting at least a week. He was accompanied by Patrick McAllen, navigator, and an aeronautical engineer understood to be named Brett Stansfield. All three men are experienced fliers. His brother Sir Jonathan Templeton has flown from England to assist in the search.

Something's set tongues wagging
in Turnham Malpas . . .

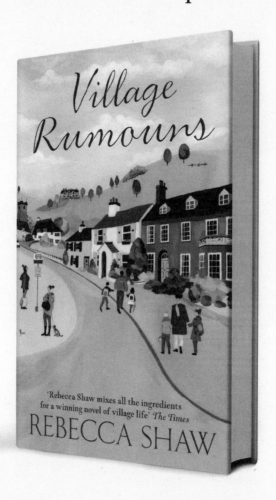

Available now in Orion hardback and eBook